A Heart MADE OF Indigo

JOURNEYS OF THE HEART BOOK 1

A Heart
MADE
OF Indigo

a historical romance by

SHAELA KAY

Other books in this series

Scoundrel In Disguise
The Rodenburg Girl

Published by Blue Water Books
Richland, WA

© 2015 Shaela Kay Odd
Visit the author at www.shaelakay.com

In loving memory of Robert George,
who always believed in his little brown-eyed Emily

Chapter 1

London, England, 1831

Katherine's stomach growled. She had not eaten since yesterday, and she knew there would be nothing today if she returned home empty-handed. Clutching the basket of red and orange flowers tighter to her chest, she walked slowly down the street, searching for customers among the passersby. A gentleman with a lady on his arm turned the corner, and Katherine smiled as she stepped towards them.

"Flowers for sale, a penny a bunch," she called, holding out a small bouquet of chrysanthemums. Confusion and suspicion flashed across their faces, and they shook their heads, hurrying on. Though she had expected their reaction, Katherine still sighed. She was met with similar responses on a daily basis, and it was discouraging.

Gathering her spirits, she turned and headed towards the heart of the city. It was late afternoon on a beautiful September day, and Katherine was certain of finding a crowd down by the waterfront. She knew she was not alone in her desire to enjoy the last few days of fine weather. The summer had lingered longer than normal, and Katherine knew it was only a matter of weeks before the frigid London winter held the city in its frozen grip. She shivered as she thought of the long, lonely season before her.

Rounding a corner, Katherine beheld the magnificent River Thames, its murky gray waters flowing through the crowded London streets like a centuries-old serpent. She slowly picked her way down to the wharf, holding her basket of flowers carefully so as not to crush them. Katherine had been right. Masses of people lined the streets leading onto and surrounding the wharf, while throngs of peddlers and beggars pushed and crowded one another in an attempt to find the best places to sell their wares. She hovered on the outskirts, hoping to sell a few bouquets before the day was over. A gruff old gentleman tossed a couple pennies at her, but he did not take the flowers that Katherine so gratefully offered him.

A tall, slender woman clad in a dark purple dress brushed past her, and Katherine glanced up. For a moment her heart leapt into her throat, thinking it was her grandmother's face beneath the knot of iron gray hair. But it was not her, and the disappointment dragged Katherine's spirits down even further.

The encounter brought Katherine's grandmother to the forefront of her mind, and she allowed her thoughts to linger on the woman who had raised her. No one would know it to look at her, but Katherine had been raised in London's high society, her father the youngest son of an earl. Her mother had been very young when she married him, and following his early death she decided to return to her own family in Bath, hoping to make

2

another eligible match. But having a young child in tow complicated matters, so two-year-old Katherine was sent to live with her father's mother Margaret Greenwood, the Countess of Rockwell. Lady Rockwell was a kind woman, and despite the disapproval she felt over her son's marriage, she determined to do right by her granddaughter. She oversaw Katherine's education, and ensured that she had the very best of everything. The two grew very close, and Lady Rockwell had great plans to introduce Katherine into high society when she came of age, but Katherine had been torn from her protection before those plans could come to fruition.

Lost in her memories, Katherine wandered around the wharf for nearly an hour. She realized too late that the sun was setting, and many of her potential customers had already gone home. Disappointed and ashamed of herself, Katherine stepped into the street and began to make her way homeward.

"Get out of the street, girl!"

She dashed out of the way just in time, dropping her basket of flowers in her haste to avoid being run over. The voice belonged to the driver of a fashionable carriage careening down the street. Its passenger stuck his head out of the window and shook his fist at Katherine as he passed. She turned to watch the carriage out of sight, and as it rounded a corner her brows came together, bitter indignation rising within her breast. How dare he shout at her in such a way! Anger and resentment burned inside her, but almost as quickly as the feelings flared to life they died, and in their stead the cold, familiar feeling of disgrace settled upon her. The encounter was a stinging reminder of her present situation, and the humiliation stabbed at her wounded heart.

3

The scattered fragments of her day's work lay all around her, the crimson blossoms trampled to the color of dried blood on the pavement. She bent to pick them up, but nothing was salvageable and she gave up in despair. Tears of anger and fear seeped from her eyes and she brushed them hastily away as she stood. *Mr. Fletcher will beat me for this*, she thought.

It was not the first time she had come to such a realization, nor reached such an end at the hands of her stepfather.

She checked her apron pocket and found the four small coins she had been able to earn that day. It was not likely to be enough to turn aside her stepfather's wrath, but at least she would not be going home empty-handed.

Home. Katherine smiled bitterly as she considered the word.

Nearly three years had passed since Katherine's newly remarried mother arrived at the estate of Lady Rockwell to claim guardianship of her daughter, but to Katherine it seemed an eternity. Neither her pleas to remain with her grandmother nor Lady Rockwell's own solicitations had any effect on the new Mrs. Fletcher. Katherine was taken away to London, and she had not seen nor heard from her grandmother since. Mr. Fletcher had forbidden any correspondence between them, and if her grandmother had ever written to her, Katherine had never known it. It saddened her, for she missed her grandmother and felt certain she was missed herself, but Katherine knew enough of Mr. Fletcher's nature never to disobey him.

Twilight descended in the narrow streets around her as Katherine made her way through the winding alleys of London. She shivered in the cool air, wrapping her arms around herself for warmth. Her threadbare dress would not survive another London

4

winter, but she did not dare ask her stepfather for a new one. Little more than an abusive drunk, he had sold or gambled away every possession they had ever owned. *Not every possession*, Katherine thought, smiling to herself.

She was nearly home now, and Katherine tiptoed up the staircase to their second-story flat so as not to be heard. But as she reached a cold hand out to turn the latch, the door swung open. Katherine gave a startled gasp and looked up at the massive silhouette that barred her entrance into the darkened room. A dirty hand shot towards her and grabbed her by the collar, yanking her into the inky blackness. "There you are!" an angry voice bellowed. Katherine's terrified eyes were no match for the darkness that engulfed her as she was pulled into the room.

Her stepfather dropped her roughly on the ground, slamming the door. She cowered there, afraid to move and draw attention to herself. A single tallow candle burned low on a lopsided table in the middle of the room. Mr. Fletcher sat down heavily and picked up the nearly-empty bottle beside the flickering light. He took a heavy draw, then turned to face her.

"Yer late," he slurred.

Katherine's heart beat frantically. He was already drunk, which meant that his temper would be close to the surface. She took a deep breath, gathering both her strength and her courage as she slowly got to her feet.

"I… I went down to the riverfront," she began, trying to keep her voice light. "There were more people, and I hoped to sell more flowers."

He grunted and took another swig from the bottle. "Good. You should 'ave more'n a few shillings this time, then."

Katherine's heart dropped, and a cold sweat broke out on her forehead. Trembling, she reached into her pocket and withdrew the four small coins. She took the few steps necessary to reach the table and dropped them in the candlelight, retreating quickly. Her stepfather stared at them, but when he picked them up and realized it was only four pence, he shot to his feet, knocking over the chair in his haste. Katherine backed swiftly away from him.

"I am sorry," she whispered desperately. "There was an accident with a carriage, and my flowers fell–" Her stepfather lunged at her, roaring as he struck a blow to the left side of her face. She gasped, searing pain shooting through her head and neck, but before she could recover he grabbed her dress and threw her across the narrow room. Katherine hit the wall solidly and landed in a dizzy heap on the floor. She tried to raise her throbbing head, but her stepfather was standing over her already, and the swift kick he dealt to her side made her double over in pain.

"That'll teach you to come home with nothin' but a few coppers!" he bellowed, kicking her again. This time Katherine could not stop the moan from escaping her lips. He cursed at her and swung his fist down.

"Thomas, please!" a feeble voice pleaded from the darkness. It was Katherine's mother. "A few coppers is better than nothing–" Her voice was abruptly cut off as Mr. Fletcher turned his rage from Katherine to her mother. He roared again as he lifted a nearby stool and threw it at her, which shattered to pieces on the floor. He followed after, kicking the cowering woman hard in the gut.

"You keep to yer own business, woman! I never wanted no

hussy wife, nor this wench of a daughter!" He swung again at her, and at the cry of pain from her mother, Katherine snapped. The months and years of humiliation and abuse rose like a burning fire in her breast, and she spoke more boldly than ever before.

"You are a monster, Mr. Fletcher. You take our money and get yourself drunk. You have stolen everything we have ever owned, and now– " She choked on her response as he lifted her to his face. His voice was dangerously low, and Katherine could smell the whiskey on his breath.

"You listen to me, girl. I ain't gonna put up wi' yer lip, an' I ain't gonna tolerate no disrespect. You best watch tha' mouth 'o yers afore I give you a beatin' you ain't likely to forget."

He threw her to the ground, expecting her to scramble away, but the fire still burned within her and Katherine was not going to let it die. She grabbed his leg and bit down as hard as she could. He roared in pain and stumbled backward, knocking over the table and extinguishing the only light in the room. Katherine struggled to get to her feet in the darkness. Her head throbbed and she was dizzy, but she heard her stepfather curse loudly and charge at her. Darting to the side just in time, he collided with the wall instead of her. A sickening crack and a loud thud resounded as he hit the wall headfirst, slumping to the floor.

Katherine crouched beside the wall and waited, hardly daring to breathe. *Five, six, seven…* she counted to twenty before she was convinced that he was unconscious. Quickly she crept to the corner where she normally slept and began to feel around. The moon had not yet risen and the room was in almost total darkness, but Katherine found the small knothole for which she was searching and reached a clammy finger down into it. The space beneath the floorboard was small, and she did not have to probe long before her finger brushed against the cold metal band. She carefully pulled the trinket out of its hiding place and breathed a sigh of relief.

Her father's signet ring was safe.

Katherine stood and moved swiftly to the door, but as she yanked on the handle, a sob escape from her mother. Katherine looked at the unconscious heap lying across the room, then quickly went to her mother's side and knelt down.

"I cannot stay, Mother, and neither should you." Her voice softened as she crouched beside the battered figure. "Come with me."

"I cannot, I cannot!" her mother moaned. "He will find me and kill me." She began to weep, and Katherine felt a surge of pity for her, but nothing more. Katherine's mother had never been attached to her, and since she usually observed Mr. Fletcher's treatment towards her daughter with silent disregard, any affection that had sprung up on Katherine's side when they were reunited had been effectively dissolved.

Katherine leaned in. "Then God bless you, Mother," she whispered.

And Katherine ran.

Chapter 2

The sign above the shop said "Abbot & Abrams, Collectibles" in red lettering. Katherine stared at it for a long time, willing herself to find the courage she lacked. She had spent the last half hour hesitating in front of the shop, afraid to face the strangers within who would surely ask difficult questions. *Perhaps there is another way…* But even as her mind formed the words she knew that there was not. Her only answer lay behind the heavy black door before her.

Katherine retreated from the doorstep as two gentlemen strode into sight. She turned her face away, wincing as the quickness of her movements sent stabbing pains shooting through her head and torso. She was sore from her beating, but if the men were sent from Mr. Fletcher she knew she would receive far worse. Her pulse quickened and her hands began to shake as she thought of what would happen to her if her stepfather found her. But the gentlemen passed by without even seeming to notice her, and she gradually relaxed as their footsteps died away. She knew she could not linger, and she tightened her grip on the precious ring held in her palm. Her grandmother had given her a means of escape—it would be senseless not to use it.

The ring had belonged to Katherine's father, but he had not been the one to bestow it upon her. When James Greenwood died, his signet ring had been given to his widowed mother, Lady Rockwell, who was supposed to destroy it, as was customary. But Lady Rockwell was sentimental, and she chose instead to keep the ring as a memento of the son she had lost. When Katherine was old enough, Lady Rockwell showed it to her, and told her stories of the man who had worn it. Her grandmother's loving remembrances brought the father she had never known to life, and the ring became a treasured keepsake that they both shared.

Katherine was shocked when Lady Rockwell gave her the ring as a parting gift, along with a fervent warning to keep it hidden from her stepfather. Only fourteen years old at the time, Katherine did not understand the reason why it should be kept a secret, but she had followed her grandmother's advice, and her stepfather knew nothing of the valuable ring she now had in her possession.

Gathering her courage about her like a cloak, Katherine took a beep breath and opened the door. A bell tinkled softly overhead, and she shut the door quietly. The shop was void of people, but full of trinkets and artifacts of a most unusual and varied collection. Beautiful china dolls, their porcelain skin glowing in the faint light from the window, sat in neat rows on a shelf next to mismatched tea cups and a large mantel clock. A beautiful writing desk lay open on a table to the side of the room, and next to it stood a large curio cabinet with clear glass panes. Beside the cabinet, its glossy wood shining in the soft light, stood a small pianoforte.

Katherine walked over to it and reverently touched the black and white keys. Her already aching heart seemed to break asunder as she thought of the music she had once known and loved. But all of that was passed; she had not touched an instrument in the three years since she had left her grandmother's house, and she did not know whether she ever would again. She sighed with longing and turned away, peering into the curio cabinet as she passed. A mink stole, a painted silk fan, and a pair of opera glasses with tiny jewels inlaid into the handle sat on a shelf inside. Hearing footsteps behind her, she turned to see a short, balding man walk into the room and stand next to the front counter. He cleared his throat and looked at her expectantly over his spectacles.

"May I help you?"

Katherine walked hesitantly over to him. "Yes, sir. I… I wish to sell a ring."

He narrowed his eyes, and she blushed as his gaze swept swiftly over her. She had spent the night in a dirty alleyway after escaping her stepfather, and she knew her appearance was appalling. Even though she had washed her face and brushed off the skirt of her dress, it did little to hide the months of dirt and neglect, not to mention the bruise beginning to bloom on her cheek. Drawing herself up to her full five-foot, four-inch height, she smiled politely. "You must forgive my appearance, sir. My family has fallen on hard times."

The man's eyebrows rose, and she smiled smugly to herself. At least she still sounded like a lady, even if her appearance suggested otherwise. He eyed her thoughtfully, clearly debating,

11

but finally he nodded. "Very well. What have you brought?"

Katherine set the large, ornate ring gently on the counter, feeling as if it were her heart upon an altar. The shopkeeper picked it up and examined it. It was a heavy gold ring, obviously a man's, and very fine. The bezel was wide and flat, with an elaborate engraving etched into the metal: a mature oak tree growing behind a large coat of arms, its branches reaching over and through the mirrored letters "J" and "G," which rested on either side of the crest. He pulled out a hand lens and turned the ring over, inspecting it. After a few minutes he laid down his lens and peered at Katherine.

"Where did you get this, young lady?" he asked gruffly.

Katherine blanched. "It was a gift, sir."

The man snorted. "A gift? Someone gave you a gentleman's ring as a gift?" He looked at her suspiciously, and she did her best to remain calm.

"Yes. It was my father's ring, but it was given to me after he died."

She spoke softly but clearly, and the man studied her. Finally he blew out his breath. "Wait here, please." He took the ring and his lens and left the room.

Katherine waited nervously, her insides churning with anxiety as the clock on the shelf ticked quietly. What if he would not purchase the ring? *He thinks I stole it*, she thought bitterly. She shook her head, willing her anger to dissipate. She did not blame him, considering the circumstances; even *she* thought it looked suspicious. But Katherine had no choice. It was several minutes before the shopkeeper returned, this time accompanied by another gentleman. Katherine stood up straight and tried not to let them see how frightened she was.

"Well, well, this is the young lady you spoke of?" The stranger addressed the shopkeeper but looked at Katherine.

"Yes, Mr. Abrams. She claims it was a gift."

Katherine could hear the distrust in his voice, and it rankled her. She turned to Mr. Abrams, a middle-aged man with graying hair. "It was a gift, sir, I assure you. It was my father's signet ring, and as his only child, it was given to me after his death."

Mr. Abrams regarded her thoughtfully. "And why did you not destroy the ring, as is customary?"

Katherine's voice was quiet, and it trembled slightly as she replied, "My father *died*, sir. It was all I had left of him."

The man before her nodded slowly. "I see. But now you wish to sell it?"

Katherine could sense that a trap was being laid for her. Their suspicion stung her already tender heart and she was more than a bit frightened. She hastily brushed away the tears that sprang to her eyes, determined to accomplish her purpose.

"As I explained to this gentleman before," she said with a nod to the shopkeeper, "my family has fallen on hard times and I am forced to part with it. I assure you that nothing but the most dire circumstances would convince me to sell it, but if you do not believe me, sir, be so good as to return my ring and I shall take my business elsewhere."

Mr. Abrams looked at her in mild surprise. "There will be no need for that, young lady; it is a fine ring and I shall be glad to purchase it." He rubbed his chin thoughtfully. "I shall give you £90 for it. Is that agreeable to you, miss?"

Katherine's eyes widened. She knew the ring was valuable,

but she had not realized it was worth so much. She felt a stab of remorse, knowing she was forced to sell such a treasured keepsake. Taking a deep breath, she pushed her sentimental feelings aside and nodded briskly.

"Yes, that is agreeable to me. Thank you, sir."

She waited as he counted out the money, but when he handed her the bills she hesitated.

"I do not have a reticule. Do you have some for sale in your shop?"

Mr. Abrams smiled and led her to a corner where a collection of ladies' articles were kept. She chose a small purse from the few available and paid him back the amount for it. She placed the remainder of the money inside and tucked it into her skirts. Turning to the two men, she curtsied.

"Thank you," she said.

The shopkeeper scowled at her over his spectacles, but Mr. Abrams smiled and nodded. The bell on the door tinkled softly again as Katherine left the shop.

The docks belonging to the East India Company were crowded and teeming with life, and Katherine looked around her, fascinated. There were vessels of all shapes and sizes, and she checked the small piece of paper in her hand again for the name of the one she was looking for. After searching for twenty minutes she finally found it, the *Sea Spray*. Several sailors and a few passengers roamed the high deck, but since it was a merchant vessel the majority of the room on board was taken up with cargo.

Katherine approached the gangplank, where a sailor was receiving orders from an older gentleman who appeared to be the captain. Katherine waited until the sailor strode off before approaching the gentleman, who had turned to board the ship.

"Excuse me—Captain Jones?"

He turned to look back. "Yes," he boomed, "what is it?"

Katherine quaked under his stern gaze, but she bit back her fear and continued. "My name is Katherine Greenwood. I purchased passage on your ship bound for India."

"Ah, yes, I heard that a young woman would be joining us. And not a mite too soon," he replied, looking up at the sky. "We sail in an hour. Best get aboard."

He continued up the gangplank while Katherine followed him, stopping just long enough to adjust the small bundle she carried in her arms. Once aboard, she was directed to a cramped cabin she would share with three other passengers during the long voyage. She stowed her belongings under her bunk and sat down. Her heart was racing, partially out of fear but mostly from excitement. *India!* Her mind thrilled as she thought of her destination, a land Katherine had longed to see ever since she was a child. Her grandmother had often spoken of India, and now Katherine was on her way there.

Katherine had never known her grandfather, the earl—all that she knew about him had been told to her by her grandmother. Lord Rockwell had been a kind, studious man whose inquisitive spirit took him all over the world. As a youth he traveled across the Continent, as well as to the Americas and the West Indies. When he married, he brought silks and spices from Asia for his bride, and his collection of art and curios grew with every

15

voyage. When he first traveled to India, he brought back tea, indigo, and ivory, but more captivating than the gifts which he showered on his wife and children were his stories of a strange, exotic land full of dark-skinned natives with musical voices, enormous elephants that people rode like horses, and tiny white monkeys dressed in clothing and hats. Lady Rockwell was not averse to traveling, and his stories so fascinated her that she accompanied him on his next journey. They spent many months in India, and Lady Rockwell grew to love it herself.

Katherine sighed as she thought of her grandmother. She was quite certain that Lady Rockwell had given her the ring for the very purpose for which it had been used, and her heart ached thinking of what it must have cost Lady Rockwell to give it up, knowing its fate. If there had been any other way, Katherine would never have parted with the beloved keepsake.

It was fortunate she received such a considerable sum for it— enough to purchase not only her passage, but a simple, well-made gown and a few items for her toilet as well. She even had a few pounds remaining, but she knew that she would need to secure employment soon after her arrival in India, or she would find herself in serious trouble. But her passage was paid, which included her berth and board during the voyage, and she was determined to enjoy the journey inasmuch as was in her power. The troubles of survival in India could wait. *India!* she thought again.

She was going to India.

Chapter 3

Though Katherine had never known her father, her grandmother had often told her she was very much like him. Gentle and shy, she was hesitant in new surroundings and around new people, but when allowed to become acquainted with them, she blossomed into a kind, affectionate girl who spoke with candor and loved unconditionally. Despite her natural timidity, she had an insatiable curiosity that often drove her beyond her reserve.

The ship on which she found herself was a good-sized vessel, and Katherine lost no time in exploring the deck. She clung to the railing and watched as the city of London grew smaller and smaller in the distance. A thrill ran through her as she realized the enormity of what she was doing. No one except her grandmother would have thought her capable of such a scheme. Outwardly, she was calm, quiet and reserved, but an inner spark lived within her breast that had always been hungry for adventure, and India was destined to be full of it.

Sailors milled about on deck, hoisting sails, coiling rope,

shouting orders, and scurrying from one task to the next. She tried to stay out of the way, but one gruff sailor shoved roughly past her when she ventured too near.

"Out 'o the way," he growled. "A ship ain't no place fer a girl. We 'ave work to do."

Katherine scurried away, towards the foredeck where it was far less busy. It was a beautiful, clear day just before Michaelmas, and the sea reflected the brilliant sapphire sky like a giant looking glass. She gazed out over the expanse of blue, letting the crisp wind blow across her face and pull pieces of hair loose from the bun on top of her head. She took a deep breath and closed her eyes, smiling.

"This must be your first time at sea," said a female voice near her.

Katherine opened her eyes and turned to see a middle-aged woman smiling at her. Katherine smiled shyly back.

"Yes, ma'am, it is."

The woman chuckled. "I thought as much. The sight of you standing there with your eyes closed and a smile upon your lips reminds me of the first time I boarded a ship, Miss–?"

"Greenwood. Katherine Greenwood," she supplied.

The woman smiled. "I am pleased to make your acquaintance, Miss Greenwood. My name is Elizabeth Jones, the captain's wife."

"It is a pleasure to meet you, Mrs. Jones," Katherine replied.

Mrs. Jones stepped beside her, and they both turned to look out over the ocean, to the distant horizon where the sky kissed the sea in azure splendor.

"No matter how many times we put to sea, it always amazes

me how vast the ocean is," Mrs. Jones said.

Katherine nodded. "It makes me feel quite insignificant."

Her companion laughed. "Indeed it does. But even though the view seems always the same, the destination is not, and that makes the beginning of every voyage new and exciting."

"I never considered that," Katherine said thoughtfully. "As a captain's wife, I am sure you have seen your share of exotic lands and countries."

"Heavens, yes!" Mrs. Jones laughed. "I have had more adventure in my forty years than many have in a lifetime."

Katherine smiled, but was silent. They stood together, gazing at the ocean around them as the sails snapped in the wind. Presently Mrs. Jones broke the silence.

"May I ask what takes you to India, Miss Greenwood?"

Katherine bit her lip. "I am going to seek a new life."

"And what, pray tell, was wrong with your old life?" Mrs. Jones asked gently.

Surprised, Katherine turned to face her, fear evident in her deep brown eyes. Mrs. Jones own eyes widened, and she quickly laid a hand on her arm. "I am sorry. I did not mean to pry, nor to alarm you. Forgive me." She laughed lightly. "I have always been told that I am too forthright in my manner of speaking. I should have held my tongue."

Katherine shook her head. "I do not mind. It is only..." Her voice trailed off and she turned, gazing back the way they had come, where the great city of London was now only a bumpy gray smudge along the horizon. As if drawing courage from the distance, she said resolutely, "I am running away. From my stepfather."

The woman beside her nodded. "I see." She glanced sideways at Katherine and added, "If the bruise on the edge of your cheekbone is any indication of his merit, I do not blame you."

Katherine instinctively reached a hand up to cover the mark, and her face flushed as she turned away. Mrs. Jones said nothing for several minutes, but at last she ventured to speak again.

"Forgive me, Miss Greenwood, I did not mean to be rude."

Katherine nodded, but kept her face averted. Mrs. Jones persisted.

"I believe it is time for tea. Would you care to join me, Miss Greenwood?" she asked with a friendly smile.

Katherine hesitated. She felt vulnerable and afraid, and her instincts warned her to run away to the safety of her own little bunk. But she was lonely. Katherine had no friends to speak of, and her heart yearned for companionship. Slowly she nodded at the woman beside her.

"I would like that, thank you. But I fear I am not quite presentable," she murmured.

"Then allow me to have a bath drawn up for you; I daresay you would like a chance to freshen up," said Mrs. Jones candidly, eyeing the untidy knot of hair atop Katherine's head.

Katherine blushed again, knowing that despite her new dress her appearance must be dreadful. But rather than taking offense at Mrs. Jones' frank remark, she ignored the sting and embraced the kindness. "Yes, I would like that very much. Again, I thank you."

Mrs. Jones smiled. "I am a woman myself, Miss Greenwood, and I know the value of a good bath as much as anyone. It always helps to calm my nerves and face my fears."

She led Katherine to her private cabin near the stern of the ship. A young lad sat outside the door, whistling absently as he whittled a piece of wood.

"Have the cook heat several kettles of water for a bath," Mrs. Jones said briskly. The lad jumped to his feet and scampered off. She led Katherine inside and invited her to sit down. Drawing the curtains, she pulled a large basin from a peg on the wall and set it in the middle of the room. Katherine sat in silence, feeling excruciatingly conscious of the trouble she was causing, fighting the urge to run from the room and hide away by herself. The captain's wife pulled a clean towel and a small bar of soap from her linen drawer and set them on a chair next to the tub, along with a comb. She smiled at Katherine.

"There now. We shall soon get you washed up, and then you will feel better."

Katherine smiled back, embarrassed. "Thank you for your kindness, Mrs. Jones. I do not wish to trouble you..."

Mrs. Jones waved her off. " 'Tis no trouble at all. It makes my heart glad to be of service. The captain and I have no children of our own, and it does me good to have a young person about to mother a bit."

Soon the water was ready and the basin had been filled. Mrs. Jones saw that all was in readiness before she took her leave.

"Thank you, Mrs. Jones," Katherine said again with feeling.

"Elizabeth, please," her new friend smiled at her. "Take your time getting cleaned up, and join me on the foredeck when you are ready." She smiled again at Katherine and left the room.

Katherine walked slowly across the ship, feeling refreshed and less self-conscious after her bath. A few sailors turned their heads to watch her as she passed, and she quickened her pace. She saw Elizabeth sitting quietly on the port side of the foredeck reading, and as Katherine made her way over to her, the captain's wife looked up and smiled.

"There you are! My dear, you look lovely—I hardly recognize you!"

The change in Katherine's appearance was indeed a dramatic one. Those who knew Katherine as she had been the last few years would not have known her, but the acquaintances of her youth, when she lived under the watchful eyes of her grandmother and the London *ton*, would recognize the sweet, shy girl in the face of the pretty young woman, now seventeen.

Though she did not possess the striking fashion of a London socialite, Katherine was quite beautiful in her own way. She had thick, mahogany hair that fell in gentle waves to her waist when it was not pulled up. Her large, almond-shaped eyes were also brown, but so dark that they often appeared black. She had a straight, petite nose and a delicate chin, and her complexion was creamy with just a hint of pink. Her mouth was a bit wide, and when she smiled a dimple appeared in her chin and her eyes nearly disappeared in her high round cheeks. As a child, she smiled and laughed often and that dimple was nearly always present, but it had grown less visible in the three years since she had been away from her grandmother's house.

"What are you reading?" Katherine asked, sitting beside her.

"*The Mysteries of Udolpho*," Elizabeth replied. "Have you read it?"

Katherine nodded. "I did not enjoy it as well as I did Ms. Radcliffe's earlier novel, *The Romance of the Forest*, but it was quite diverting."

Elizabeth eyed her approvingly. "Do you enjoy reading?"

Katherine smiled. "Indeed I do. Books are wonderful companions."

"I agree that they are quite pleasant to pass the time, but I would think that someone such as yourself would enjoy the company of other young ladies more," Elizabeth hinted.

Katherine was silent, and Elizabeth decided not to press the matter. They were quiet for several minutes before Katherine spoke.

"Have you traveled to India often?" she asked.

Her companion smiled. "Yes, indeed. I have been to India more times than I can count."

"What is it like?"

"Hot."

Katherine laughed. "That is what my grandmother says. She said it felt as if she were stepping into a furnace when she first arrived."

Elizabeth chuckled. "It certainly feels that way at times. It is a land unlike any other I have seen. It is lush and green, and more beautiful flowers and birds I have never seen in my life. And the people! Such beautiful dark skin and ebony hair. They are quiet, calm, and polite, but there is a certain stubbornness about them that is surprising at times."

Katherine looked out into the wide expanse of the sea, a soft smile upon her lips. "Grandmother says there are enormous elephants that walk along the streets, twice as big as any carriage."

Her friend nodded. "Elephants, as well as horses, cows, donkeys, pigs—in cities such as Bombay and Calcutta, the streets are full of animals and people all the time."

"And in the smaller villages?"

Elizabeth shook her head. "I am afraid I cannot tell you. The captain and I have never stayed in India for long, and our visits are always confined to the busy port cities where the captain docks his ship."

Katherine sighed dreamily. "I have longed to see India my whole life. Grandmother promised to take me there someday, but she never had the chance."

"Did she die?" Elizabeth asked gently.

"No," Katherine replied slowly. "But I have not seen her since my mother remarried."

"And how long has that been?"

"Nearly three years."

The older woman watched her carefully, but Katherine supplied no other information. Intrigued, Elizabeth decided to try a different approach.

"Your grandmother sounds like a wonderful lady."

Katherine's face softened. "She is. Kind and generous, but firm. I am very blessed to have been raised by her; I know many are not so lucky."

"You were raised by your grandmother?"

"Yes. My father died when I was two years old, and while my mother went back to her own family in Bath, I was sent to live with my grandmother. She taught me music and drawing, how to speak French, German, and Italian, proper poise and etiquette, and to be polite and graceful. She taught me to be a lady," Katherine finished with a small smile. Elizabeth stared at her.

"Good heavens! I could see that you had had a proper upbringing, but I never dreamed you were a true gentlewoman. Pray, what is your grandmother's name?"

Katherine shifted uncomfortably in her seat. "Margaret Greenwood, the Countess of Rockwell."

"Lady Rockwell!"

Katherine nodded.

"If your grandmother is a countess, why on earth did you ever leave her, my child?"

"I had no choice," Katherine sighed. "I did not want to go; I thought I would always be with her. I never dreamed that my mother would remarry and come to take me away with her, but that is what happened."

"Did you not ask to stay with your grandmother?"

"I did. Grandmother, too, asked that I might remain with her. But Mr. Fletcher insisted."

"Mr. Fletcher is your stepfather?"

Katherine nodded.

Elizabeth was thoughtful. Katherine's story was intriguing, and she felt an even keener interest in her young friend. Katherine was silent, staring out at the endless expanse of water with a sad look on her face. As the minutes stretched by, Elizabeth could feel Katherine withdrawing into herself, and she knew that their conversation was over.

"I am sorry, my dear," she said gently. "I am sure it has been difficult."

Katherine nodded again, not trusting her voice to speak. They sat in silence for several minutes more, until Katherine excused herself and retired to her cabin.

Mrs. Jones did not see her the rest of the day.

Chapter 4

Despite Katherine's enthusiasm for adventure, she had a hard time adjusting to life on the ship. A week into the voyage they encountered some rough seas, and soon she was horribly ill. Sick, miserable, and confined to her bunk, Katherine wished she had never stepped a foot off land.

Elizabeth visited Katherine often, spooning soup into her mouth and bathing her face after she retched. Watching Katherine's pale face grow thinner and thinner worried her, but she trusted that with calmer seas Katherine would recover. She was right. After a week the storm blew itself out, and the tossing and tipping of the ship ceased. Desperate to see the sky again, Katherine ventured up to the deck as soon as she was able.

The sun was warm but the wind brisk, and she shivered in the cool air. Elizabeth adjusted the shawl around her shoulders and led her slowly over to a pile of crates, tied down on the starboard side. Katherine sat down and drew a deep breath, trying to smile.

"You have been so good to me, Elizabeth. I do not know what I would have done without you."

Her friend smiled and squeezed her hand. "I am glad to see you out of your bed at last. I am sorry you have been so ill, but it is best to get one's sea legs underfoot as soon as possible. I do not think you will be so ill again when the next storm rolls in."

Katherine groaned, and Elizabeth laughed. They looked out over the water, watching the waves froth and foam into little white peaks. Not a sign of land could be seen in any direction.

"Does it ever frighten you?" Katherine whispered.

"Does what frighten me?"

"This." Katherine gestured to the vast nothingness around them. "Days and weeks on end without any sight of land. Are you ever afraid that you will be lost at sea?"

"I was, once," Elizabeth said. "Early in my marriage. But the captain is a good man, and an excellent sailor. When I was frightened of the sea, I put my trust in him, and my fear subsided."

Katherine stared soberly out at the waves. "I wish I had someone on whom to rely," she murmured, more to herself than her companion. Elizabeth did not answer.

Gradually Katherine regained her strength, and in time, she was able to tend to her various duties. Though the sailors and servants did much of the work, the captain's wife had her own responsibilities to attend to, such as the captain's washing and mending. As the few passengers on board were likewise expected to care for their own laundry, Elizabeth taught Katherine how to do so aboard the ship. It was hard, exhausting work, and the strong lye soap stung Katherine's eyes and turned her hands raw. After clothing was laundered it was strung along ropes tied across the deck to dry. Katherine had discarded her worn out dress before the voyage, but Elizabeth made her a gift of an old dress and a work apron so that she had something to change into when her own clothes needed laundering. They darned socks and mended tears while they talked about England and India and all the lands between.

Day followed day, week followed week. When they had been at sea for nearly three months, they stopped at the island of St. Helena to take on fresh water and supplies. Since Christmas was only a week away, the captain traded goods for a half-dozen crates of oranges and some firecrackers. Katherine was excited to celebrate the season, even if it would be in a somewhat unorthodox fashion.

The day of the blessed holiday dawned bright and warm, with only a few fleecy clouds in the sapphire sky. "Happy Christmas, Katherine!" Elizabeth greeted her as she emerged onto the deck. She held out a small package, and Katherine took it with a smile.

"Happy Christmas, Elizabeth! But what is this? You have done so much for me already, and I have no gift for you." She frowned slightly, but Elizabeth laughed merrily.

"Your company has been the most delightful gift I could hope for. And this is nothing, simply a token to remember me by."

Katherine carefully unfolded the stiff brown paper, and a small cake of lavender-scented soap fell into her hand, along with a slip of paper that read, "For Katherine, that you may always remember our meeting. With love, Elizabeth Jones."

Katherine laughed. "It is wonderful! Thank you, Elizabeth." The older woman smiled so broadly that the wrinkles around her eyes nearly doubled. The two friends embraced, and Katherine ran to place the gift amongst her things in the cabin. When she returned, the oranges were being passed around to all the sailors and passengers. Katherine tore the tough skin off, breathing in the sharp, clean scent of the citrus. She ate the fruit slowly, savoring every bite.

"Mmm," she murmured to Elizabeth, who sat beside her outside the captain's cabin. "I have not had an orange in ages; it tastes heavenly!"

"I am glad we were able to secure some," her companion replied. "It will help ward off the scurvy. We are halfway to India, but our supply of fruits and vegetables will be minimal until we arrive."

The captain invited everyone on board to gather on the deck while he read aloud from the book of Luke. He then offered a solemn prayer, thanking God for their blessings and asking Him to bless them with safe passage. Katherine's heart was deeply stirred, and she felt the simple service was as great as any sermon she had attended back in England.

The rest of the day was filled with singing, dancing, and merry-making amongst all of those on board. Several of the sailors brought out pipes and flutes, and many of the passengers danced to the jigs they played on their instruments. Katherine smiled as she watched, tapping her feet in time to the rhythm and laughing at the antics of some of the less coordinated passengers. The ship's cook managed to create a few enormous puddings for their supper, and as the sun set the captain ordered the firecrackers lit.

The crate were opened, and the sailors sent them fizzing into the sky with gusto. They burst overhead in a kaleidoscope of color, illuminating the ship and its occupants in brilliant flashes of light. Katherine climbed into her cramped bunk that evening feeling like it had been one of the most beautiful Christmases she had ever celebrated.

The days stretched endlessly on after the holiday. The novelty of life aboard the ship had worn out long ago, and Katherine grew restless of the monotony. After four months at sea she felt as if she would go mad. Daily she paced the deck, from the bow to the stern and back again. She counted the sails and calculated the lengths of rope tying them to the mast. She followed the sun in its track across the sky and the stars in their course at night, while the horizon remained ever empty. The food was invariable as well. Salted pork and boiled beans, or beef and mealy bread were often what they ate for every meal. Katherine began to wonder if life in India would be worth the trouble and length of the voyage.

To help pass the time, Katherine and Elizabeth talked a great deal. The captain's wife had a few precious books on board, and they read them aloud to one another every day.

"What I do not understand," Katherine once stated, after they had finished reading William Shakespeare's *Romeo and Juliet*, "is why Juliet so rashly takes her life when she finds that Romeo is dead. Surely she had other interests before; why did her existence suddenly and entirely depend upon him?"

Amused, Elizabeth asked, "Have you never been in love?"

Katherine blushed. "No, indeed. I did not have many acquaintance in my youth, and once I returned to my mother's house any connection between us was dissolved."

"Did you not make any new friends?"

Katherine shook her head. "No. There was a rift between myself and any other young people." Her eyes darkened. "It did

31

not take long for Mr. Fletcher to drink and gamble away my mother's fortune. And once we were removed from polished society, the company around us changed. I may have looked like a pauper, but I was still a lady. As such, I had no place in either social circle."

Elizabeth knew Katherine's entire history by now, and considering the home Katherine had shared with her mother and stepfather, she did not blame her for running away. She had once questioned, however, why Katherine did not go straight to her grandmother for protection.

"Naturally I considered that," Katherine had answered wistfully. "But I knew it was the first place my stepfather would go looking for me, and since I am not yet of age, I knew I would be forced to return with him."

Katherine also knew, of course, that she may have been allowed to stay with her grandmother, but not unless her stepfather had been able to extort Lady Rockwell out of a considerable fortune in return. As much as Katherine longed to return to the love and safety of her former home, she did not want to see another farthing wasted at the hands of her reprobate stepfather. Katherine had therefore dismissed the idea of seeking her grandmother's protection, and once that decision was made, the only remaining choice was to sell her precious signet ring and buy passage to one of the colonies. She felt it was only natural that she should choose India, a land she had heard so much about and had longed to visit ever since she was a child.

A few weeks later they landed in South Africa, at the Cape of Good Hope. Katherine and Elizabeth went ashore for a few precious hours to stretch their legs, but all too soon it was time to return to the ship. Katherine watched the shoreline with hungry eyes as they sailed away, not wanting to lose her view of land. But Elizabeth assured her that it was their final stop before landing in India.

"We are making good time," she remarked enthusiastically. "I expect that we shall arrive in Calcutta in another month."

Her prediction was correct. On a cool, sunny day in early March, Katherine and Elizabeth sat working on the foredeck when shouts of "land, ho!" reached their ears. Katherine looked up from the stocking she was mending, straining her eyes as she searched the horizon. But there was nothing to disrupt the seemingly endless ocean. Then slowly, as if rising out of the sea, a thin gray line came into view, its flat haziness nearly blending in with the water.

"There it is, my dear! Your first glimpse of India." Elizabeth rolled up her mending and tucked it away. She turned to Katherine with a smile. "Are you ready to see your new home?"

Katherine laughed lightly. "I do not know that I shall ever be ready, from what I have heard. But I am certainly ready to get off this ship."

Her friend laughed. "I have no doubt you are."

Katherine smiled at her affectionately, but a pang of sadness shot through her as she thought of the parting that must soon take place. During the weeks and months on board the *Sea Spray* the two women had grown very close, and Katherine was not looking forward to saying goodbye. The last six months had been the happiest in Katherine's life of late, and much of that was due to the lady sitting beside her. Since her arrival on the ship, Katherine's smile had gradually resurfaced, and her friendship with Elizabeth Jones had even resurrected her laugh—a deep, throaty sound that voiced comfort and contentment to her very core.

Elizabeth stood and beckoned to Katherine. "Come, let us gather your things. We will arrive in port soon and the captain will want us to be ready."

Katherine turned to gaze at the gray line in the distance again, now growing in size and shape. Soon they would land on what would now be her home, but she could not determine if the knots in her stomach were more from excitement or fear. With a sigh, she gathered her mending and followed her friend.

Chapter 5

The ship had to sail up the Hooghly River a considerable distance before arriving at port in Calcutta, and therefore Katherine was able to see much of the Indian landscape before disembarking. The first thing she noticed was the heat. Although the temperatures had been growing steadily colder when they left England in late September, the further south they sailed the more moderate the climate became. Now as they approached land, the tempering effect of the sea lessened, and Katherine began to feel the tropical heat in its fullness. Wisps of hair that had blown loose from her bun now stuck to her forehead, and she felt a trickle of sweat between her shoulder blades seeping slowly through her dress. She drew her handkerchief and wiped her brow, craning her neck to see the shoreline.

A thick mangrove forest grew right up to the edge of the coast, the stilt-like roots reaching into the water like hundreds of huge claws. Small brown monkeys watched from the treetops as the ship approached the mouth of the river, and now and then a flock of brilliantly colored birds burst from the canopy and flew off into the distance. Katherine watched it all, enthralled.

The ship slowly made its way upriver, where the muddy water cut a crooked swathe through the thick forest. As the ship sailed further from the seashore, the rumbling and crashing from the waves became only a dull roar in the distance, and smaller, more distinct sounds became apparent. The snap and rustle of the thick green foliage as monkeys climbed and swung from the branches competed with the calls from dozens of birds, and now and then a splash from the river indicated the presence of fish and other small creatures. Katherine watched and listened in fascination, until suddenly a hush fell over the forest, and she searched the emerald tangle for the cause. She gasped as a massive striped cat crept out of the undergrowth and lapped at the water's edge before melting back into the shadows.

The port in Calcutta was a large, bustling maze of docks and ships. Merchants, sailors, British officers, Hindu servants— people of every shape and size and color swarmed about in self-concerned importance. Katherine took in the scene before her with delightful anticipation, eager to see all she could. Sailors were unloading cargo from their own ship, so she stood out of the way on one side of the deck.

Elizabeth Jones had a brother employed as the steward over an indigo plantation in Calcutta. As he often came to meet his sister when he knew her husband's ship was due in port, Elizabeth had promised Katherine that she would ask him if a situation could be found for her at the plantation which he oversaw. Katherine was grateful to her friend for the offer, and was both excited and nervous to see how the plan unfolded.

In the meantime, Elizabeth suggested they get a room at the

Empire Hotel on Strand Road. Katherine readily agreed, anxious to see more of the city. The captain was engaged in business with many of the Indian merchants; a task that would take days, perhaps even weeks, to accomplish. He was therefore unable to accompany them, so with the first mate serving as escort, the ladies disembarked and went in search of transportation. The hardened sailor carried their belongings, and hailed a group of men carrying a covered platform as they passed by. The men stopped and set the litter down. Katherine stared.

"What on earth is that?" she exclaimed.

Elizabeth laughed. "A palanquin. It is the primary means of transportation within the city."

Katherine was amazed. The first mate helped the ladies get settled under the canopy, gave the men directions to the hotel, and soon the two women were on their way.

They traveled north on Strand Road to Tank Square, where the great Government House and many of the public buildings were located. Enthralled, Katherine watched the city around them pass, and Elizabeth watched Katherine with amusement. Hundreds of dark-skinned natives in airy white clothing swarmed the streets, but interspersed among them were the brilliant red uniforms of East India Company soldiers. Carriages, horses, dogs, cows, palanquins, camels, and even a few elephants crowded the streets. Katherine's eyes grew wide as one of the massive beasts lumbered slowly past them. Everything she saw fascinated and delighted her, and Katherine was anxious to discover more about this land she would now call home.

They arrived at the hotel, and having paid the men who brought them hence, Elizabeth dismissed the palanquin.

Katherine looked up at the massive white building before them. The deep covered porch was supported by tall pillars that reached clear to the second story. Marbled steps led up to a pair of beautifully carved doors, where Elizabeth was waiting patiently for her. Katherine smiled sheepishly and joined her friend.

The hotel was very grand, even by London's standards. Elizabeth arranged to have a room for each of them and a private parlor to share during their stay. A Hindu servant in a traditional *dhoti*, or loincloth, carried their belongings for them and showed them to their rooms.

"I will send a message to my brother," Elizabeth said when they were alone in the parlor. "Then we can have some supper."

She made quick work of her note, and gave it to the clerk in the lobby to post for her. The ladies then crossed the street to a restaurant, and Katherine partook of her first Indian meal.

The menu consisted of many foods she knew from England: roast fowl, puddings, dates and figs, broiled beef, creamed vegetables, and a selection of fruit. But there were also several items with which she was unfamiliar.

"What is this dish called?" she asked Elizabeth, helping herself to a bright yellow broth with chunks of vegetables and meat in it.

"That is a curry," her friend explained. "Eat it with some rice, but be careful—they are sometimes quite hot."

Katherine took a small taste, and a wide smile spread across her face. "It is delicious!" she said. "Spicy, but also sweet." She finished the curry and reached for another dish.

"That is a fish stew," Elizabeth offered. "It is a bit strong for my taste, but not disagreeable."

Katherine did not care. To be eating genuine food after months of mealy provisions! Every dish was like ambrosia to her tongue.

They finished their meal and returned to the hotel. It had been a long day, filled with new and exciting things, and Katherine was tired. Her mind was filled with all she had seen, the wonders and delights crowding out the worry she felt for her future. India was everything she ever dreamed it would be and more, and she fell asleep with a smile on her face.

Katherine awoke early the next morning. Breakfast consisted of tea, rice, fresh fruit, and a cold curry, which she and Elizabeth ate in their little parlor. Just as they were finishing the meal, a servant came to inform them that there was a Mr. Henry Wilson waiting in the lobby. Katherine's stomach gave a nervous little flip at these words, but Elizabeth smiled.

"Let me speak to my brother alone for a moment, and we shall call for you directly," she said to Katherine.

Katherine nodded, and retired to her room. She paced across the length and back again, now stopping to look out the window, now into the glass, now sitting at the writing desk, now once again on her feet, pacing. After ten minutes, a soft knock came at the door. She answered the summons, and a young Hindu servant indicated that she was wanted. Her knees shook, and she took a deep breath to steady her nerves as she walked down the short hallway to the parlor.

Elizabeth and her brother turned as she entered, and she

curtsied to them as they stood to greet her. Mr. Wilson was tall and smartly dressed, with graying hair and kind eyes. Elizabeth smiled her encouragement at Katherine as she made the introductions.

"Miss Greenwood, this is Mr. Wilson. Henry, this is the young lady I told you of."

"How do you do, Miss Greenwood?" the gentleman asked.

"How do you do, Mr. Wilson." Katherine was so nervous her voice came out barely above a whisper. She cleared her throat and tried to calm her racing heart.

"My sister tells me that you are looking for a position," he continued. "Have you been trained as a lady's maid?"

The question caught Katherine by surprise, and she stumbled on her response. "Not exactly, no. I know their duties, of course, but I have never been one myself." She blushed, clasping her hands firmly in front of her.

"A housemaid, then?"

Katherine was ready this time. She lifted her chin and said, "Sir, I have two able hands and a willing mind. I can and will do anything that may be required of me, in whatever position I can secure." She spoke with confidence, and was rewarded with a look of mild surprise from Mr. Wilson.

"Indeed!" He was silent for a moment as he studied her, then his eyes relaxed and he turned to his sister. "Elizabeth, I believe I can find a position for her as you requested." He turned to Katherine and asked, "Can you be ready with your things in a quarter-hour?"

"Of course."

"Wonderful! I shall await you downstairs."

With a nod to each of them, he excused himself and left the room. The moment the door shut behind him, Katherine collapsed into a chair, her relief nearly bringing her to tears. She turned to her friend, who was smiling warmly at her.

"Oh Elizabeth, however can I thank you? I am sure Mr. Wilson would never have looked at me twice had I sent inquiry to the plantation myself. I know it is you to whom I owe my good fortune."

Her friend laughed. "Nonsense! You are a very capable young lady, and I have no doubt you could have secured employment yourself, had it been required of you." Her look softened, and she squeezed her young friend's hands to keep them from trembling. "I am very happy for you, my dear, and I believe you will do well where you are going. Now, let us gather your things—Henry does not like to be kept waiting."

Fifteen minutes later, Elizabeth stood waving as the carriage carrying her brother and Katherine drove out of sight. The farewell between the two friends had been a tearful one. Elizabeth promised to inquire after Katherine when she next came to port, but as that would likely be more than a year in the future, the thought did not give Katherine much comfort.

Upon finding herself seated across from Mr. Wilson, Katherine's nerves began to tie themselves up into knots again. She had never been in such a situation before—how was she to proceed? Her benefactor remained silent, so Katherine thought it best to do the same.

They traveled south and east through the city of Calcutta, through the area known as White Town. Here, the British residents and East India Company employees lived in their "marble palaces," as the natives called them. Rows of massive white houses built in the neoclassical style stood proudly along the streets. Deep covered porches, or porticoes, stretched across the front of every building they passed, while tall, smooth columns converged in delicate arches on the second level. Most of the high, flat roofs of the buildings were lined with balustrades and urns for decoration.

In stark contrast to the English residences, tiny mud huts with woven grass roofs butted up against them on every side. These were the homes of the countless servants who waited on the wealthy British. Hundreds of people and livestock thronged the streets, and Katherine was again amazed at the eclectic masses that swarmed around them.

After traveling in silence for ten minutes, the gentleman seated across from Katherine cleared his throat. "Miss Greenwood, my sister informed me that you are unfamiliar with the area and therefore with the plantation for which we are bound. Would you like me to tell you about it?"

Katherine smiled, grateful for his offer. "Yes, sir. I would very much like to know what my new home is like."

"Please, call me Wilson," he said, smiling at her. "That is what the majority of the household calls me." She nodded. "We are one of the oldest indigo plantations in the province, albeit one of the smallest. The plantation amounts to roughly 2000 acres, all of which we own and cultivate ourselves. We employ 250 laborers and contract with two factories in Bengal. Most of our workers are natives, including the majority of the household staff. Besides myself and the cook, you will be the only European we employ."

Katherine reared back, surprised at this news. Wilson went on without a pause. "You will be employed as a maid-of-all-work. The restrictions imposed by the Hindu caste system make it difficult to maintain a small household staff, and it will be most helpful having a servant in the home who can handle any task put before her. Though the cook may require your services at times, you will report to me."

"Is there no housekeeper?" Katherine blurted. She flushed. "I beg your pardon," she murmured, "please, continue."

Her companion studied her. "No, Miss Greenwood, we have no housekeeper. The plantation, as I said, is small, and the house is even smaller. It is my responsibility to run them both."

"Of course."

Wilson cleared his throat. "You will sleep with the other servants in their quarters off the kitchen, and you will have every second Tuesday off, at which time your wages will also be paid." He paused. "Do you have any questions?"

Katherine smiled to disguise her uneasiness. She was suddenly very much afraid. What if she was unable to perform her duties as expected? Would she be dismissed? What then?

She swallowed the fear that threatened to erupt in a sob. "No, I believe you have answered them all. Thank you for explaining things to me. And thank you for accepting my services." She choked out the last sentence with difficulty and dropped her eyes to her lap, where her hands were clasped so tightly together her knuckles were white.

A look of surprise flashed across Wilson's face, followed by one of curious concern. "Of course. But accepting your services was simply a matter of business. Our household has been understaffed for some time, and my sister's note came at a most opportune time. I had already planned to travel to town this week in order to secure additional help."

He watched her thoughtfully, an unspoken question on his lips, but as she did not look up nor continue the conversation, he let it slip away. The rest of their journey passed in silence.

Chapter 6

It took them an hour to reach the plantation, and Katherine did her best to enjoy the ride. She had never been outside of England, and everything was new to her. The sky was bluer, the vegetation greener, the air hotter. Katherine drank in the sights that rolled past the carriage window with hungry eyes. She had dreamed of India since she was a child, and she could hardly believe she was actually here.

The plantation lay southeast of Calcutta, and therefore she saw much of the city before the crowded streets gave way to rolling fields dotted with teak and mahogany trees. The subtropical landscape was lush and green, and every once in awhile a flash of color from some exotic plant or flower would come into view. Katherine had never seen any place more beautiful in her life. Scatterings of small huts lined the road intermittently, and Katherine leaned towards the window with eager curiosity as they approached one such dwelling. They passed several natives, and although the carriage drove by before she could get a good look at them, Katherine noted their dark skin in heavy contrast with the lightweight robes draped around their bodies. A group of small children ran out of a hut, and she drew back, shocked to see that they wore nothing. She blushed and averted her eyes. India was certainly very different from England.

Soon the trees began to gather more closely together, and Wilson sat forward in his seat with an air of expectancy. Katherine saw this, and the fear that had temporarily subsided came back in full force. She watched out the carriage window for some sign of the plantation, and was soon rewarded with a pleasant yet unexpected view.

Whatever opinion or idea Katherine had formed in her mind of what the estate would look like, it was nothing compared to what lay before her. The bungalow style house was a long, low building surrounded by high trees and low-lying bushes. A deep portico supported by dozens of smooth, white columns stretched across the entire front of the building. High, arched doors and windows opened directly onto the porch from the rooms within, and the large overhanging roof was thatched with reeds and grasses. Katherine was at first surprised and then delighted. While nearly completely lacking in English style and design, the house so perfectly fit into its surroundings that Katherine at once felt it was how she had always pictured it to be. Pulling up to the front, a native servant came out of the house and opened the carriage door for them. Katherine alighted first, followed by Wilson.

"This way, if you please, Miss Greenwood," Wilson said.

He led Katherine into the parlor and invited her to sit down. Katherine became more nervous and fearful every moment, and she clasped her hands in her lap to keep them from trembling. Wilson noted all this with another look of bewilderment but said nothing. He rang the bell, and a young girl about fourteen years of age answered the summons. Wilson rattled off a string of words in Hindustani, and the girl bowed, leaving the room. Presently she returned bearing a tray of tea and some biscuits, for Katherine and her companion.

Wilson spoke hardly a word to her, and every time Katherine glanced at him, she noticed that he was watching her with a curious look in his eyes. She drank her tea and ate her food mechanically, her anxiety growing with every passing moment.

"What are you doing, Miss Greenwood?" he suddenly asked.

Katherine was so surprised to hear him speak after such a long and thorough silence she nearly choked. Coughing, she searched her mind for an answer, but he continued.

"You are clearly not a servant. It is evident you never were one. Your tone, your address, your very countenance speaks gentility. If you are indeed a lady of birth, and I do not doubt that you are, I am at a loss to understand what has led you to masquerade as hired help."

He paused, and Katherine looked anxiously up at him. He set his teacup down, a look of serious concern on his face. "I am afraid, Miss Greenwood, that I have no employment to offer you unless you can explain to me the nature of your circumstances."

Katherine's heart sank. She looked across at the older man and tried vainly to keep her voice from trembling. "Please, is there nothing I can do? I will do anything." Her voice was quiet in her desperation, and for a moment Wilson did not speak.

"Miss Greenwood, unless you can tell me why you came to India and what it is you intend to do here, I am afraid there is nothing I can do for you," he repeated.

His voice was gentle, and when she looked at his face she saw only concern and bewilderment. Katherine suddenly realized that he looked very much like his sister, Elizabeth Jones. The memory of her friend gave her courage, as well as faith in the man sitting opposite her. If Elizabeth trusted him, could she not as well? She took a deep breath and clasped her hands together.

"I... I am not sure where to begin," she hesitated.

Her companion relaxed. "Why not start at the beginning? Where were you born? Who are your parents?"

Katherine stared nervously at her hands. She glanced up at Wilson, who smiled his encouragement. She took another deep breath.

"I was born in Somerset, England, in 1814. My father was the youngest son of the Earl of Rockwell, and my mother was the daughter of a wealthy merchant from Bath. ... "

By the time Katherine had finished her history, the sun was low in the sky. She sat in silence, staring out the large french doors that led outside as she waited for Wilson to speak. He had been silent during the whole of her explanation; the only indication that he heard her was the slight lowering of his brow at certain points. Finally Katherine turned to face him. Telling her tale had completely drained her. She had been living from moment to moment for so long, not knowing her fate from one day to the next, and she was exhausted. She was tired of trying to sort out where her life was going and what her future would be, and for a moment she wished that the last three years had simply been a bad dream; that she would shortly awaken and find herself amidst the velvet curtains and rich tapestries of her grandmother's house.

Finally Wilson spoke, breaking her reverie. "I see that you have had a difficult time of it, Miss Greenwood. Far more difficult than I could have imagined." He paused, thoughtful. Katherine watched him nervously, but he was not silent for long. Presently he turned to her with a smile.

"I believe I may have a solution for the unfortunate position in which you now find yourself," he said. "Master Mendenhall is away on business at present, but his sister is at home, and I feel quite certain that she would be happy to entertain you here as her guest for a time."

Katherine blinked. "Oh, I could not possibly impose on Miss Mendenhall—why, she does not know me at all!" She flushed. "I am well aware of the precarious nature of my circumstances, but there is no need to trouble Miss Mendenhall about them. I am quite sure she will not wish to have me."

"And I am quite sure that she will," he countered, with a twinkle in his eye. "Please excuse me for a moment." He stood and left the room before Katherine could protest further, leaving her embarrassed and anxious and more nervous than before.

After twenty minutes Katherine could sit still no longer. She stood and paced in front of the portico while she awaited his return. The sun was setting, and the sky had paled from the brilliant cerulean of the afternoon to a soft, muted blue that blended seamlessly into the gold and crimson sunset on the horizon. Katherine heard the door open behind her and she turned, her stomach fluttering.

Wilson held the door open as a young lady about Katherine's age stepped into the room. She was very pretty, with chestnut hair piled in elaborate loops and curls on top of her head. She had a heart-shaped face and a little pointed nose that turned up at the tip, and that, combined with the scattering of freckles across the bridge, gave her a jolly, impish appearance. She had large blue eyes and creamy pink skin, and her figure was fine. She smiled warmly at Katherine, revealing a row of even white teeth. Her appearance and air were overall so friendly, so welcoming, that the knot in Katherine's stomach eased significantly, enough to allow a smile in return. The young lady held out her hands to Katherine as she approached, and the latter took them timidly.

"My dear Miss Greenwood! How delighted I am to make your acquaintance." Her eyes crinkled at the corners when she smiled, and Katherine felt herself relax.

"How do you do, Miss Mendenhall?" Katherine bobbed a curtsy but her hostess waved her off.

"Please, call me Sarah. We are going to be such friends, you and I, I am sure of it!" She led Katherine over to the sofa as Wilson retired, shutting the door behind him.

Katherine was still a bit nervous as she sat down, but Sarah either did not notice or did not care. She spoke to Katherine as if she had known her all her life. "Wilson has told me everything. He is *such* a dear man, and he did right in coming to me, for of course you must stay here." Her face suddenly took on a tragic air. "I have been languishing of boredom for weeks, but now that you are here we shall have such merry times. Wilson said you are new to India, is this true?"

"Yes, I have just arrived."

"And what do you think of it?"

Katherine smiled. "I am not sure. I have not seen much of the country yet, but from what I can tell it looks very interesting."

Sarah pursed her lips and looked thoughtful. "Yes, India is very interesting, I suppose. But I think I would rather be in London. Oh, how I long to see it!" She gave a sentimental little sigh, and Katherine smiled in spite of her surprise.

"You have never seen London?"

"No, I was born here in India. My brother Charles promises that he shall take me to London someday, but he has not had the time. He is always so busy with business, you see." There was a hint of pride but also a little sadness in her voice, and Katherine suspected that despite the nonchalance with which she spoke, Sarah felt the sting of her brother's inattention. Katherine wondered what sort of man he was. Judging from what Sarah had said, she gathered that he spent much of his time working.

Sarah stood and beckoned for Katherine to follow her. "Come, let me show you to your room."

Katherine started to object. "You are very kind to let me stay, but I do not want to impose."

"Tsh! It is no trouble at all. Did I not tell you I was pining for company? You are an answer to prayer and I insist that you stay with me." She smiled warmly at Katherine. "I shall tell you all about India and you shall tell me all about London and we shall get along splendidly."

Katherine laughed. There was something so sweet and likable about Sarah that she could not help it. Her new friend slipped an arm around her waist and the two of them walked out of the room together.

Chapter 7

Sunlight was just beginning to peek into her room when Katherine awoke the next morning. She yawned and stretched her arms, thinking over the dream from which she had awoken. It was a memory, really, one she had not thought of for many years. It recalled an instance from her childhood when she first heard about the land in which she now found herself.

She was very young, only five or six years old, and her grandmother was having tea with a friend who had just arrived from India. Katherine had crept into the room undetected and was hiding behind the thick velvet curtains at one of the windows, listening to their conversation. Lady Rockwell and her friend were discussing the Indian tea plantation in Serampore where her friend's son lived. Fascinating words like "Bombay" and "elephants" fell on Katherine's ears as she stood listening, entranced, until the tête-à-tête concluded and her grandmother and guest departed. Katherine awoke at this point, and her memories swirled and mingled with her thoughts of the preceding day.

She and Sarah had spent the prior evening getting further acquainted, and Katherine liked her new friend very much. Having spent little time with anyone her own age while growing up, Katherine was of a more sober mind and reflective nature, but Sarah was all bubble and charm; she loved everyone and everyone loved her. She reminded Katherine very much of a young sparrow—chirping and hopping about in happy excitement, but flitting from one thought to the next in an instant.

Katherine smiled as she nestled further into the linen bedding. She had not slept in a real bed in years, and she reveled in the luxury. Rolling over, she was surprised to see a new gown laid out for her on a chair near the foot of the bed. She climbed out of bed and went to examine it. A small envelope addressed to her lay on the nearby writing desk, and Katherine picked it up, reading the short note inside.

My dearest Katherine,

I hope you will forgive me for taking the liberty of having a gown brought in for you. I know you expressed a desire to have some dresses made, but until that can be arranged, please accept this one as a gift from

Your devoted friend,
Sarah

Katherine fingered the smooth folds of the light blue fabric and smiled. The gift spoke volumes about Sarah's generous nature, and Katherine was grateful to have made such a friend.

She slipped into the dress and smoothed her hair in the glass. Sarah had been appalled to learn that Katherine had been dressing herself and fixing her own hair for the last two years. She insisted on assigning one of their servants to Katherine as her personal maid while she was a guest in their home, but since the young lady was not present at the moment and breakfast would not be served for another hour at least, Katherine decided to have a look around.

Her room was at the end of the hallway on the west side of the house. Next to the door was a large wooden wardrobe, and beside it a cabinet containing a few books and curios. Directly across from this, a set of arched wooden doors opened onto the portico that stretched the entire length of the front of the house. Between these two walls stood the large four-poster bed, and at its foot a small campaign desk was tucked against the wall. A wood and rattan chair where the gown had been laid completed the furnishings. It was a small but comfortable room, and the white walls and high ceiling gave it a large, airy feel.

Katherine walked over to the curio cabinet and opened the glass door. A tiny carving of an elephant sat atop a low pile of books, and Katherine picked it up. She turned the cool, creamy ivory over in her hands, admiring the detail. Setting it down, she picked up the top book, *The Swiss Family Robinson.* A smile broke over her face, for it was one of her favorites. She took the book and went out onto the covered porch, seating herself in one of the large wicker chairs. Opening the cover, she read the first line: *The tempest had raged for six days, and on the seventh seemed to increase.* How she had thrilled to those words as a child! Such adventure and excitement! She thought of the adventure in which she now found herself, and wondered what other twists and turns her life would take while in India.

A soft knock on the bedroom door behind her caused Katherine to turn. A Hindu girl about fourteen years of age and wrapped in pale robes entered the room. Katherine recognized her as the girl who had served her tea on her arrival. She arose and went to greet her.

"Good morning, you must be…?"

"Bhavani," the girl said, smiling timidly.

Katherine smiled. "I am very pleased to meet you, Bhavani. That is a very pretty name."

The girl stared back at her, smiling mutely. Katherine tipped her head.

"Do you understand what I am saying?" she asked. Again, the girl simply stared at her. Katherine frowned. How was she supposed to communicate with her? She thought for a moment, then sat down in the chair beside the desk, facing the girl.

"Bhavani," she said, pointing to her. Katherine then laid a hand on her own chest. "Miss Greenwood," she said with a smile.

The girl shook her head. "*Memsahib*," she said. Katherine raised her eyebrows.

"Memsahib?" she asked, pointing to herself.

The girl nodded emphatically. "Memsahib," she said again.

"Very well. I suppose I shall be Memsahib," Katherine said with amusement. The girl smiled and asked a question in her native tongue, pointing to Katherine's head. Katherine nodded.

"Yes, thank you, I would like some help with my hair."

Thirty minutes later, Katherine was shown into the dining room for breakfast. The double doors across from her were opened onto a large covered patio facing the rear of the plantation, and Katherine was delighted to see they would be dining al fresco. Sarah sat at the table and smiled as Katherine joined her.

"Good morning, Katherine! I hope you slept well?"

Katherine smiled. "Yes, thank you. It is a bit warmer in India than I expected, but I was quite comfortable."

"You will grow accustomed to the heat. And how becoming that gown looks on you! I was sure that shade of blue would look lovely against your dark hair, and I was right." She smiled in self satisfaction and waved off Katherine's thanks. "Now, would you care to join me for some breakfast?"

Two native servants arrived carrying silver trays heaped with fruit and freshly baked scones, which they set in the center of the table. Dishes of churned butter, preserves, and sweetmeats surrounded them. Katherine's mouth watered as she looked at the tantalizing spread.

A mischievous grin spread across Sarah's face as she poured tea for Katherine and herself. "I confess, I asked Cook to make an extra special meal for your first morning here. Most days we just have tea and toast."

"Tea and biscuits are perfectly fine with me," Katherine declared, generously spreading a scone with butter and preserves. "Although I would not say no to a breakfast like this on occasion."

"Are you pleased with your room?" Sarah asked anxiously.

"Very much."

"And Bhavani?"

Katherine hesitated. "She seems very nice, but how am I to

communicate with her? I do not think she knows any English."

"Oh no, the servants here do not speak any English," Sarah said nonchalantly. Katherine stared at her.

"How do you communicate with them?" she asked incredulously.

Sarah laughed. "They know what to do. And Wilson can speak to them—he is usually the one to handle them anyways. But I will teach you a few words of Hindustani to help things along."

"Bhavani called me *memsahib*. What does that mean?"

"It is a Hindu word meaning *great lady*, or something to that effect. It is a term of respect for the ladies of the house," Sarah explained.

"I see. So, you are the *memsahib* in the house?"

"Yes," Sarah beamed. "And now, you are as well!"

Once the meal was finished, Sarah asked if Katherine would like to be shown around the bungalow and the gardens near the house. Katherine eagerly accepted the invitation and Sarah called for an escort to accompany them. A tall Indian servant carrying a large gun joined them as they set off. Katherine glanced at the man out of the corner of her eye as he followed at a discreet distance behind them, and casually asked Sarah why she felt they needed an armed escort.

"Why, to protect us, of course."

"From what, pray?"

"Tigers," Sarah said matter-of-factly. Katherine gave a start.

"What! Do they hunt so close to the plantation as to warrant the need for protection?"

"Not usually," her friend replied. "But they are such

frightening creatures, and I do not wish to encounter one alone. Charles shot one several years ago; he uses the skin as a rug in his study, but I cannot abide to go in there and see it. They frighten me," she finished with a shiver.

They continued to converse as they walked. Sarah led Katherine down the patio steps and out onto the small lawn. The bungalow was surrounded nearly on all sides by large trees, which lent a great deal of shade to the house. Bright flowers burst forth from shrubs which were scattered across the grounds, and in the distance, dark brown fields of churned earth shimmered in the heat.

"Is it always this hot?" Katherine asked, wiping the perspiration beading on her neck with her handkerchief. Sarah laughed.

"No, more often it is even hotter. This is the hot, dry season, but soon it will be the hot, wet season, and *that*," she said with emphasis, "will be much worse."

"How do you bear it?" Katherine asked, incredulous.

"*Punkahs*."

"Pardon?"

Sarah laughed again. "*Punkahs*. See? There, on the portico."

They had come around the side of the house to the front lawn, and Katherine saw that Sarah was pointing to a long pole suspended from the ceiling, with a short length of fabric attached below it.

"It is like a giant fan," Sarah continued. "A servant pulls on the cord—there—and the *punkah* waves back and forth to allow for air flow. Although," she made a face, "sometimes it feels more like the bellows of a furnace than a refreshing breeze."

58

They continued across the lawn and entered through the front doors. It was only ten in the morning but already the air outside was stifling, and Katherine was glad to get in out of the immediate heat. Once inside, Sarah led her friend down the hall to the right. Though comfortable, the bungalow was not very large and the inside tour did not take long. Katherine had already seen the sitting room and dining room, and apart from those and the bedchambers, there was only a small study "where Charles conducts his business," and the library. Katherine gave a little gasp of delight when they entered the latter.

"Why, you have a pianoforte!"

Sarah looked pleased. "Yes, we do. Mother was very accomplished and she loved to play. She was so heartbroken at leaving her music behind in England, so Father bought a small instrument and had it brought out for her when they settled here. Do you play?"

"I used to," Katherine answered wistfully. "But it has been so long…" Her voice trailed off as she ran her hand gently over the polished wood. Sarah smiled.

"Well, let us see if you remember how. I should dearly love to hear how a proper concerto sounds."

Katherine needed no second bidding. She sat down at the instrument and put her hands on the smooth, white keys. She trembled slightly with excitement, but did not hesitate as she began to play. Voices and memories floated through her mind as the music swelled around her. Closing her eyes, she let her fingers remember the music she had learned so many years ago. She made a few mistakes, though she did not play for long. As the last notes of the song died away, she slowly opened her eyes, bringing her mind back from its wanderings. Sarah was watching her with bright, fascinated eyes.

"Oh Katherine, that was beautiful! I have often dreamed of what it must sound like, but I never imagined it to be so lovely as that."

Katherine was surprised. "Do you not play?"

Sarah sighed heavily. "Indeed, I wish I could say that I do. But I cannot. You see," she settled herself comfortably on a nearby chair, "Mother loved to play. Music was like air to her, and the house was always full of it. But when the cholera broke out..." Sarah's voice trailed off, and Katherine understood. After a moment, Sarah cleared her throat. "Father died as well. So did our brother, Edmund. Charles was eleven at the time, but I was just a baby, only three years old. I do not have any memories of my parents, but Charles remembers how much Mother loved to play, and it made him sad to hear the pianoforte. I begged him for lessons as I grew older, but he flatly refused. Sometimes I would come in here and attempt to play, but after awhile I stopped doing even that."

"Did it make your brother angry?" Katherine asked.

"No, for if it did I could have managed him. When Charles gets angry he blows up in one big fizz, but then he is as meek as a kitten and just as sweet afterward. No, Charles did not get angry, but it made him sad. He would come in and stare at me with such mournful, haunted eyes, and I could not bear to see the pain in them anymore." Sarah was quiet, and Katherine thought about on what she had said. After a moment, Sarah brightened.

"But now that you are here, we shall have music again! Oh, I knew you were sent to me for a reason!"

"Oh, but I couldn't!" Katherine cried, shock coloring her tone. "Not after what you just told me about your brother. He obviously does *not* want any music in this house, and as his guest I would not dream of causing him pain or discomfort."

"Nonsense," Sarah declared. "Charles is not even at home, and besides, you are not *his* guest, you are *my* guest. Charles did not like to hear me play, but I do not think he would mind hearing from someone who could actually make music. He used to love listening to Mother."

Katherine was not convinced, but Sarah seemed determined, so she let the matter drop. They explored the rest of the library, which, aside from the sitting room, was the largest room in the bungalow. Floor to ceiling bookshelves lined the walls, and Katherine read the titles with great interest.

"What a wonderful collection you have!" she said, pulling a well-worn volume from the shelf and examining its pages.

"Yes, our library is quite extensive," Sarah replied in a bored tone. Katherine looked at her, amused.

"You do not care for reading?"

Sarah made an impatient gesture. "Why should I? There is nothing more boring than sitting alone in a room with a book." Katherine laughed. Placing the book back on the shelf, she decided to come back another time, when she could peruse the titles at her leisure.

Having finished the tour, the ladies betook themselves to the sitting room, where they passed the remainder of the morning in happy conversation consisting of whether or not the current fashion for puffs and leg-of-mutton sleeves would last very long, and if the coming monsoon season would be a very terrible one.

Chapter 8

"Are you sure you do not wish to accompany me?" Sarah implored as she looked at her friend. Katherine smiled wanly, and Sarah pouted. "Oh, I know it is horrid of me to ask when your head aches so, but it is dreadfully lonely to ride to town by oneself. I never do so if I can help it."

The fortnight since Katherine's arrival had been a pleasant one, and the two of them had planned on driving into Calcutta that morning to do a bit of shopping, but Katherine awoke with a headache and had declined to go. Normally Sarah would have been content to stay at home and postpone their excursion, but since she was expecting a new fashion magazine and Katherine's dresses were due to be picked up, she was keen to make the trip into town, albeit by herself.

"Well, I suppose I shall still go. Besides," she brightened a bit, "perhaps your headache will be gone by the time I return and we can pour over *The World of Fashion* together."

She waved to her friend, assuring her that she would return in the afternoon, and set off in the carriage. When she had gone,

Katherine retired to her room to rest and nurse her aching head.

After an hour's repose, Katherine felt much better and determined to explore the library in greater depth. The house was quiet, and the library quieter still. She entered the stillness and breathed in the warm, dry air. The smell of dust and books filled her lungs, bringing a smile to her lips. Books had always been her friends, most especially because she had so few human counterparts growing up. She perused the shelves, not quite sure what she was looking for. She found a few familiar favorites, and far more that looked interesting, but nothing seemed to satisfy the longing within her. At last she faced the truth of her feelings: she did not want books, she wanted music.

The pianoforte stood nearly in the middle of the room, somewhat closer to the far wall and the large window there. Katherine crossed over to look at the view, gliding her hand along the smooth wood of the instrument as she passed. The window was partly obscured by a large tree, but beyond the trunk was a view of the distant indigo fields, where the tender young plants were just pushing up through the dark brown earth. Katherine admired the view only for a moment before turning to face the instrument behind her. Her heart was racing as she sat down in front of the keys. *Surely no one will mind if I play for a little while*, she thought. *Sarah is away, and who else is there but the servants?* She lovingly touched the ivory keys as she contemplated what songs she had committed to memory. Remembering one of her favorites, she placed her hands and began to play.

The lilting sounds of Franz Schubert's *Serenade* floated around her, the soft cadences almost haunting in their poignancy.

Katherine opened her heart, releasing the feelings that had been trapped inside of her for so long, her hands trembling with the effort to control their expulsion. She closed her eyes and gave herself up to the music, letting it wrap around her like a warm embrace. Katherine played with more feeling than she had ever played before, and as the final notes died away, a tear rolled down her cheek. She felt cleansed, and the hope that had begun to blossom in her heart grew to fill the empty space left by the fear that had been washed away. Placing her hands once more on the keys, she glanced up for a moment, and froze.

A man stood in the doorway, watching her.

He wore a dark blue coat that was tailored to accent his tall, lean frame. An abundance of chestnut hair covered his head, but his face was clean shaven. He had a strong jaw and a chiseled face, with gray-green eyes and a straight nose. He was very handsome, and had he been smiling he would have been handsomer still. He stood motionless, and Katherine held her breath as she waited for him to speak. But he remained silent, and every moment that passed seemed like an eternity. Finally Katherine stood, and her movement seemed to break a spell.

"Who are you?" he asked, his voice deep and quiet.

Katherine swallowed. "Katherine Greenwood, sir."

He did not answer; his eyes still trained on her face, his unsmiling lips still pressed in a line. Katherine trembled under his gaze, wishing the floor would open up and swallow her whole. Finally he spoke.

"And can you tell me, Miss Greenwood, how you came to be in my library, and playing my pianoforte?"

Katherine suddenly realized that Charles Mendenhall—for

she was sure of his identity the moment she saw him—had not the slightest idea who she was, nor that she was a guest in his home. Her face flushed crimson, and she clasped her hands in front of her.

"Oh, dear, I am so very sorry. Sarah is away–" She took a breath and tried to steady her nerves. "That is, Miss Mendenhall was so good as to invite me to stay, and I am sorry to discover that she did not inform you of the arrangement."

She twisted her hands together nervously, and the corner of his lips turned up in the hint of a smile, but the expression did not reach his eyes.

"Ah, yes, that certainly sounds like something Sarah would do." He clasped his hands behind him. "And my sister is away, is she?"

"Yes, she left this morning to go to town. She promised to be home this afternoon, and I had no idea of your returning today or I would have pressed her to stay."

"Of course." He studied her for a moment more, then took a step forward and gave her a somewhat forced smile. "Forgive me for my rude inquiries, but you caught me completely by surprise, and I momentarily forgot my manners. I am Charles Mendenhall," he said with a slight bow, "and I am pleased to make your acquaintance, Miss Greenwood."

"Thank you, sir," Katherine dropped into a curtsy, but knew not what else to say. Thankfully, Charles excused himself and she was able to escape to her room, where she hid in mortification until Sarah's return a few hours later.

Charles fled the library for the safety of his study. He took off his jacket and tossed it across a nearby chair, then sat down, troubled. He had been surprised—stunned, actually—when he arrived home and heard the sounds of the pianoforte floating through the air. There had not been real music in the house since his mother's death, and for a moment he was transported back in time, the pain and sorrow almost as real as the memories that flooded his mind. He knew that it could not be Sarah playing, and he half wondered if he might find the ghost of his mother sitting at the instrument she knew and loved so well. But as he stopped in the doorway to the library, he saw instead a young lady completely unknown to him. She was about his sister's age, but he could not recall having ever seen her before. She was beautiful, for one thing, and beautiful young Englishwomen were a rarity in India. No, he was sure he had never met her. And yet, as he watched her, he recognized something familiar. She played with great feeling, completely unaware that she was being watched, and the passion that flew from her fingertips bespoke a heart unleashed. *This girl has known fear, and loss, and heartache,* he thought. In a flash of pain he realized that this is what he recognized in her: another soul with as many wounds as his own.

He was still deep in thought when there was a knock at the door. When he did not answer, his steward opened the door and stepped inside, a liberty that few servants would take. But Wilson had always been like family, and Charles never bothered about ceremony with him.

"Master Mendenhall, I am glad to see you have arrived home safely."

"Hello, Wilson," Charles answered mechanically, not looking

at him.

"I am sorry I was not outside to greet you. The last word you sent indicated you would not be home until tomorrow or the day after." He waited, but Charles made no response. "Do you require any refreshment?"

Charles waved him off impatiently. "No, no, Wilson, I am well."

His steward watched him thoughtfully. "You do not seem well, sir."

Charles looked at him for the first time since the man had entered the room. Their eyes locked, and for a moment neither one spoke. Finally Charles sighed.

"What can you tell me about Miss Greenwood?" he asked, turning once more to look out the window. Wilson cleared his throat.

"She was invited to stay by Miss Mendenhall, and has been with us a fortnight, sir."

"She told me nearly as much herself. But who is she? Where did she come from? I have never seen her before; Sarah has never mentioned her to me."

"That is likely because Miss Mendenhall did not know Miss Greenwood herself before her arrival." Charles turned to him with a questioning glance. Wilson briefly explained how she had come to the plantation. "My sister, Mrs. Jones, recommended her to me, and personally vouched for her character. While she did not tell me the whole of Miss Greenwood's history, she indicated to me that she was a gentlewoman by birth who had fallen on hard times. I learned the rest from Miss Greenwood herself, after her arrival."

Charles looked thoughtful. "And my sister offered to let her stay?"

Wilson hesitated only for a moment. "I confess to have put the idea in her mind, sir. Once Miss Greenwood explained to me her situation, I related the events to Miss Mendenhall and suggested that she invite her to stay for a time. She is lonely when you are away, sir, and the two have become good friends."

Charles was nodding. "You did right, Wilson. That will be all, thank you." His steward inclined his head in acknowledgment and left the room.

Charles sat for a long time in his study. The encounter with Katherine had unnerved him, and he was not sure if he was more upset or intrigued by this new development. The more he contemplated the situation, the more uneasy he became. But what about Miss Greenwood made him uneasy? He was not entirely sure. Finally he drew a deep breath and stood. There was nothing to be done for it at the moment, and only time would tell what her presence at the plantation would mean for him.

"Oh Katherine, Charles is home!"

Sarah came bursting into Katherine's room with no other introduction than this. She was breathless in her excitement, and Katherine smiled wryly.

"Yes, I am well aware of that fact, you ninny. He came across me as I was playing the piano this morning, and I cannot tell you who was the more surprised between the two of us."

Sarah's eyes grew round and her tone serious. "You were

playing the piano?"

"Yes."

"And Charles heard you? He saw you?"

"Yes."

"And? What did he say? What did he do?"

Katherine contemplated their meeting. Even now, she could not quite fathom the look on his face. "He did not say or do anything. He just... looked."

Sarah let out an exasperated sigh. "Well, how did he look, then?"

"I am not sure," Katherine said slowly. "He stood very still, and he did not smile, but I do not think he was angry. It was almost as if he were looking through me," she finished with a shrug.

"But did he not speak to you?"

"Not at first. After awhile he asked who I was, and why I was here." She made a face at her friend. "I thought you would have sent word to him about that!"

Sarah waved her off. "Oh, Charles can never be bothered about things at home when he is away on business. Besides, I was not exactly sure where he was and I knew he would be returning soon, so I did not bother."

Katherine frowned at her. "You could have warned me that he might be coming home today."

Sarah laughed. "I did not know any more than you did! But the facts remain that he is home now, and he has heard you play, and he was not angry." Sarah pondered all this, tapping a dainty finger against her chin. "I wonder if he would mind if you played for us in the evenings?" she mused.

Katherine looked stern. "Whether he minds or not is not the question. *I* certainly do not expect to play for him again anytime soon, of *that* I can assure you."

Sarah shrugged, then jumped into a relation of the events that transpired while she was in town, the principle of which was the acquirement of Katherine's gowns and an encounter with several of the regimental officers. Katherine smiled at her friend, and gladly set aside the events of her own morning. But as she dressed for dinner later, the look on Charles's face haunted her mind. She struggled to define what she had seen in his eyes. It was not anger, of that she was almost certain, but whether it was more a look of longing or one of sadness she could not decide. *Well, I shall see him again soon enough,* she thought. *I wonder how he will look tonight?*

She did not have to wonder long. When Katherine entered the sitting room a short while later, he was standing in front of the patio doors conversing with his sister. At her approach they both turned, and Sarah walked forward to greet her friend.

"Here she is! Katherine dear, this is my brother, Charles Mendenhall."

Charles bowed slightly, his expression friendly but guarded. "Yes, I believe we had the pleasure of meeting earlier, did we not, Miss Greenwood?"

"Yes, indeed. How do you do, sir?" Katherine curtsied, trying not to look as nervous as she felt.

"I am well, thank you," he replied, studying her face. Katherine turned to Sarah, who was chattering about something, but when she glanced back at Charles she found that he was still watching her. She blushed. He did not look as stern as he had that afternoon, but Katherine could tell he was nearly as disconcerted as she was. She was searching her mind for something to say should he speak to her again, but dinner was announced, and she had not the opportunity.

With a well-laid table before them, the party seemed to relax a bit. Sarah and Charles were obviously very close, and Katherine watched them throughout the meal with amusement. Their hair was the same rich brown, and something about the shape of their eyes bespoke familiarity, but otherwise they did not bear much resemblance to one another. Their personalities were vastly different as well: Sarah chattered and scolded and laughed continuously, as bubbly and swift as a brook. Charles, on the other hand, was more temperate in his conversation and address. He smiled and laughed by degrees, but his overall manner was steady and constant, more like a deep-flowing river. Katherine found herself studying him throughout the meal. His eyes were greener than she originally thought, and when he smiled the right side of his mouth rose up a bit higher than the left, and the slightly crooked result gave him a somewhat rakish appearance. He was certainly the most handsome man Katherine had ever encountered, and she flushed with embarrassment every time he caught her looking at him.

Charles was equally as interested in watching Katherine as she was in watching him, but with their earlier meeting still fresh in his mind, he was hesitant to engage her in conversation, lest she unsettle his nerves once more. But despite his best efforts, his eyes were continually drawn to where she sat, quiet and observant, and his opinion of her beauty rose considerably. He had noticed enough in the library to ascertain that she was very pretty, but his senses had been in such a muddle that he hardly registered anything beyond that. Through his guarded glances over dinner he noted the smoothness of her skin and the gentleness of her smile, and the blush on her cheek when their eyes met lent a lovely color to her creamy complexion.

After the meal the trio retired to the sitting room, and Sarah turned her attentions to Katherine. "You were very quiet at dinner, my dear."

Katherine laughed lightly. "That is because you and your brother had enough to say for all of us."

Charles chuckled. "Oh no, do not lump me together with that chatterbox! I was merely deflecting her attacks." He was far more relaxed than he had hitherto been, and his eyes danced merrily as he gazed fondly at his sister, who swatted him playfully on the arm.

"Well, we cannot all be silent and stone-faced. Besides, how do you expect me *not* to talk once you are finally home to talk *with?*"

"You were not alone for long this time, I gather," Charles replied, with a meaningful look at Katherine.

"Indeed not," Sarah cried happily. "Katherine was an answer to prayer." She smiled fondly at her friend, then turned a teasing glance at her brother. "In fact, she has been such a delightful companion that I did not even miss you."

Charles laughed, and settled himself more comfortably in his chair. His voice and manners were easy and relaxed as they conversed, but whenever his gaze fell upon Katherine, the façade slipped and the same haunted look from the library filled his eyes. She was surprised to note how often his eyes were turned on her, but she was equally conscious of how frequently her own eyes were drawn towards him, almost against her will. The fact that he caught her gazing at him on more than one occasion kept her in a constant state of embarrassment.

Sarah had exhausted nearly every subject appropriate to the situation when she suddenly turned to her friend. "Katherine dearest, do go in and play for us. I am absolutely bursting with anticipation to hear you again."

If she had thrown a bucket of water on her companions, their reactions would have been scarcely less astounding. Charles sat bolt upright, the color draining from his face. Katherine was so shocked at Sarah's sudden declaration she actually dropped her teacup, which bounced off the saucer she held in her hand and dumped its contents onto the rug at her feet. Sarah had obviously expected their reactions; she sat and smiled benignly as if nothing had happened.

Charles had recovered somewhat by the time Katherine retrieved her now empty teacup and a servant had been summoned to clean up the mess. But although his color had returned, his face was stone and he sat rigidly in his chair. Katherine stole a sideways glance at him before responding to Sarah's request.

"I am afraid I am not quite disposed to play at present," she said.

Sarah pressed again. "Why not? You play so beautifully. Does she not, Charles?"

Katherine's eyes darted to his face, and though she saw a muscle in his locked jaw flicker, he responded with nothing other than a quiet, "Indeed."

Katherine stared at him, recognizing the expression he had worn earlier in the day. Alone in her room, she had struggled to decide whether his look held more sadness or longing, but seeing it again now she knew that neither emotion was the most dominant. It was clearly neither sadness for the past, nor longing for the familiar that warred within their emerald depths. It was pain—clean, raw, undiluted pain—and she had no desire to deepen the wound she saw there. She turned to Sarah with a firmness in her mind and heart she was unaccustomed to feeling.

"No, Sarah. I will not play the pianoforte."

Her friend looked surprised, and glanced at her brother, who remained mute and immovable. Sarah shrugged, and began to chatter about something else entirely. But the serenity of the evening had been shattered, and Katherine soon afterward excused herself for the night. As she left the room, she stole a glance in Charles's direction and found him looking at her. His face was still stern, his lips unsmiling, but in his eyes she saw an unexpected change, and a new emotion filled them.

Gratitude.

Chapter 9

If Charles said anything to Sarah about her behavior or their conversation, Katherine never knew of it. All she knew was that in the days following, no talk of music or the pianoforte arose in any conversation. She and Sarah went for walks and carriage rides, they talked and sewed, and Katherine was even sent to the library to choose a book for them to read aloud, but never once did Sarah suggest that she play, and Katherine did not ask, however deeply she longed for it herself.

In the days following that first evening together, Charles avoided Katherine and his sister almost completely. He confined himself to his study almost from sunrise to sunset, and he took his meals alone. Whether this was really due to his having "much business to attend to" as Sarah rationalized, was unknown, but Katherine suspected that it was as much to avoid any possibility of another such disastrous meeting. She was surprised to find herself thinking of her absent host often, and comparing the stiff, brooding man she had initially encountered with the handsome, amicable brother who joined them for dinner. She wondered at the drastic differences between the two men, and wished she could unravel the mystery behind them.

As time passed, Charles slowly began to join them again. At first it was only for dinner. He would arrive just as the meal was announced, and disappear into his study the moment it concluded. But soon he was meeting with them before the meal as well, and as his displeasure wore off, his amiability began to show once more. In time he was almost as lively a companion as his sister. Katherine found pleasure in his company, and grew fond of the friendly banter and easy laughter he brought to the sitting room. His manners and address were always pleasant; he still laughed and smiled and quizzed his sister, and towards Katherine he showed nothing but a growing regard. But she often caught him glancing at her with that same unfathomable look in his eyes, and she wondered what it meant.

One evening after dinner, Sarah suggested a game of cards. Katherine readily agreed, and Charles good-naturedly joined them. A servant was summoned to set up the card table, and the game of Speculation was decided upon.

"I confess to be somewhat rusty," Katherine acknowledged with a smile. "Grandmother always preferred Cribbage."

"Then I shall be sure to take advantage of your inexperience," Charles said, flashing his crooked smile. Katherine laughed.

"You will do nothing of the sort," Sarah commanded, slapping his arm playfully. "What atrocious manners," she mumbled, looking over her cards.

"What other sorts of things did your grandmother prefer?" Charles asked, beginning the round.

"The country, for one thing. Grandmother detested town life, and consequently we never went to London for the season. We stayed at home, where it was quiet and comfortable."

"And where is home?"

"In Leicestershire. I was raised there, on my grandmother's estate."

"And do you feel the same as your grandmother about London?"

"Of course not," Sarah interjected. "Why on earth would she prefer the country to London?"

Charles laughed. "Not everyone has the same taste in society as you do, my dear sister." He turned to Katherine. "Am I correct?"

Katherine smiled. "Yes, indeed. London is a bit too busy for my taste. Strangers make me nervous, and the city is so loud and dirty. I much prefer the countryside."

Charles was nodding. "I feel precisely the same way," he said. "My sister has been begging me for years to purchase a fashionable home on Esplanade Row. But I prefer to stay here on the plantation."

"Have you never lived anywhere else?"

"Never."

"Then it is only natural you would wish to stay. All that you love, or have ever loved, is here," Katherine observed.

The familiar uneasiness stole over him as Charles looked at Katherine. The quiet, gentle girl before him had a way of unraveling his defenses and seeing directly into his heart, wounds and all. Part of him resented the intrusion—the knowing look which he sometimes saw on her face, and the feeling of vulnerability that came with her discernment. But a growing part of him almost looked for opportunities to be vulnerable, to connect with the mahogany-haired beauty at his side. Charles had rarely felt such understanding from another person, and the experience both gratified and unnerved him.

"Yes, quite," he said at length, suddenly busy with his cards. "Sarah, I want that queen—what will you sell her for?"

The round continued and each led by turns, although Katherine generally lagged behind. When they had tired of the game, they went outside to sit in the cooler night air. Katherine looked out across the lawn, to the distant fields where the young indigo plants grew. Moonlight glinted off the glossy young leaves like thousands of tiny stars. She sighed.

"All my life I have dreamed of India," she said quietly. "I still cannot believe I am actually here."

"I do not understand how you can prefer all this," Sarah waved vaguely at the land around them, "to the sights and sounds of London."

Katherine's smile faded. "There are some sights and sounds I should be glad never to see nor hear again," she murmured, wrapping her arms around herself. Sarah was instantly contrite.

"Oh Katherine, I am so sorry. That was a careless comment and I apologize. Of course you would wish to escape your stepfather's house." She shivered, though the night was warm. "I cannot imagine the horrors you endured."

Katherine shifted uncomfortably in her seat, obviously desirous of changing the subject. Charles cleared his throat.

"What about India fascinates you so?" he asked.

Katherine turned gratefully towards him, and her eyes lit up. "Why, everything! The people, the architecture, the climate–"

Sarah interrupted. "How can you possibly enjoy this abominable heat?"

Katherine laughed. "I am sure that I will tire of it soon enough. But at present, everything is so new, so different from what I have been accustomed to, that it is all magnificent to me."

Charles regarded her thoughtfully. "India is certainly an intriguing place. I have lived here all my life and still find beauty and wonder in the land around me."

"How fortunate to have been raised in such a paradise," Katherine mused. Charles laughed.

"Not everything is wonderful," he said with amusement. "I could live without the bugs, for one matter, and for another, the heat and humidity *do* get rather tiresome."

"But surely the splendors of India far outweigh the inconveniences…?" Katherine's voice trailed off, and she looked from brother to sister expectantly, hoping to receive encouragement. Sarah looked at her doubtfully, but she was satisfied in Charles.

"Indeed. There are few things I have seen or heard of to rival the history and magnificence of the great Moghul empire. The polished marble of Taj Mahal and the rock temples near Bombay are incredible to behold. The land itself is amazing as well, from the great Sundarbans along the coast to the massive Himalayas in the north; it is a land full of beauty and mystery, one that I am proud to call my home."

Katherine felt something stir within her as she listened to him speak. His portrayal of India spoke to her heart in exactly the same manner as her grandmother's descriptions always had, and she knew that Charles, at least, could understand the growing love she felt for the country. She had never known the value of a friend who thought and felt as she did, who understood her heart and her fascination with the land in which she now held residence. It was a comforting feeling, and she smiled shyly at him.

"I do not understand either one of you," Sarah mumbled. They laughed, and the comfortable silence that followed bore testimony to the deepening friendships between them.

Chapter 10

A month had passed, and Katherine was now quite settled at the plantation, and quite intimate with her new friends. She had once mentioned to Sarah that she would like to begin her pursuit for employment, but Sarah had been so shocked and feigned offense so greatly that Katherine did not dare bring it up again. To be perfectly frank, Katherine felt more at home in the cozy bungalow than she had anywhere else—excepting her grandmother's house—and she was in no hurry to leave it. She decided that so long as her friends wished her to stay, she would remain indefinitely. Her future in India could wait.

One afternoon, Katherine found herself alone in the sitting room. The air inside the bungalow was heavy and hot, and while it at least offered protection from the glaring sun, it was stifling nonetheless. In addition to the one on the portico, each of the communal rooms within the house had a wide *punkah* suspended from the ceiling to allow for air movement, but there was not a servant employed in waving it at the moment. Katherine walked through the open sitting room doors onto the covered patio, hoping for a breeze to cool her perspiring brow. She leaned against one of the smooth columns and gazed out at the flowering indigo fields, now hazy with pink blossoms.

"Is it not beautiful?"

Katherine turned to see Charles standing in the doorway behind her. She smiled and turned her face back to the view before them.

"Yes, it is. India holds far more beauty than I ever imagined."

He came and stood beside her, gazing out across his plantation with a softness in his eyes. " 'I could be content to see no other verdure than its own,' " he quoted softly. Katherine laughed.

"I believe Mr. Keats was speaking of England, sir," she teased gently. Charles laughed, and turned to face her. He smiled into her eyes, and Katherine's heart gave a funny little jump.

"Yes, he was. But his words are still true for my application of them."

They were silent for a time as they looked at the beauty around them, each lost in their own thoughts, each wondering what the other was thinking of. The early afternoon sun slanted across the lawn, and the distant fields shimmered and danced in the heat waves that rose off the earth.

"Katherine, I feel as though I owe you an explanation." She turned to face him, and found a shadow of the same haunted look lurking in the back of his eyes. But it did not fill his gaze nor his mood completely, as it had those times before. He looked at her intently, and for once Katherine did not blush, nor did she look away. She felt a connection with the tall, handsome man beside her, and the thought both thrilled and frightened her at the same time.

"When we first met, that morning in the library, I am sure you thought I was possessed." He turned his gaze to the growing fields, and Katherine waited patiently for him to continue. When he did, he kept his eyes trained on the distant horizon. "I suppose I was, in a way," he said quietly. He looked at her. "Has Sarah told you about our mother?"

Katherine nodded.

"What has she told you?"

"That she was very fond of music, and played the pianoforte beautifully. And that she died." Katherine's voice was soft, and Charles smiled sadly.

"No, she was not *very fond* of music—she *lived* for music. I cannot remember a day of her life when she was not singing or playing. And yes, she played the piano very well. It was almost an extension of her soul. When she played," he turned and looked out over the view, struggling for words. "When she played," he said more slowly, "it was as if her spirit left her body and became a part of the music in the air. Whenever I heard the sounds of the piano, I was not hearing individual notes and melodies—I was hearing *her.*"

He continued to gaze out across the hills, and Katherine turned her thoughts to that morning in the library. She recalled the feeling of freedom, the release she had felt in letting her heart flow through the music, and she thought she understood how his mother must have felt.

He turned, and Katherine looked up into his face. Pain, sorrow, loss, fear; a dozen emotions fought for dominance in his eyes. But it was wonder—and again, gratitude—that won out and shone down upon her. When he spoke, his voice was husky with emotion. "When I heard you playing that day, I thought I heard my mother. And hearing her was something I had never expected to experience again."

Katherine did not know what to say. Suddenly embarrassed, she turned her face from his gaze. He continued to watch her, but it was some minutes before he spoke again.

"Tell me about your mother."

Katherine looked back at him, surprised at this turn in the conversation. "I do not know what to tell you of her," she hesitated.

"Was she never a part of your life?"

Katherine was silent, sifting through the swirling mass of emotions his question elicited. "I have no early memories of my mother," she finally replied, speaking slowly. "My grandmother did not approve of my parents' marriage, and though she never spoke ill of my mother, I knew she did not have a high opinion of her. During all the time I lived with my grandmother, my mother never wrote to me; she never visited; she never seemed to care."

She glanced up and saw Charles watching her intently, a look of sympathy in his soft eyes. She continued quickly, trying to smile.

"I did not mind. My grandmother had been my guardian for as long as I could remember, and I am convinced that she loved me as greatly as any mother ever loved a child." Her smile faded. "The first time I remember seeing my mother was when she and Mr. Fletcher came to take me away with them. She was young and pretty, and I believe she tried to be kind, but she was more interested in her new husband than in the daughter she barely knew. Even when things became difficult..." Her voice trailed off into silence. Charles waited patiently for her to continue.

After several minutes Katherine cleared her throat. "There were times when she tried to intervene. But for the most part, she stood silently by and watched." A spasm of pain flashed across her face, and Charles drew a breath, his own heart aching at the sight. Her large brown eyes filled with tears, and she looked up at him, pleading.

"Can I be blamed for not loving her?"

"Of course not," he answered quickly, but she sighed.

"I know I am wicked to say so. But I do not miss her at all. All of my affection was bestowed upon my grandmother. It is for her that my heart breaks."

"Tell me about her," Charles said gently.

"I love her more than anyone in this world," Katherine responded quietly. "She is brave and kind and affectionate. She loves beauty; art and music fill her world, and she taught me to love it as well." Her eyes filled with tears again.

"You miss her."

It was not a question. Katherine nodded, not trusting her voice, and the movement caused a tear to overflow and run swiftly down her cheek. She reached up and brushed it quickly away, painfully aware that Charles was watching her. She forced a smile that she did not feel and turned to look at him. His gaze rested on her face as gently as a caress, and she blushed. He smiled softly at her.

"I would be honored if you would play for us this evening, Katherine."

Katherine searched his face for a long time before she

answered. Whatever she saw there must have satisfied her, for she nodded her head in mute reply. Charles smiled at her again, then bowed his head and returned to the house.

Dinner that evening was a gay affair. Sarah had been discussing the menu with Cook earlier in the week and decided on several new dishes for them to try. While not entirely inedible, they left much to be desired. Charles grimaced in exaggeration whenever he took a bite, and Katherine laughed at the stern rebukes he continuously received from his sister.

"I declare, Charles, you are as bad as you were when you were a child!" Sarah announced in exasperation. Katherine chuckled, and Charles turned his head to wink at her.

"What do you expect?" he countered, a look of martyrdom on his face. "This may likely be my last night on earth due to your experimentation, and all you can do is scold me. Have some compassion, my dear sister!"

Sarah pouted. "I will not, and you would do well to thank me for this dinner. If Cook had had his way, we would be eating boiled pork again."

This time Charles grimaced in earnest, and he did not tease his sister any more for some time. Finally, when the meal concluded and the servants arrived to clear away the dishes, he sat back and grinned at her.

"Sarah, despite my reservations, I must confess that was a fine meal, and if I am not kept awake half the night with indigestion, I shall thank you in the morning."

Katherine laughed as Sarah rolled her eyes. They stood and made their way onto the patio, the evening air being cooler outdoors than inside. They conversed quietly for a time, but Katherine became more nervous as the night wore on. Did Charles really want her to play for them? Should she go inside and begin? Propriety demanded that she wait to be invited, but they did not stand on much ceremony here, and she felt at quite a loss to know what to do. She bit her lip in agitation, and had almost resolved to forget the whole thing when Charles turned to her with a smile.

"Do you have any other favorite composers, besides Schubert?"

Katherine was not entirely surprised at his question, but Sarah's eyes grew wide.

"Johann Sebastian Bach is another favorite of mine, as is Mozart."

"Ah, you favor the Austrian composers to our own Englishmen?"

Katherine laughed lightly. "I suppose so. Something about the continent must inspire greatness."

Charles laughed softly. "I am not sure that I agree with that statement, but perhaps you can convince me. Go on—play for us some of their greatness."

Katherine looked across at Sarah, who was practically vibrating with suppressed excitement, her clear blue eyes bright with anticipation. Katherine smiled, then stood and walked back into the house.

The door to the library was directly across the short hall in front of the dining room, and with the doors open she would easily be heard. She sat in front of the instrument for several moments as she contemplated how to begin. Finally she decided on Bach's *Prelude* and began to play.

The rhythmic melody grew and faded by turns as the song progressed. She allowed herself some liberty in her expression of the music, but she did not let herself go as she had before. The music flowed effortlessly from her fingertips, and she smiled as she recalled how often she had practiced the piece in earlier years. After Bach she played Mozart. She loved his sonatas, and despite her earlier restraint she found herself getting lost in the music once more. By the time she came to the last movement of Sonata No. 11 she was unaware of anyone or anything around her. Its rapid pace matched her breathing and the beating of her heart. Her fingers flew over the keys, hitting their mark with exactness before bounding on to the next. Despite the recent years when she had no piano on which to practice, she played as if she and the instrument were one. Her body and soul came alive as they released the music that had lived on inside of her.

She finished the song, her chest heaving, her hands trembling, her mind slowly returning to the time and place and room. How long she sat there she was not sure, but eventually she felt a pair of eyes trained on her face and knew that Charles had come in to listen to her. She turned to him, and as their eyes met she once again felt a connection between them, stronger than before. There was pain and longing in his eyes still, but also wonder and delight. She was glad to see that her playing seemed to have eased his suffering rather than add to it.

Charles walked over to the piano and looked down at her. His green eyes were gentle, and he smiled softly into her brown ones.

"Thank you," was all he said, but the look in his eyes spoke infinitely more.

She smiled and inclined her head, and an unspoken understanding passed between them. The library would no longer be empty; from now on, it would be filled with music.

Chapter 11

From that evening forth, Katherine was free to play the piano whenever she wished. Sarah would bring her handiwork into the library and work quietly in a corner while Katherine gave herself up to the music. Many mornings and afternoons passed in this fashion, and Charles often opened the door to his study in order to hear better. Sometimes he even came and stood in the doorway to listen, but he rarely spoke. As the days passed, the pain in his eyes gradually faded until it was a mere shadow. Katherine noticed this and was glad.

One day Sarah pounced on Katherine as they were having breakfast. "You know I love to hear you on the pianoforte, Katherine," she said, "but I absolutely must insist that you refrain from playing this morning and help me prepare for our guests this afternoon."

Katherine grinned sheepishly at her friend. "Of course. I am sorry I have been so preoccupied, but you do not know how much good it does my spirit to make music again."

Her friend smiled at her. "I am sure that it does. And the

music has done heaps of good for Charles as well. I can hardly recognize him anymore!"

"Has it?" Katherine asked, feigning disinterest as she sipped her tea.

"Goodness, yes. Not that he was ever really a bore, but he somehow seems more alive now." She paused thoughtfully. "I do not think I have ever seen him so animated and happy before."

Katherine kept her eyes down as she listened. She, too, had noticed a change in Charles's behavior, but without knowing what he was like before her arrival, she could only compare his mannerisms to what they were a month ago. Even in that short amount of time she had noticed a greater liveliness in his step and a more readiness in his laugh, and it gave her pleasure to know that she had helped to bring about the change.

"Where *is* Charles this morning?" Katherine asked.

"Oh, he had to go over some business or other with Wilson. But he promised me that he would be finished in time to greet our guests this afternoon, and I am going to hold him to it."

"Do you know yet how many we are expecting?"

"Let me see…" Sarah said, tapping her chin quizzically. "There are Colonel and Mrs. Whittaker, Captain Strong, the lieutenants, and probably half a dozen more officers."

"Does that not seem like a rather large group to be gathered here?" Katherine asked, smiling.

"It *may* be a bit crowded," Sarah agreed, "but I did not have much choice in the matter. I could not very well invite Lieutenant Bradford and not Lieutenant McArthur, and it would have been strange to ask some of the lesser officers and *not* Captain Strong, though he is a bit tiresome. So you see I had no choice but to issue an invitation to them all," she concluded matter-of-factly.

Katherine laughed. She had not yet met many of the officers, though she had seen their crimson-clad figures around town on occasion. Although she was a little nervous about meeting so many of them at once, she was looking forward to the afternoon very much.

Sarah rang the bell and a few servants came in to clear the table. As they were leaving, she called out to the elder of the two in Hindustani, asking that she join them in the sitting room. The girl bowed and followed them as the two young ladies went to begin their preparations.

"Are you quite sure, Wilson?"

Charles's brow was furrowed, and he looked at his steward with an expression of someone who knows he is going to hear bad news.

"Quite sure, Master Mendenhall. I have gone over the accounts several times, and without cutting back the staff or decreasing the workers' wages, I cannot find any way of making up the difference."

Charles sat back in his chair and sighed heavily. "We cannot do either of those things, Wilson. You know that."

"I do, sir."

The younger man leaned forward again, rifling through the sheaf of papers in front of him. "I was counting on the price of indigo to be as high as in years past, if not higher. And with such a plentiful harvest anticipated, it would have been enough—at last!" He drew a paper out from the stack and scanned it quickly. "Yes," he said, more to himself than to his steward, "it would have been enough." He dropped the paper and slumped back in his chair, rubbing a hand across his eyes.

"We must hope that the price of indigo climbs again before the harvest is in," his steward said gently.

Charles blew out his breath in aggravation. "Yes, we must hope. But if it does not? If a buyer cannot be found for the second harvest? Tell me, Wilson, what shall I do then?"

"I believe you have another choice, sir," he said quietly.

"It is not one I am keen to make, Wilson," Charles said sharply.

The older man watched him quietly for a moment, then he picked up the paper Charles had dropped and read it through to himself again.

"Perhaps Mr. Kerns will give you an extension?"

"No, I have already spoken with him. He granted me an extension last year but he is not willing to do so again." Charles could not keep the bitterness from his voice, and Wilson slowly set the paper down.

"I am sorry, sir, if my counsel has led you into difficulties."

Charles looked across at his steward and smiled gently. "No, old friend, I am the one who is sorry. Your counsel has never led me wrong. Your advice and companionship have been invaluable to me; I should not have implied otherwise. Forgive me."

The older man inclined his head, and Charles sighed. It was true—Wilson had always had the best interest of his young master and the estate in his heart. But years ago he had counseled Charles to sign a mortgage on the plantation, in order to cover the numerous expenses and debts resulting from the deaths of Charles's parents and brother. While there had not seemed to be any way to avoid it at the time, over the years it had become a festering sore spot for Charles. His plantation was small, and while he usually made a good harvest, there was never much money left after clearing his own expenses and providing a comfortable living for himself and his sister. During the last ten years he had managed to make every payment, with the exception of last year. An early rainstorm had nearly wiped out his young indigo plants, and only half of those resown survived to harvest. Mr. Kerns, the mortgage lender, had grudgingly allowed a year's extension but had doubled the amount of the final payment. Charles had saved as much as he could from the money earned at auction last year, but unless the price of indigo rose a great deal higher, and a buyer could be found to purchase their smaller, second harvest, there would not be enough money to make the final payment in October.

Charles sighed again. He was a man of action, and he desperately wanted to find a solution to his problem right away. Nothing could be done at the moment, however, so it was with a troubled conscience that he set the papers aside and dismissed his steward.

After Wilson withdrew, Charles sat gazing out the window, lost in thought. It was not long, however, before he began to feel uneasy.

Something was wrong.

He stood and opened the door to his study, listening. It took him a moment to pinpoint what had unnerved him, and he smiled to himself as he realized what it was.

There was no music.

He turned down the hallway and entered the sitting room, where Sarah and Katherine were putting the finishing touches to their decorations. Sarah looked up as her brother came into the room.

"Charles! I am so glad to see you have emerged. Have you finished your business for the day, then?"

"I have," he responded. "But pray, what mischief are you two up to?"

"Oh, Charles," his sister scolded, "surely you recall that we have invited the officers to tea? You promised me that you would join us."

"Is that all?" he laughed. "I was under the impression you had designed to open a hothouse in the sitting room. Are so many flowers really necessary?"

"I was telling her so myself," Katherine said with a smile. "I do wonder if we shall be able to converse through the foliage." Charles chuckled, but Sarah looked hurt.

"Come now, sister, do not be offended. The flowers are lovely. But I must agree with Katherine, I think there are far too many crowded into this single room. Take some into the library," he suggested. "I daresay we shall spend some time in there."

Sarah called for assistance, and the servants followed her as she took a bowl overflowing with blossoms out of the room. Charles walked over to Katherine, who was arranging some jasmine in a vase. She looked up as he stepped beside her.

"You will play for us, won't you?"

His voice was soft as he looked down at her. Katherine's heart stuttered in her chest and she blushed, taking a step back. "Of course," she replied. "I am always happy to play the pianoforte."

"Yes, I know," he agreed. "You play for us every day."

She looked up at him, concerned. "Does it bother you that I play so much? Does it disturb your work?"

"On the contrary," he said. "In fact, I came out of my study with the express purpose of discovering why you were *not* playing. I had not recalled that the officers were invited to tea until Sarah mentioned it. My mind has been less agreeably engaged of late." His brows drew together and he was quiet for several moments. Katherine wondered what was troubling him.

The servants returned just then to retrieve more flowers, and Katherine heard Sarah's voice calling to her from the library. Charles bowed, excusing himself, and she did not see him again until their guests arrived a few hours later.

"I understand that you are lately arrived from England, Miss Greenwood."

Katherine was sitting on the settee next to Captain Strong, a sober-faced young gentleman who looked as though life was a vale of tears. He had already explained to Katherine that he had been on the verge of entering the ministry, but had decided on a military career instead. In her opinion, he was ill-fitted for either occupation, but for the sake of his would-be congregation, she felt glad he had chosen the army.

"Yes, I have only been in India since March."

"And what part of England are you from?"

"I am lately from London, but I was raised in Leicestershire."

"Have you any family here?"

"No, sir."

He looked at her quizzically. "None? Then what induced you to come *here?*"

Katherine was saved from answering this by the approach of another young officer.

"Miss Greenwood. Captain." The newcomer bowed to each of them in turn.

"Lieutenant," Captain Strong returned the greeting. "Miss Greenwood, may I present Lieutenant Marcus Bradford." She smiled and nodded, and the lieutenant gave her a somewhat sheepish grin.

"Forgive my interruption, but I could not help but overhear what you were saying to Captain Strong. You were raised in Leicestershire?" he asked.

Katherine looked up at him. He was handsome; a tall gentlemen of about five-and-twenty, with broad shoulders and a trim waist. Vivid blue eyes looked down at her from under a strong brow, over which grew hair so dark it almost looked black. He had a chiseled jawline with a defined cleft in his chin, and his face was clean shaven.

"Yes, sir, near Sutton. Do you know the country?"

He smiled broadly. "Not as well as you, I am sure. I hail from Northampton."

"Indeed! Then we are neighbors."

Marcus chuckled. "It would seem so."

Katherine asked after his family and neighborhood, and soon they were engrossed in conversation. When Captain Strong excused himself with an air of mild annoyance, Marcus seated himself beside her. They spoke of London, and the country, and what each of them admired and missed about their native land. Soon the conversation turned to other socially acceptable pleasantries.

"Are you fond of music, Miss Greenwood?"

"Yes, indeed."

"Do you play, and sing?"

"I sing a little, but I prefer to let the instrument be voice whenever possible."

He smiled. "Then I hope we shall have the pleasure of hearing from you this evening."

A burst of laughter interrupted them and they turned to the source. Several officers were gathered around Sarah, who smiled and nodded and laughed by turns. Although often surrounded by admirers, she was not a flirt; her nature was simply so cheerful and vivacious that men and women alike were drawn to her like moths to a flame. She turned and saw Katherine and Marcus watching her. Excusing herself, she came to stand before them.

"Katherine, darling, will you not play for us?" she asked.

"An excellent idea, Miss Mendenhall," Marcus agreed. "We were just discussing Miss Greenwood's musical talents and I am quite impatient to judge them for myself."

Katherine readily agreed, and the trio, along with several other guests, walked down the short hall to the open library. Charles was in discussion with Colonel Whittaker and looked up as the company divided, but made no move to follow them.

Katherine stood at the piano and searched through some sheet music left on the stand. When she and Charles reached their understanding, Sarah had pulled out her mother's old music, and

Charles made a gift of some new music as well. Katherine found what she was looking for, and seating herself, began to play. Those who had followed her into the room stood loosely around the instrument or seated themselves in nearby chairs. Marcus stood beside her.

The piece she had chosen was soft and gentle, and an informal air filled the room and its occupants. A few low conversations broke out among the guests, and after several minutes Marcus leaned down to speak to Katherine.

"You play beautifully," he said, appreciation coloring his tone.

"Thank you," she replied, her concentration unbroken.

"How long have you played, and by whom were you taught?" Marcus pulled a nearby chair next to the bench and sat down beside her. She glanced at him and smiled.

"I do not know, exactly. I have been playing ever since I can remember." Her voice became a little softer. "My grandmother taught me."

"She must be a talented musician."

"Indeed she is—or was, I suppose I should say. As she grew older, her hands began to trouble her. She could not play the pianoforte or the harp very much at all after that."

"And so you played for her." The statement was full of admiration.

Katherine smiled. "Yes, I did. Sometimes she would tutor me, turning the afternoon into a lesson. But often she would simply listen." Katherine grew quiet, and although she continued to play, her feelings grew more somber, and the tone of the music changed.

Marcus noticed her subdued air and was silent. The song ended, and a scattering of applause from those in the room brought Katherine's mind back to the present. She tried to shake off the aching loneliness she felt, and turned to Marcus with a somewhat forced smile. He smiled back, still applauding.

"Excellent, Miss Greenwood. Shall you play another?"

She inclined her head in assent, and began again. The piece she chose was lighter, with fancy trills and brighter chords woven throughout. It was not easy to converse through, which was largely the reason Katherine chose it for her second. Thinking of her grandmother left her feeling vulnerable, and she wanted to get her emotions well under control before attempting to speak again.

The song ended, and Katherine immediately began another. Her feelings were spiraling out of control, and she was desperately trying to reign them in. Sarah had engaged Marcus in conversation, and the two of them stood a little way off from where Katherine sat. She was playing Beethoven's 17th Sonata quite forcefully, and many of the guests wandered back into the sitting room in order to continue their conversations, which could hardly be heard over the pounding of the keys.

"You are not often this passionate in your execution," a voice sounded in her ear. She was startled, and her fingers slipped on the notes. The blunder further unnerved her, and she hesitated for a moment before finding her place on the page and continuing.

"What has troubled you so?" Charles was watching her face intently, his expression searching.

"Nothing, sir." She tried to smile as she forced her heart away from her fingers. After several minutes passed in silence, she glanced at his face. He looked thoughtful, and Katherine looked away before he could read too much in her face. Finally she sighed.

"I was thinking of my grandmother, that is all."

He nodded in understanding but said nothing. Katherine continued to play until the end of the movement, but instead of continuing with the next she let the notes die out in complete silence. The room was now empty except for the two of them, and she sat and stared at the keys before her, a thousand memories and emotions whirling through her mind. Tears rose unbidden to her eyes, and she struggled to maintain her composure without much success. Charles reached out and handed her his handkerchief, which she gratefully accepted.

"I am sorry, I did not mean to upset you further," he said gently. But Katherine was shaking her head.

"You did not upset me. I let myself get carried away, thinking about her. I should have known it was not a wise course to follow." She wiped her eyes and her nose and attempted to smile at him. But as she looked up into his face, her smile faded. His eyes stared unflinching into her own, and the expression she saw in them reflected her own feelings. The connection that had been growing between them seemed to deepen.

"You do not have to pretend, Katherine. I understand," he said quietly. "The pain that is caused in remembering our loved ones is acute. And yet, we do not want to forget them." He smiled sadly at her, and her breath caught in her chest. "So we gladly drink the bitter cup, because we remember how it once was sweet. And we cling to that sweetness, hoping the dregs of a happier time will linger still."

Katherine stared at him, amazed. He had described her

feelings perfectly, as if he had read them straight off her heart. It was a strange, yet comforting feeling to be so well understood. She looked away, and another tear slipped down her cheek. Before she could reach to brush it aside, Charles's hand lifted to her face and gently wiped it away. The gesture was more like a caress, and once again Katherine looked up into his face, surprised. They continued staring at each other, lost in their own thoughts, bound by the connection they both felt. Finally Charles took a breath and looked away. The tension between them faded, though it did not disappear completely. Somehow Katherine felt it never would.

After a moment, Charles turned back to her with a gentle smile and motioned to the open library doors.

"We seem to be neglecting our guests, Miss Greenwood. Shall we indulge in their company once more?"

His manner was cordial, but he seemed more distant than he had been only moments before. Katherine was not sure if she was grateful for the change or not. She was not in very great control of her emotions yet, so she tried to think of the sudden switch as a chance to check her mind as well as her heart. Realizing that he was waiting for an answer, she forced herself to smile and nodded in agreement. She took the arm he offered and the two of them walked out of the library together.

Chapter 12

Charles could not sleep. He tossed and turned for what seemed like hours, then finally gave up and crept out of bed. He put on his dressing gown and silently made his way to the library. Stepping softly onto the polished floor, he walked to the large window and stood looking out of it for a long time, trying to sort through the tangled emotions within his heart. He had been careless—too careless—and thinking of his behavior that evening filled Charles with dread. He could not deny the growing attraction he felt for Katherine, but whether or not she felt the same he was less certain of. She was always gentle, always kind, and sometimes she looked at him with a tenderness in her eyes that sent his mind racing and his heart soaring. To be sure, she blushed quite often when he looked directly at her, but he had noticed that she colored just as quickly when Wilson spoke to her, or when she conversed with Sarah over seemingly trivial matters. She was often guarded in her responses, and it left him wondering what she was really thinking inside that pretty little head of hers. But last night he had gone too far. He had allowed his regard to show too plainly, and he was afraid that Katherine might respond in kind. Playing with his own emotions was one thing, but endangering Katherine's heart was something he vowed he would not do.

He sighed. The connection he felt with her was growing ever stronger, and the thought worried him. He was not the master of his own fate; not yet. It was a privilege he knew he must earn, and thinking of Katherine made him more determined than ever to win his freedom and then her heart. He wanted more than anything to make her happy, to do everything in his power to draw out that laugh and that smile he had come to love.

He blew out his breath in frustration, suddenly angry. *Blast Mr. Kerns!* he thought. If he had not doubled the price of the last payment, Charles would not have anything to worry about. The plantation would be safe, he would be free to woo and win his lady and his life would be complete once more. But the uncertainty of his own future removed that choice from him, and he groaned inwardly. What if the price of indigo did not rise? What if a buyer could not be found for the second harvest? If either of those possibilities became a reality, he would not have enough to make the final payment. His mind grew uneasy as he thought of the repercussions. The plantation would be seized and he and Sarah would be thrown out. He simply could not risk involving Katherine in such a precarious future. There were, of course, certain choices Charles could make in order to secure both financial comfort and his beloved plantation, but they were not pleasant to think about, and Charles practically refused to acknowledge their existence at all.

He sighed again. He would have to be more careful. Until he

was free of his legal obligations, he could not allow himself to pursue matters of the heart. Not only that, but he would not allow Katherine to waste her heart on him if he was not free to return her affection. Tired and disheartened in both mind and spirit, he made his way back to his room and sank, exhausted, into a dreamless sleep.

Katherine's mind was troubled, and sleep had alluded her from the moment she lay down. Her feelings for Charles had been growing with each passing day, but until tonight she did not suppose he returned her affections. Her cheek still burned where his hand had brushed against it, and the feelings his touch had aroused in her heart made Katherine feel at once both elated and distressed. She had never before been in love, but she knew not how else to describe her present feelings. Aside from the awkwardness of their initial meeting, she had never felt so comfortable in the presence of anyone before. His quiet, gentle nature suited her own somewhat reserved temperament, and the playful manner in which he interacted with his sister made him even more endearing. Handsome, kind, observant; he seemed perfect in every particular. But it was more than his manners which drew her to him. He understood her so perfectly, so completely; his friendship was more valuable to her than she could scarcely admit to herself. Yes, when she considered the particulars, Katherine was quite certain she was in love with Charles Mendenhall.

But why would he be in love with her? *Was* he in love? The

question gnawed at her. Katherine was not sure. She was convinced he felt *something* for her, something more than just friendly camaraderie, which she had at first suspected. She also knew that he could feel the connection between them as surely as she, though perhaps her partiality made her more aware of it. There had been times, however, when she had seen a look burning in his eyes, or when they had understood one another without a word being spoken that led her to believe that he felt it, too. And yet, if he felt more than a friendly fondness for her, why did he not speak?

Katherine realized that her heart was beginning to run away with her, and her mind brought her firmly back to reality. *Because you are a penniless young girl, with no family, connections, or even great beauty*, it told her. The thought stung, though she knew it was true. Charles was no pauper, but neither was he among the extremely wealthy. He had a modest income and a comfortable estate, but those were hardly the makings for a love-match by any standards. Charles would have to marry prudently, not only to secure his own comfort, but to increase the chances of his sister forming an eligible alliance herself. Katherine did not blame him for this, but her heart ached nonetheless.

She sighed. His manners towards herself were very likely the result of a feeling of obligation for her attentions. She would have to tuck away her private feelings and try not to let Charles see how much she cared for him. She would not put him in the awkward position of courting one eligible young lady while knowing that another young lady (his own sister's intimate friend, at that) was in love with him. The thought of Charles paying his addresses to another young lady, whomever she may be, made her heart sick, but she smothered the feeling before it could bring her to tears. She had no claim on him, and she would not stand in his way of pursuing the proper course for his own life.

Still troubled in heart and mind, Katherine tossed and turned for what seemed like hours, until she at last fell asleep.

Katherine awoke to the clatter of a tea tray as Bhavani set it down on her desk. The early summer sunshine was pouring through the windowpanes and Katherine sat up, her mind foggy with exhaustion. She was embarrassed to find that it was later—much later—than she normally awoke. She was sure she had missed breakfast, which was most likely the reason her maid was bringing her something to eat. Smiling at Bhavani, she nodded her thanks.

Katherine was sipping her tea when there was a knock at the door. Sarah peeked her head in and, seeing Katherine awake, let herself into the room and plopped down on the bed

"I am glad to see you are finally awake. Breakfast was such a dismal affair by myself!" She turned onto her back and sighed dramatically.

"Did not your brother join you?"

Sarah rolled over and propped her chin in her hands. "No, he did not. He dined early and left for town straightaway. Business, you know," she added. Katherine smiled in sympathy.

"I am sorry you had to dine alone. You could have woken me —I did not sleep well last night, but I did not realize the hour was so late."

Sarah shook her head. "No matter. You are awake now, and what fun I have planned for us!" She sat up, her eyes dancing with delight. "I propose a picnic in the Botanical Gardens—there! Is it not a good plan?"

Katherine clapped her hands. "It is a marvelous plan! I have longed since my arrival to see the gardens. We sailed past them as we arrived in port."

"They are quite splendid, as you will soon see for yourself. Are you ready, then? Let us call for the carriage."

Taking her gloves and parasol, Katherine joined her friend at the front entrance. A servant was loading a large basket of food into the carriage, while another helped the ladies climb inside. Sarah and Katherine were accompanied by a Hindu escort named Rahul, as well as their native driver. Having ensured that nothing was forgotten, Sarah gave directions to the driver, and the company set off.

The Botanical Gardens were on the western side of the river, just downstream from the docks. It would take them a little over an hour to arrive at the *ghat,* at which point they would employ a boatman to ferry them across the river. Katherine watched the beautiful Indian landscape out of the carriage windows while Sarah chattered about the success of their tea party the prior evening. Katherine was only half interested in what her friend was saying, until something Sarah mentioned caught her attention.

"Lieutenant Bradford seemed quite taken with you," Sarah said with a sly smile.

"Did he?" Katherine turned to her friend with genuine

surprise.

Sarah laughed. "Of course he was! You sat and conversed with him for the better part of an hour, and he accompanied you when you went in to play. He does not usually pay such particular attentions to any single young lady."

Katherine blushed. "Perhaps it is because I am newly arrived. Strangers always arouse interest amongst established social circles, you know."

"Perhaps," Sarah agreed, but her smile seemed to say she thought otherwise.

Katherine mulled this over. Her thoughts had been so consumed with the encounter she had had with Charles that she had not considered the rest of the evening much at all. She turned her attentions now to the memory of Marcus Bradford. He was certainly very dashing; tall and dark with a handsome figure. He had a ready smile that brightened his already brilliant blue eyes, and such a friendly demeanor as to put anyone at ease. Katherine tried to recall exactly what they had spoken of, but more than particulars she remembered the comfortable manner in which they conversed. While she did not detect any particular regard in his manner of address, she did recall the eagerness which he showed in becoming acquainted with her. Katherine pondered on this for the remainder of their journey.

They drove through the southern end of Calcutta but skirted most of the city. Passing the docks, the carriage made its way down Garden Reach Road and stopped before a broad flight of steps that led down into the water. Several similar *ghats* could be seen up and down the riverfront, where people came to bathe and where small boats could launch. The ladies alighted from the carriage, and Rahul was sent to seek out a ferryman to take them across the river to the gardens.

He soon returned and led them to a small, crescent-shaped boat a short distance from the *ghat*. It was commanded by a bare-chested native wearing a large turban and wielding a long pole. Though quite accustomed to the sight now, Katherine always wondered at the strange manner of dress that the natives employed, even if she did envy them their lighter garments in the rising heat. With the picnic basket carefully stowed aboard, the ladies were helped into the boat by Rahul, who then boarded as well. Once situated, they pushed off from land and were soon gliding their way across the river.

From where they launched, the Hooghly River was only a quarter of a mile wide. The river was calm and their guide confident, so it did not take them long to cross. The sun beat down mercilessly, and even beneath her parasol Katherine felt the piercing heat begin to warm her brow. She pulled off her glove and reached her hand over the side of the boat to dip her fingers into the water, which cooled her somewhat.

"How often have you been to the gardens?" she asked Sarah, who was fanning herself under her lace-trimmed parasol.

"Not very often. I do not like to venture so far on my own, and Charles has so little time to spend on such excursions." She sighed.

"What keeps him so busy?"

"Well, our plantation produces a fair amount of indigo each season, but not all of it is contracted. If the remainder is to be saved from the auction, Charles must find a purchaser for the second harvest himself, and he often has to travel a fair distance to do so. Of course, Wilson is primarily responsible for overseeing the accounts and managing the estate, but Charles cannot bear to be idle. He is very much involved in all matters concerning the plantation. He prefers to keep Wilson at home and travel about himself."

Katherine nodded. She knew that Charles was fiercely proud of the plantation he had helped to build, so it made sense that he would wish to be an active part in the management of it.

Peering ahead, she saw a cluster of towering palm trees, their fronds wide and glossy, waving over the river shoreline. Their guide steered them close to the garden *ghat* to allow them to disembark, and Rahul stepped ashore. Helping the ladies out of the boat, he spoke to the boatman in their native tongue, indicating that he was to wait for them. The ladies waited under the shade of their parasols while Rahul gathered the basket, then the trio set off.

Chapter 13

Entering the park from the water, they climbed up a bank and found a manicured path running parallel to the river. Huge palm trees grew betwixt mahogany and bamboo, and the tiny white blossoms of jasmine could be seen on every hand like fallen stars. They followed the gravel walk a short distance until they came to a crossroads where four paths joined. Not knowing or caring in which direction they traveled, they chose the middle path and started down it.

They meandered past flowering bushes and tall trees. A small lake to their left was filled with lilies, and butterflies fluttered around them in the humid air. Soon they came to a beautiful monument. A set of perfectly round marble steps led up to an intricately carved urn sitting atop a short pillar, and just beyond it stood a large greenhouse.

"Oh Katherine, you simply must see inside the Orchid House! You will love it," Sarah exclaimed when they drew within view.

Walking around to the main entrance, the ladies entered the greenhouse, and Katherine gasped in delight. Thousands of the most beautiful flowers she had ever seen surrounded them. Tiers of potted plants lined the path, from which every shade of green erupted. Young palm trees, spiny cacti, majestic lilies, and delicate orchids mingled together along their rows. Katherine walked the path slowly, trying to take in the beauty that surrounded her.

"Is it not magnificent?" Sarah asked.

Katherine turned to her with a smile. "It is breathtaking! Such beauty..." Her voice trailed off as she leaned down to examine a creamy orchid blossom that arched over the walkway. The ivory petals were smooth and perfect, with a burst of magenta at their lip. Katherine leaned down and gently kissed the bloom. Sarah saw her and laughed.

The greenhouse was beautiful, but it did not hold their attentions for long. The humid air inside was suffocating, and although the midday sun beat down on them as they emerged, a welcome breeze cooled their perspiring brows. Opening their parasols again, they continued their exploration of the garden.

They wandered from path to path, stopping to admire the flowers and vegetation that grew in abundance around them. Several other people were enjoying the garden as well, and murmured greetings to those who passed nearby punctuated their conversation. Despite the cultivated lawns and graveled paths, the garden had a certain wildness to it, and it suited Katherine wonderfully. Her heart swelled within her at the overwhelming beauty that surrounded them, until she felt as though it would burst clear from her chest. Her love and admiration for this strange new land was growing stronger every day.

Crossing an arched stone bridge, they found a shady spot to

spread out their picnic on the manicured lawn. Rahul unpacked the basket, first laying down a large blanket for the ladies to sit upon. Once everything was ready, he took his own lunch and settled himself a short distance away; far enough to allow privacy for his mistress, but close enough to be called upon if needed.

The luncheon consisted of cold pork, chicken sandwiches, cucumber salad, dates, figs, strawberries, and a large pudding. A bottle of fresh lemonade served to quench their thirst and round out the meal. The ladies ate everything with the hunger and delight which fresh air and exercise always arouse in the young, and the picnic was judged to be a great success. Having eaten their fill, Rahul was summoned to repack the basket, and they set off to see the crowning jewel of the park: the Great Banyan Tree.

The banyan's massive canopy was visible from quite a distance, looking more like a small grove than a single tree. As they approached, the chirping and chattering from scores of birds filled the air. Katherine's eyes widened as they drew near.

"This is a single tree?" she asked incredulously.

"Yes," Sarah replied. "It is over 100 years old, and still growing."

They stood in the shade underneath the giant tree. Hundreds of roots grew downwards from the branches overhead, like pillars in an arboresque cathedral. Katherine walked between them, awestruck.

"I would not have believed such a tree existed had I not seen it myself," she confessed. Sarah smiled wryly.

"Miss Greenwood, I do believe you have fallen in love with this garden."

Katherine laughed. "Can I be blamed for my choice? This

place feels like Heaven itself. I would be content to live out all my days wrapped in the embrace of this garden." She threw an arm around a nearby aerial root and kissed it soundly. Sarah laughed.

They walked around the tree for a while longer, enjoying the shade of the thick green foliage. A sudden shower swept across the park, and they watched the rain from the protection of the tree's enormous canopy. The squall was over in a quarter-hour, at which point they decided it was time to go home. The ladies and their escort made their way back through the garden to the *ghat* on the river. The boat they had crossed in lay moored a short way up the beach, its guide asleep in the bow. Rahul woke him, and soon they were on their way. Katherine looked back at the garden and the lush green palm fronds waving in the afternoon breeze. She breathed a sigh of contentment and smiled, then turned to face the approaching shoreline.

By the time they were once again settled in the carriage it was late afternoon, and they decided to stop at a tea room in Calcutta for refreshment. Pulling up in front of an establishment on Park Street, the two young ladies alighted and entered through the open front doors.

The tea room was crowded. Indian merchants with their dark skin and light, airy clothing, Sepoys in crisp red uniforms and large turbans, smartly dressed Englishmen with business associates; the spacious establishment seemed filled to capacity. A native servant wearing a large turban approached them, and Sarah kindly asked for a private parlor where they could partake of some light refreshment. He bowed and led them through the tangled maze of patrons and servants to a small room with a round table at its center. No sooner had the ladies sat down and the servant been dispatched to bring them tea than another person entered the room.

"Why, Lieutenant Bradford! What a pleasant surprise," Sarah said.

He bowed, a broad smile on his face. "Miss Mendenhall, Miss Greenwood, I am delighted to see you again. I observed you as you came in, and wanted to come pay my respects."

"That is very kind of you," Sarah replied, with a glance at her friend. Katherine ignored her look. "Would you care to join us?"

Marcus was only too happy to oblige, and a lively conversation soon sprang up between the three of them. Upon learning that they had been across the river to the Botanical Gardens, he insisted on hearing their opinion of it.

"Have you not seen it yourself?" Katherine inquired. Marcus shook his head.

"Alas, I have not. Though I have been to Barrackpore Park on several occasions, and it is very fine."

"Barrackpore! Oh, how I long to see it!" Sarah lamented. Marcus laughed.

"And you, Miss Greenwood? Have you a desire to see Barrackpore Park as well?"

Katherine colored slightly. "I confess that I am not familiar with the name. Is it another garden hereabouts?"

"Not a garden only, Katherine dearest," Sarah answered. "It is a very large park, with a menagerie, an aviary, and even a theatre."

"And you have been there often, sir?" Katherine asked the lieutenant.

"Yes, the regiment is regularly at Barrackpore. It is the residence of the Governor General, and he frequently requires our assistance. We often engage with the regiment at Serampore in our various duties and training exercises. I would be honored to escort you to the park whenever you have a wish to see it." He spoke to them both, but he was looking at Katherine. She smiled shyly and looked down.

"I shall have to speak to Charles about it," replied Sarah.

"Is it far?" Katherine inquired.

"Not very," Marcus answered. "Barrackpore Park lies but 14 miles north of Calcutta, across the river from Serampore."

"Yes, but as our plantation lies south and east of Calcutta, it adds to the distance considerably," Sarah fretted. "I am not sure that Charles would approve of such a distance.

"Perhaps I can speak to him myself?" Marcus suggested.

Sarah smiled. "It certainly could not hurt matters. You must call on us soon." She looked meaningfully at Katherine, who blushed but took the hint.

"Yes, do come visit us," she echoed.

Marcus smiled. "I shall come at my earliest convenience, then." He stood and bowed to the ladies. "I must take my leave to return to my party. Please pay my respects to Mr. Mendenhall," he added.

The ladies finished their tea and paid the bill, and climbing into the carriage once more, headed back through the streets of Calcutta, towards home.

Chapter 14

Supper and Charles were waiting for them by the time they arrived. "Ah, here you are!" he exclaimed as they entered the sitting room. "Wilson informed me that you two had ventured on an excursion to the Botanical Gardens today, and I was beginning to wonder whether or not I would be dining alone."

"We stopped in town for tea," Sarah replied, removing her gloves. He nodded.

"I thought as much." He turned to Katherine, who was standing near the door. "And how did you like the park?"

"More than I could have imagined," she replied. "Such beauty! I was very sorry to leave it all."

"I daresay you shall visit there again."

"Of course. But future visits will not hold the enchantment, the wonder of newness that this first visit held. The garden will be beautiful still, and I may discover new things in the park, but hereafter I will be expecting and anticipating such beauty and discovery. It will be enjoyable, yes, but it will not be magical again."

Charles was nodding. "I see your point. And I can understand your feelings. We shall have to conjure up some new place for you to explore," he finished with a grin.

"Barrackpore Park would be just the thing, would it not?" Sarah interjected.

Charles looked at her in surprise. "Yes, Barrackpore would certainly captivate Katherine's attentions. But it is not likely that we shall visit there soon. The rains are coming, and then the harvest will be in. We shall have to content ourselves with something nearer to home than Barrackpore."

Sarah pouted, but not for long. The excursion to the gardens had done her a great deal of good, and she was full of laughter throughout the meal. Katherine, however, was feeling the effects of a day spent in the hot Indian sun and was more subdued during supper. When applied to for musical entertainment following the meal, she declined. Charles raised his eyebrows, looking at her with surprise.

"I believe that is the first time I have heard you decline an invitation to play for us, Katherine. Is something the matter?"

She managed a small smile. "No, indeed. I am only tired. I am not accustomed to being out in such heat as this."

Sarah was mortified. "Oh, Katherine! I am so sorry I did not think of your comfort before." She drew near her friend and took her hand. "Does your head ache? Are you feeling ill?"

Katherine confessed that her head did indeed ache, and Sarah immediately called for a servant. After a few words in Hindustani the girl scampered off. Sarah turned to Katherine with a look of tender concern. "We shall sort this out directly, and you will feel much better in the morning." Katherine started to protest, but her friend insisted on her retiring.

Charles agreed with his sister, his deep voice rendered even more persuasive by its gentleness. "You do not look well, Katherine. You had best go to bed."

Too weary to object further, Katherine allowed herself to be ushered to her room. Once there, Bhavani helped her undress and bathed her head gently with lavender water. Exhausted from the late evening before and the long day in the sun, she was soon fast asleep.

Katherine awoke early the next morning, before the sun. Her sleep had been deep and dreamless, and it left her quite refreshed. She slid into a gown, calling on Bhavani to do her laces, then stepped out onto the portico. The sunrise was turning the sky pearly blue, and she sighed in contentment. The air was still cool, and she longed to walk around the grounds before the heat made it impossible, but she shivered as she remembered Sarah's reason for always having an escort. The threat of a tiger attack, however unlikely, was enough to check her desire, and she was just about to return inside when a movement to her left caught her attention. A man was walking briskly across the lawn, whom Katherine recognized even from a distance. In two steps she was off the porch and walking quickly towards him.

"Mr. Mendenhall!"

Charles turned, surprised. His astonishment increased when he saw who had addressed him, and he quickly closed the distance between them.

"Katherine! What is the matter?" He looked at her with alarm, concern etched across his brow. She saw this and a thrill of pleasure went through her, though she lost no time in assuring him that all was well.

"Nothing, sir. I am sorry to alarm you—I only meant to stop you before you had gone too far." She blushed at her own forwardness as Charles's face relaxed in a smile.

"I am glad you did. But what are you doing awake at this early hour? Surely you are not unwell?" His voice and looks spoke concern, but Katherine shook her head.

"I am well, thank you. I awoke early and sat outside to enjoy the sunrise. But then I saw you, and thought perhaps you were taking an early morning walk, and I wondered if I might join you." Standing so near to him in the quiet, dim light felt more intimate than she had anticipated, and she suddenly saw the impropriety of her request.

"I... I am sorry to impose. I do not wish to intrude," she stammered, uncertainty clouding her tone. "I should not have stopped you. Forgive me," she said as she turned to go, but his voice stopped her.

"You are not intruding, Katherine. I would be glad of your company, if you wish to join me." His voice was soft and his eyes were warm, and in that moment Katherine knew she would follow him anywhere.

They continued across the lawn, making their way towards the northern border of the plantation. The morning was quiet and the air still, and the silence between them was a comfortable one. Katherine smiled to herself as she considered the differences between life in India and life in England. In England, if she were caught walking alone in the pre-dawn light with a man, the scandal caused by such an event would ruin her reputation and label Charles a scoundrel. But life in India was far more relaxed. Sarah had once explained that while the British had attempted to recreate England on the subcontinent, the Anglo-Indian life was neither wholly British nor wholly Indian, but a unique culture all its own. With so few English families living there, it was necessary to make adjustments to the rules and models of society. The result was a comfortable, relaxed society that surprised Katherine greatly upon her arrival, but to which she had quickly grown accustomed. Knowing that both she and her reputation were safe in the company of the handsome man walking beside her, Katherine reveled in the quiet stillness of the morning air.

Approaching the vast fields of indigo, Katherine broke the silence.

"I was always under the impression that indigo was blue," she mused as they stepped down the narrow path between two rows of plants. Charles chuckled.

"Indigo *is* blue."

Katherine looked at him, puzzled. She reached out and gently fingered the pale pink flowers on the plant beside her. "But these blossoms are pink."

"The blossoms are pink, yes. Some are even white. But indigo, as you know it, does not come from the blossoms."

"Does it not?" she asked, surprise coloring her tone.

In reply, Charles reached out and plucked a single, dark leaf from the shrub. He tore it in half and firmly rubbed his fingers along the torn edge, then held out his hand to Katherine. She peered at his fingers, which were streaked in a dark, nondescript

122

color. As she watched, he rubbed his fingers together again and the streaks began to turn blue.

"Why, it is the leaves!" she exclaimed in surprise.

Charles laughed. "Yes, it is. There is a substance in the leaves which reacts with the air, and in turn becomes blue. It is a fascinating phenomenon. As a child, I thought it was magic." He smiled wryly.

"And how does one extract the dye from the leaves?" she asked with interest.

"I can show you, if you'd like," he offered. She eagerly accepted his invitation, and they turned in the direction of a small building lying just beyond the fields. Charles spoke as they walked.

"The plants are harvested by cutting the branches and removing the leaves. The factories that produce our indigo require only that we pack the leaves into crates and ship them off; they extract the dye themselves. But for the smaller, second harvest, we make the indigo here on the plantation. Once the leaves have been removed from the branches, they are laid out to dry in the sun for several days. The dried leaves are then crushed and mixed with water. The mixture is boiled to thicken it, then strained and pressed into cakes before drying."

Katherine was thoughtful. "I think I understand. And the cakes of indigo are used to make dye?"

"Yes."

They had reached the outlying building, and Charles opened the door leading into it. Katherine ducked under the low, thatched roof and entered the room. The building consisted of one enormous room, and was larger than it appeared from the outside.

Several large barrels stood in a row along the far wall, their tops and sides stained dark. A number of huge iron cauldrons were gathered together near them, and to the left of the door hung several dozen empty burlap sacks, and to these Charles led her. He pulled one down and opened it. Reaching inside, he retrieved a shriveled fragment of a leaf and handed it to Katherine. It was thin and crisp, and she handled it gently.

"This is what the leaves look like once they are dried." He pinched off a corner and ground it to powder in his palm. At first it was a pale, dusty blue, but as he rubbed it further, the moisture from his hand turned it a brilliant sapphire. Katherine watched, fascinated.

"Does the dye wash off?"

He laughed. "Unfortunately, no. That is the nature of dye." He smiled crookedly at her, and she blushed. He led her across the room and out another door to the rear of the building, where several fire pits stood empty.

"Those large pots you saw inside will be filled with water and the crushed leaves," he explained. "Then they will be placed here and boiled down."

"How long does it take?"

"The entire process takes several weeks."

"And then the cakes of indigo are sold?"

"Yes. We have two factories in Bengal that purchase the majority of our indigo leaves, but there is a fairly large amount of dye that we produce ourselves for which buyers must be found."

Katherine was nodding. "Yes, Sarah explained that to me. Is it very difficult?"

"Sometimes. I often have to travel great distances in order to sell the remainder of the harvest, or else the indigo is sent to auction."

They had been walking slowly around the building, and Charles now stepped a few paces from her and crouched down to where a small irrigation canal flowed. He did his best to wash away the effects of his demonstration, but when he stood and returned to her side Katherine laughed.

"How long will your hands be blue?" she inquired with amusement.

He chuckled. "A week, at least. Sarah will scold me to high heaven when she sees it, but it could not be helped." He looked down at her and smiled.

Katherine smiled back, and they continued on their way. She glanced up through her lashes at the man walking beside her. His thick brown hair was in careless disarray, and she suddenly had the desire to reach up and run her hands through it. She blushed as she considered the action, embarrassed lest he guess the direction of her thoughts. Most of the time she felt comfortable and safe in his presence, and could spend hours in his company without noticing the passage of time. But then there were moments when he looked at her with such gentleness, and spoke with such tenderness that she felt herself come undone. It was in those moments that her heart threw caution to the wind, and she longed to be wrapped in his arms and in his love for the remainder of her days. If his was a love that could be nurtured and eventually won, she would have gladly paid the price. But she knew what Charles's affections were worth, and also that she had nothing with which to purchase them. No dowry, no connections; she had nothing but her love to offer him, and she knew it would never be enough.

Charles was silent as he walked beside her. She wondered what he was thinking, and soon he satisfied her curiosity by asking her a question.

"Are you happy here, Katherine?"

His question surprised her. "In India? Of course." She spread her arms out, gesturing to the open expanse of fields surrounding them, now filling with Hindu and Muslim workers. "England has its beauties, but nothing compares with this."

He nodded, smiling. "I feel exactly the same way. I know that Sarah longs for London, for a change of scene and society. But I cannot imagine leaving India. It is my home."

They walked in silence for a few moments more. Presently he spoke again.

"Did Sarah ever tell you that I went to England?"

Surprised, Katherine shook her head. "No, she did not. She mentioned that you have promised to take her someday, but she said nothing of you having already been."

Charles grimaced, then laughed. "Yes, Sarah has never forgiven me for not taking her with me. It was a few years after our mother and father died. I was fourteen, but she was only six, and I did not want her to risk the voyage at so young an age. I had been pressured to sell the plantation and move to England with my sister, but I did not want to live in a land I had never visited, even if it was my native soil."

"And how did you like England?"

Charles was thoughtful. "At first, I liked it immensely. It was all so new and exciting. But I had not been there many months before I began to long for my home in India." He looked at

Katherine and smiled. "Can you blame me?"

She shook her head emphatically. "No. I cannot imagine leaving India now that I have come here."

This time it was Charles's turn to be surprised. "Have you really no desire to return to England?"

"No, not at all."

He was thoughtful as he considered her answer. "But what can keep you here? What will you do if you stay?" He stopped and looked at her, determined to hear her answer.

"I do not know," she murmured, halting beside him. "I know that I must find some sort of employment, for an income will be necessary if I remain here." Her voice trailed off, and she looked up at him. He was watching her keenly.

"Is that your only course—to find suitable employment?" He gazed at her earnestly, as if searching for a particular answer.

Katherine dared not voice the hope she entertained in regards to him, for she knew it to be impossible. Unsure what answer to give, she merely shrugged. When he did not reply, she looked up into his deep green eyes and felt her face grow warm. He was watching her intently, his eyes boring into her own as if he could see directly into her soul, searching for some hidden truth. Her heart began to pound and her breath caught in her throat. His look deepened, and he studied her face, his gaze finally coming to rest on her slightly parted lips. He took half a step towards her and she trembled, feeling lightheaded.

"Katherine." His voice was soft, and it matched the quiet morning air. She stared at him, not daring to breathe as she waited for him to speak. Suddenly his face clouded and he drew back, and Katherine watched, confused, as his manner abruptly changed. He took a deep breath and stepped away from her, gazing out at the distant view. He ran his hands through his hair, clearly agitated, but finally he turned to face her. He wore a stiff smile and his manner was aloof.

"Forgive me," he said. "I did not realize the lateness of the hour, and you must be hungry. Shall we go in for breakfast?"

She nodded, trying desperately to hide her disappointment as she fell in step beside him. Summoning all her courage, she smiled up at him, and they walked silently back to the house.

Charles excused himself as soon as he had escorted Katherine into the sitting room, and for once Katherine was happy to see him go. She needed a few moments alone to untangle the confusing mess of emotions within her breast. He did not join her again, and when Sarah entered the room before the meal she indicated that Charles had explained he was preparing to leave on another business trip and would probably dine alone. Katherine's heart sank.

"Is he often away at this time of year?" she asked.

"Not usually," Sarah mused. "I was quite surprised when he told me that he was going away again." She shrugged. "But I am sure that his business must be important and incapable of delay, else he would remain at home."

Katherine nodded numbly. She felt certain that he had guessed her secret, and the thought that she had driven him away stung. To be forced to leave one's own home because of the unwelcome presence and attentions of a guest! Her cheeks burned with humiliation. She knew it had been imprudent to call out to him earlier that morning. If she had only let him go his own way and returned to her room herself, he might now be dining with them. Instead, she had chased after him and nearly thrown herself in his way. How base! How presumptuous! She was disgusted with herself for her behavior.

Not only did she regret her actions, but guilt pricked her heart as she considered that *he* chose to leave instead of asking *her* to remove herself. Knowing that Katherine had nowhere else to go had likely prevented his suggesting it, and she suddenly saw new meaning in his questions regarding her plans. Katherine was mortified. She would have to leave. As soon as possible, she must find a position and be gone from the plantation. Her heart shrank from the idea, but her mind was firm.

Her reverie was interrupted as they were called in for breakfast, and she did her best to put on a smile for Sarah, who still loved and wanted her, it seemed. The thought gave her some comfort, and she sat down to the meal determined to enjoy the time she had remaining with her friend.

Chapter 15

"Lieutenant Marcus Bradford to see you, miss," Wilson announced.

Sarah looked up from her needlework as the gentleman stepped into the room. "Lieutenant Bradford! How delightful to see you again."

"My pleasure, as always, Miss Mendenhall," He bowed and cocked his head. "It seems as though Miss Greenwood is practicing this morning," he said with a grin.

Sarah smiled. "As she does most mornings. Will you not sit down?"

He took the chair Sarah offered, and a servant was dispatched to inform Katherine of their visitor. The sounds of the pianoforte issuing from the library were abruptly cut off, and soon Katherine's figure appeared in the doorway. Marcus stood as she approached.

"Lieutenant Bradford, how very nice to see you again."

"The pleasure is mine, I assure you, Miss Greenwood," he said. Marcus returned to his seat and Katherine joined Sarah on the settee.

"I had hoped to meet with your brother as well," he said, addressing Sarah. "Perhaps between the three of us we might convince him to facilitate an excursion to Barrackpore Park."

"Sadly, you are but two hours too late. Charles left on business this morning, and I am not sure when he plans to return."

Marcus nodded. "An unfortunate circumstance, but I hope that he will have safe travels and return in due course."

Sarah nodded her gratitude.

"And how are the affairs in your own regiment, sir?" Katherine inquired.

Marcus flashed a grin. "At the moment, spirits are unusually high. The officers have just been made aware of a ball to be held at the lower assembly rooms on Esplanade Row. A general invitation has been issued to the officers in several regiments, and there is a notice posted on the assembly room doors."

"A ball! How wonderful! When is it to be?" Sarah asked.

"On Thursday next."

Her face fell. "Oh dear, I am not sure if Charles will have returned by then."

"I am very sorry to hear it," Marcus declared. "I wish him a speedy return, that your pleasure might not be detained." He glanced at Katherine as he said this, who looked down in embarrassment.

This happy news, while keenly agreeable to Sarah, left Katherine feeling torn. The ball sounded wonderful, but she would certainly be prevented from attending such events once she debased herself to the level of a servant. She felt uneasy at the thought of putting it off her search for employment, fearful that her head might surrender to her heart if Charles returned before she had secured a position. Not knowing how long it would take her, she determined to begin as planned, but entertained a hope that nothing might come to fruition until after the ball.

While Katherine struggled with her thoughts, Sarah was tapping her chin thoughtfully. "I cannot say for certain," she said, "but perhaps Charles will return in time. I was very surprised at his going, so I do not think he intends to stay away long."

Marcus turned to Katherine. "And you, Miss Greenwood? Does a ball sound agreeable to you?"

Katherine smiled. "Indeed it does, Lieutenant. I have not attended a ball in ages, and it would be wonderful to dance again."

"Do you dance as well as you play?" Marcus asked.

"I am sure I do not play nor dance as well as some young ladies," she replied, laughing.

"And I am sure that you are too modest, Miss Greenwood," he said with a smile. "In the event that your escort arrives in due course, I would be honored if you would accept my hand for the first two dances, and allow me the pleasure of judging for myself."

Flattered, Katherine stammered her acceptance. Sarah gave her a knowing look, which only flustered her more. She turned the attention from herself by asking Sarah a question.

"Are there many balls and parties held at the assembly rooms?"

"Not usually at this time of year. But after the rainy season, when the weather cools down, there are assemblies held quite often. I am glad we shall have something to look forward to next week."

"The regiment as well," interjected Marcus, smiling wryly. "Several of the newer soldiers are unused to the Indian climate, and the officers are tired of their grumbling. It will be a nice change of pace."

"Do you know who is organizing it?" Sarah asked.

"I understand from Colonel Whittaker that the Landon family is hosting, along with the Cumberland and Robinson families," he replied.

The conversation continued, and each young person took part by turns. Marcus flattered, Sarah teased, and Katherine blushed. They got along splendidly, and the remainder of the morning passed very quickly. Finally Marcus stood to take his leave.

"Thank you so much for coming to call," Katherine smiled at him.

"It was a pleasure I could not long postpone," he said gallantly. Then, leaning forward, he murmured in her ear. "I look forward to dancing with you, Miss Greenwood. If you dance half so prettily as you blush, it shall be the highlight of my evening."

He drew back and looked down on her flushed face, but before she could summon a response, he bowed and was gone.

Left alone once more, Sarah turned to Katherine with a teasing smile. "There, you see? I told you Lieutenant Bradford was quite taken with you, and if you cannot see that now, you are a simpleton."

Katherine forced herself not to blush as she answered. "Perhaps there is some partiality on his side, but I am convinced that his attachment is nothing serious."

Sarah laughed and embraced her friend, smiling at her fondly.

"Dearest Katherine, you underrate your natural charms! You are too modest, too kind, too innocent for your own good. If you were not so convinced that there lies nothing in your power to seriously attach any number of young men, I should be quite concerned of your being taken in."

Though unintentional, Sarah's words stung. Whatever her friend said, Katherine's charms had no power to secure the man she loved—not without a considerable fortune or desirable connections to go with them. She shook her head, and laughed to keep herself from crying.

"You are the dearest girl in the world, but since I have never heard you speak an unkind word to anyone, I am convinced that your natural generosity and affection for those you love overpowers your sense of discernment in this case."

Sarah was laughing as Wilson came to announce dinner, and she linked her arm with Katherine's as they left the room.

The day following Marcus's visit brought another caller to the plantation. Mrs. Whittaker came to talk over the ball, and to offer herself and Colonel Whittaker as escorts for the young ladies. Naturally, they were delighted to accept. Sarah looked at Katherine with a twinkle in her merry blue eyes after their visitor left.

"This is Lieutenant Bradford's doing," she said slyly. "How else would Mrs. Whittaker have known of Charles's absence?"

"Perhaps Charles stopped to call on the colonel before he left town," Katherine replied, not looking up from her needlework.

Sarah laughed and shook her head, and gaily began making plans for the ball. Sarah insisted that Katherine order a new gown, and no amount of protestation on Katherine's part had any effect on her friend. When with flushed cheeks and downcast eyes Katherine finally confessed that she had not the funds for such an expense, Sarah promptly insisted on paying the bill herself.

The dress was ordered, and the following week passed in feverish excitement. Between discussions over hairstyles, gowns, and suitors, Katherine managed to find time alone to look over the *Calcutta Gazette.* She found a few advertisements that interested her: one for an assistant to a recently-arrived seamstress, and the other as a companion to a middle-aged woman, who was planning to open a school in Dinapore. Katherine did not know how to respond to the notices without arousing Sarah's suspicions, so she determined to tuck them away for the time being, and revisit them after the ball.

The day before the dance brought Katherine's gown to the plantation, and even the sweltering heat could not lessen the young ladies' excitement. In the early afternoon, a hired carriage pulled up in front of the house, and before they could reach a consensus as to who might have been conveyed therein, the door opened and Charles walked into the sitting room.

"Charles!" Sarah cried. She ran and embraced her brother, who laughed at her exuberance.

"I pity the men who have not such a sister waiting to greet them when they arrive home." He smiled at her affectionately, and she laughed.

"Oh Charles, I am so glad that you have returned! For what do you think: there is to be a ball at the lower assembly rooms tomorrow night!"

"A ball! Well, if you are glad, then I am glad as well. It is fortunate that I arrived home today and can escort you both there. If you had missed it due to my absence, you may not have welcomed me so cordially as you have hitherto done." He smiled teasingly at her, but Sarah waved him off, sitting down again.

"Oh, we would not have missed the ball on account of your absence. Colonel and Mrs. Whittaker promised to escort us to the assembly rooms if you were away."

Charles's face registered surprise for only a moment, but then he smiled. "I am glad to hear it. But now that I am arrived, their escort will not be needed." He was silent for a moment before turning to Katherine.

"How do you do, Miss Greenwood?" he asked politely.

His tone was cordial but distant, and she had not missed that he had addressed her as "Miss Greenwood" instead of "Katherine." It seemed as though all familiarity and warmth had disappeared as quickly as he had last week.

"I am very well, sir, thank you," she replied, matching his tone.

"I am glad to hear it." He smiled politely and walked across the room to look out onto the covered porch. Katherine resumed trimming her bonnet, but watched him out of the corner of her eye. He paced in front of the double french doors for a few moments, then turned to address his sister.

"How did the Whittakers know of my absence?" he asked casually.

"Did you not call on the colonel before you left town?" she answered innocently, with a glance at Katherine.

"No," he said slowly, his eyes darting between the two of them.

Sarah shrugged. "Oh, well, then I expect Lieutenant Bradford informed them after he came to call on us," she said with exaggerated disinterest. Katherine's face burned, and she did not dare look up from her work. Charles noticed this and frowned, but soon he recovered his composure.

"Lieutenant Bradford came to call, did he?" Charles asked, picking at a plate of biscuits on a side table. He laughed lightly. "Ah, yes, I expect that Captain Strong was with him. I have been anticipating a visit from him and did not have time to inform him of my departure last week."

"No, the captain did not accompany him. Lieutenant Bradford waited upon us alone." Sarah was busy trying to unpick a knot in her embroidery and did not see Charles's eyes flicker to where Katherine sat.

"Indeed!" He tried to make his tone disinterested, but Katherine saw a muscle in his jaw tighten. Her heart gave an excited thump. Perhaps he had not lost *all* regard for her.

"Well!" he suddenly exclaimed brightly. "I believe I shall see what Wilson has been doing in my absence." He strode swiftly to the door and opened it. "Oh, and Sarah," he turned to look back at his sister. "Be sure to have a note sent out to Colonel Whittaker. I will escort you and Katherine to the ball myself."

He was gone. Sarah turned to Katherine with a dramatic sigh. "I fear that we shall not have the pleasure of an hour long carriage ride in Lieutenant Bradford's company," she said with melancholy. Katherine looked up, surprised.

"But we would have been taken by the Whittakers, not the

137

Lieutenant."

A mischievous grin appeared on Sarah's face. "Yes, but whom do you think would have accompanied them?"

Katherine blushed, but then she laughed and tossed her head, doing her best to imitate her friend. "I do not care in what manner we get to the ball," she declared, "so long as I never have to sit down once there."

Sarah joined in her laughter, and they continued their preparations for the following evening.

Chapter 16

The next morning dawned bright and hot, but for once Katherine did not care. She was alive with excitement, and even Sarah's teasing remarks at breakfast could not dampen her spirits. They would have to leave the plantation early in order to arrive at the assembly rooms on time, so shortly after dinner the young people retired to dress.

Katherine had frowned at the extravagance of a new ball gown the week prior, but as Bhavani helped her on with the dress, she was glad to have something so pretty to wear. The ivory colored crepe was embroidered with small pink rosebuds around the wide hem, and it set off her dark hair and dark eyes beautifully. Bhavani cinched up her corset and slid the gown over her head, fastening it behind her. She pulled and combed Katherine's hair and piled it on top of her head, weaving a cluster of delicate orchid blossoms into her coffee-colored tresses. The flush of youth and excitement set off her creamy complexion nicely, and Katherine stood before the mirror to admire herself when Bhavani had finished.

"*Sundara*," her maid shyly announced. Katherine smiled.

"Thank you, Bhavani. I would not be so without your help."

The young girl beamed.

Katherine was breathless with excitement when she entered the sitting room a short time later. When she saw that Sarah had not yet finished her toilette and Charles was the only other occupant, her face grew warm, and she wished that she had remained in her room. Charles turned to look at her from his place by the window, and his unsmiling gaze reminded Katherine of the first day they met.

He looked more handsome than ever, in a formal black tailcoat and trousers. His necktie and vest were of white silk, and a black top hat was tucked under his arm. Katherine saw that he was clean shaven as usual, and his chestnut hair was neatly combed and recently trimmed. He stared across the room at her, his vivid green eyes boring into her own. Her pulse quickened, wondering what he would say. Finally his face relaxed into a smile.

"Miss Greenwood, you look absolutely charming," he said.

Katherine felt a tinge of disappointment. He had addressed her as "Miss Greenwood" again, and his compliment was hardly significant. But she forced herself to smile in response and dropped a small curtsy. "Thank you, sir. You look very well yourself."

He laughed. "It does not much signify what I shall wear this evening. I am not a dandy; I simply aspire not to mortify my sister with my lack of fashionable taste." He turned away as he spoke, and Katherine felt her spirits sink further. The door opened once more and Sarah swept into the room.

"Oh good, we are all assembled," she said. She turned to Katherine and exclaimed over her friend. "My dearest Katherine! You are positively radiant. That dress is absolutely perfect for your coloring and figure. Is she not the picture of beauty itself, Charles?"

Charles nodded absently, and Sarah turned back to her friend. She linked her arm through Katherine's and spoke close to her ear as Charles went to call the carriage. "I daresay you shall receive a much prettier response from Lieutenant Bradford," she whispered. Katherine blushed in reply, and the two young women followed their escort out of the room.

Charles's heart felt wrenched in two as he watched Katherine dance down the length of the hall. No sooner had they entered the crowded assembly rooms than her attentions had been captured by Lieutenant Marcus Bradford. He secured her hand for the first two dances, and Katherine's smiles had barely been bestowed on anyone else throughout the evening. Charles had danced with a few young ladies, but he could not recall who they were nor what they had talked of. He saw only Katherine. Katherine leaning on Marcus Bradford's arm. Katherine laughing at the wit of something Marcus said to her. Katherine smiling up at Marcus as she curtsied following a dance. Charles felt ill with jealousy.

He laughed darkly to himself. He had been a fool to think that his recent absence would have lessened the effect of her charms. If anything, it had done the complete opposite. He had never wanted anything as greatly as he wanted her, and nothing felt so further from his grasp. He had fled, not only to escape his weakening willpower, but also to find a purchaser for his unencumbered harvest—one that would provide him with sufficient funds to pay off his mortgage. He had found some interest, and a promising prospect to be had in Balasore, but nothing could be decided upon until after the harvest was in. So he had returned, determined to keep Katherine at a distance and thereby ensure the safety of her heart in case his plans came to naught, but he had not counted upon Marcus Bradford.

He cursed inwardly and drained his glass. Another set was beginning to form, and for once Katherine stood without her regimental shadow. He crossed the room, determination etched in every feature.

The room was crowded and hot, and although she was enjoying herself, Katherine was glad to have a moment's reprieve from dancing. She had only been able to cry off by begging Marcus to get her a drink. As he went to fetch her some refreshment, she fanned herself and tried not to think about Charles.

He had spoken hardly a word to her during the hour long carriage ride into town, and since their arrival she had scarcely seen him. Of course, Marcus had attached her nearly from the moment she entered the room, but her eyes were intermittently drawn to wherever Charles was throughout the evening. She saw him dance with a few pretty young women, and her heart nearly broke. She had no claim on him, and therefore did not feel the bitterness of jealousy; only sorrow that she had nothing to offer which might invite and secure his affections for herself.

She glanced towards the corner where she had last observed him, but he was not there. Disappointed, she scanned the room for his tall, fine figure. When she could not find him, her brow furrowed with concern.

"Whom, may I ask, has the pleasure of being sought by such pretty eyes?"

Katherine jumped as Charles's voice sounded low in her ear. Her pulse quickened and her face flushed. She turned to look up at him, and found that his handsome face was only inches from her own. For a moment, she merely stared at him, trying to remember how to breathe. At last she found her voice.

"You, sir," she said candidly.

Surprise and pleasure flickered across his face, but he narrowed his eyes as he smiled at her. "Flattering words, but I cannot believe them. You have been engaged the whole of the evening to Lieutenant Bradford."

She blushed. "Lieutenant Bradford solicited my hand when he called on us last week."

Charles nodded. "He is a fortunate man. I have been envying him his partner these last two hours, and I am now determined to deprive him of your company."

She thrilled at his words. Charles was acting anything but distant now. Could it be possible that she had merely imagined his cool civility over the last two days?

Charles bowed and held out his hand to her. "May I have the pleasure of this dance?" He gazed with unyielding determination into her eyes, and Katherine felt herself come undone. She nodded and placed her hand in his as he led her to the floor.

The musicians were just beginning as they found their places in the set. Charles's eyes were locked on Katherine's face as they first moved together, then apart in the steps of the dance. Katherine felt her color rising, and she glanced away from him to reassemble her nerves. She saw Lieutenant Bradford standing against the wall, a glass of lemonade in one hand and a look of confused concern on his face. She felt a twinge of guilt as she watched him, and she turned her eyes back to Charles. He smiled wryly at her.

"Do you regret your decision to stand up with me?" he asked as they drew together.

She blushed, embarrassed at being caught. "Not at all."

He glanced past her and chuckled. "Lieutenant Bradford certainly does."

Her color deepened but she said nothing. The dance drew them apart for a moment, but when they converged once more he smiled and said, "I had no idea of your being such an excellent dancer. Does it give you as much enjoyment as your music?"

She smiled. "Not nearly, but I do find dancing to be a pleasant diversion."

He nodded. "I must agree with you there. Dancing has never been a favorite past time of mine, but I think it may be because I did not have a partner to suit me. At the moment, I feel as though I could dance all night with pleasure." His look deepened, the burning intensity in his eyes nearly unraveling her senses.

She shook her head, confused. Charles's current behavior conflicted so greatly with much of his treatment towards her of late that she knew not what to think. He mistook her reaction and raised an eyebrow. "You do not believe me?"

Embarrassed at having been caught in personal reverie, she replied, "That is not why I shook my head."

"Why, then?"

"I was simply thinking of something else."

He laughed. " 'Ay, there's the rub,' " he quoted softly. "I, who does not usually enjoy dancing, finally find myself paired with a talented, beautiful young lady, and her mind is engaged elsewhere." His eyes darted to where Lieutenant Bradford was talking with another officer. Katherine knew not what to say, and so was silent. The dance continued, and they did not speak again. When it finished, he escorted her to a seat near the veranda, then bowed and excused himself.

Katherine could not determine if she was more disappointed or confused. Charles's behavior left her heart feeling vulnerable and her mind indignant. His flattering words and intense looks sent her heart racing and her hopes soaring, but almost the next minute his cold, indifferent manner validated her mind's rationale that she was a simpleton to believe he had any serious designs on her. Her head and her heart ached from the constant fluctuation, and she rubbed a hand against her forehead, exhausted.

"Miss Greenwood, are you unwell?"

She looked up into the anxious eyes of Marcus Bradford. He held a glass of lemonade in one hand and a look of concern on his handsome face. Sitting down beside her, he took her hand. "You do not look well. What is wrong?"

Katherine feigned a smile. "It is nothing, I am only a bit warm."

"It is no wonder, in this hall," he murmured as he stood.

"Come, let us walk out onto the veranda. There is a light breeze that may do you some good."

She took the arm he offered her and they walked slowly through the open doors. The temperature was not much cooler outside, but as Marcus had indicated there was a light breeze, and it cooled her brow and helped to clear her mind. She looked up into Marcus's grave face. His eyes were serious and his jaw was tense with concern. She smiled, hoping it would help him to relax.

"This is better. Thank you, Lieutenant."

"Is there nothing more I can do?" He shook his head and flushed a little. "I believe I set your lemonade down inside. Shall I get you another one?"

She nodded. "Yes, please."

"Then I shall procure one at once." His mouth turned up at the corners. "Just promise me you will be here when I return."

She blushed in embarrassment but managed a small laugh. "You may count on it, sir."

He nodded and turned to go back inside. She watched him stride purposefully through the crowd, and something stirred in her mind. *Lieutenant Bradford is a fine young officer*, she thought. *He is kind and witty, and his partiality is clear.* Looking through the doors, she scanned the crowd for a sign of her friends. She saw Sarah dancing gaily with a young officer, but there was no sign of Charles. She sighed. Perhaps her heart needed to learn a lesson from her head. She watched Marcus coming towards her with a glass in his hand, relief evident in his expression as he saw her standing where he had left her. She smiled in genuine gratitude as he stepped beside her.

146

"Thank you," she said with feeling. His face lit up in a radiant smile, and he bowed.

"Anything for you, Miss Greenwood," he said gallantly. "I am at your service."

She smiled, and the rest of the evening passed pleasantly in his company. When at last he handed her up into the carriage, she felt content with the course of the evening. Sarah sat down beside Katherine, and Charles took his place across from his sister. Aside from a few remarks about the evening in general, he did not speak to them the entire ride back to the plantation. Katherine felt a twinge of regret, but her mind kept her heart firmly in its place. She was no Juliet: her future happiness did not depend entirely upon Charles Mendenhall. She recalled the looks of admiration and the gentle compliments she had received from Marcus during the course of the evening, and it helped to soothe her wounded heart. For the first time, she considered that perhaps Sarah was correct in her assumption about Lieutenant Bradford's attentions, and if it were so, Katherine may never need to procure employment at all. The thought made her smile.

Chapter 17

The day following a ball is almost as delightful as the dance itself, for it brings young people together to talk over the event. Sarah and Katherine were walking around the small lawn doing precisely that the next morning when a servant was dispatched to bring them inside. They hastily made their way to the sitting room, where Charles was waiting for them. He turned at their approach.

"There you are!" he greeted them. He held a piece of paper in his hand and had a somewhat amused air about him. "I wanted to inform you, Sarah, that Aunt Ellen is coming for a visit. I have had a letter from her this morning."

"Aunt Ellen! Oh, how wonderful. It seems ages since she was here last." Sarah clapped her hands in delight. "Will she be coming into port soon?" she asked.

"Her letter indicates that she will arrive sometime in September or October."

Sarah laughed. "I expect she wants to wait for cooler temperatures." Turning to Katherine, she explained. "Aunt Ellen is our father's widowed sister. Her home is in England, but her son has a tea plantation outside of Serampore and she spends much of her time here in India. We have not seen her for a few years, and I wondered if her traveling days were over, but I am glad to hear it is not so."

Charles chuckled. "Aunt Ellen is as hearty and stout as a lad of nineteen," he declared. "I do not think she shall ever give off traveling."

Sarah noticed that Charles still held a letter in his hand. "Was there any other news?" she asked him.

"Not from England," he said. "But I have had a letter from Mr. Grant."

Sarah raised her eyebrows. "Mr. Stephen Grant?"

"Yes."

"What can he possibly have to say?"

"Only that his daughter has lately arrived in Calcutta, and he hopes that myself and my fair sister will wait upon her soon."

"Priscilla Grant is in Calcutta?" Sarah exclaimed. "I never thought to see her again! How very unexpected. Does he give any explanation for her return?"

"None whatsoever." He smiled wryly at his sister. "But I am sure you will lose no time in finding out."

Katherine laughed at the indignant look on her friend's face. Sarah had an eager ear for gossip, and the fact that an event as large as this had occurred without her prior knowledge was a keen blow. Turning to her, Katherine asked, "Who is Miss Grant, pray?"

"Miss Priscilla Grant is the only child of a wealthy family from Calcutta. Her father, Stephen Grant, came here when our parents were alive. Miss Grant was born a few years after their arrival, but was sent away to be raised in London. She has spent nearly her entire life there, and has not been to India for many years." She paused, thoughtful. "I wonder what brings her back?"

"You and Katherine may call on her this morning and find out if you like, but I have business to attend to." Excusing himself, Charles left the room.

"What sort of young lady is Miss Grant?" Katherine asked.

Sarah tapped her chin thoughtfully. "I cannot say for certain, since it has been many years since I saw her, but she was very nice when last we met. She is quite fashionable. Tall and slender, with rich golden hair and very pretty manners. She and Charles spent considerable time together when she was last in India, but I was not out yet. I shall be happy to see her again, though." She turned to Katherine with eyes suddenly aglow. "And she can bring us all the latest news from London!"

Katherine laughed. "She sounds very interesting. Born in India but raised in England. I wonder which one she prefers?" she mused, thinking of the conversation she and Charles had had on the subject.

Sarah smiled. "I would guess England. She could have come any number of times to India, but instead she preferred to stay in London."

"Perhaps she was afraid of the journey."

"Perhaps." Sarah's brow was furrowed. "Still, it seems very strange that after all these years, she chose to return at this time. I wonder what brings her back to Calcutta?" she said again. "What do you think? Shall we call on her today?"

Katherine nodded her head emphatically. "Yes indeed. I

should be very happy to make her acquaintance."

"And I shall be very happy to hear some new gossip," Sarah declared with an impish grin. They laughed, and went to fetch their bonnets and gloves.

"It was very kind of you to call," Priscilla said as Katherine and Sarah sat down.

The ladies were assembled in the drawing room of the Grant's enormous house in White Town. Katherine had been quite impressed as they drove through the gate, and her opinion of Priscilla Grant was at first not any less favorable.

Sarah's description had not done her justice. She was tall and willowy, with clear ivory skin and full, pink lips. She had large blue eyes rimmed in thick dark lashes, and a mass of golden hair was piled atop her head. Perfect ringlets framed her angelic face and softened her statuesque appearance. Outwardly she was loveliness personified, but there was a calculating look in her eyes that made Katherine uneasy.

"I confess that I was very surprised when Charles told us you were lately arrived," Sarah hinted. Her voice trailed off suggestively, hoping that their hostess would offer some explanation. But Miss Grant only sighed dreamily.

"Dear Charles! Why did he not attend you this morning? I should be very happy to see him again," she said with an arch smile.

"He is much involved with business at present," Sarah excused, "but I am sure he would be happy to call on you as soon as he is able."

"I hope your journey was pleasant?" Katherine asked politely.

"When is such a journey ever pleasant?" Priscilla laughed. "Our dear Miss Mendenhall cannot know what it is like, but I am sure that *you* will agree with me that sea voyages are detestable."

"There are certainly many things unpleasant about them," Katherine agreed.

"Unpleasant!" Priscilla drew back surprised. "No, indeed. I said detestable and I meant it." Recovering herself, she asked, "And what brings you to India, Miss Greenwood?"

Katherine hesitated. "I have long desired to see India. I have heard nothing but praise of this country since I was a girl."

"Have you any family here?" Priscilla asked with a shrewd look. Katherine was spared from answering by a laugh from Sarah.

"My dear Miss Grant, this will never do! Never mind Miss Greenwood's own reasons; what brings *you* to India?"

Their hostess turned to face Sarah, and Katherine gave her friend a grateful smile. Priscilla smiled a bit condescendingly and answered, "My father wished me to come."

Sarah frowned. "Was there no other reason?"

"Perhaps you feel that the request of a parent is not reason enough."

This time it was Sarah's turn to blush. "No, indeed. Forgive me, I only thought it might have been something more particular. But of course you would want to oblige your father. Is he in good health? How is your mother?"

"They are both very well, thank you." Priscilla smiled angelically, and all sign of displeasure disappeared. Katherine wondered at her erratic manners.

"How did you leave London?" Sarah inquired after a few minutes.

Priscilla sighed dramatically. "I left London disappointed. Three seasons have been enough to convince me that there is not a single gentleman in all of England worthy of the bestowal of my affections," she lamented.

"Indeed!" was Sarah's polite response. "Have the seasons been ill-attended, then?"

"No, not at all. But London seems to attract far less of the *true* gentility anymore." She gave Sarah a knowing look over her teacup, and Sarah nodded, trying to look as though she understood.

Priscilla continued. "And I am afraid I left a few broken hearts behind as well. Though *I* never encouraged any intimacy, there were several young men who were very attached to me. But they were such insolent, prattling things! I confess that I could barely be civil to the last one when he offered for me. I knew then that I had to get out of London, and the arrival of Father's letter came at a most advantageous time." She smiled benevolently.

Priscilla's portrayal of London society seemed hardly sensible, and Katherine had not missed the warmth with which she had asked about "dear Charles." She wondered if there was more to Miss Grant's sudden appearance in India than a disenchanted season.

The remainder of the morning passed pleasantly enough. Sarah could not discover any further reason for Priscilla's unexpected appearance in India, but she was fully satisfied in her desire to hear about the latest fashions from London. Priscilla's pale pink dress was beautifully tailored in the latest style, with a dropped waist, a full skirt, and short, puffed sleeves. She laughed at Sarah's endless questions, and made her a present of some recent fashion magazines. Katherine was quiet but attentive during most of the visit. Miss Grant hardly spoke to her, and Katherine rarely supplied anything to the conversation except when directly applied to for comment. When it was discovered that she was musical, Priscilla turned her large, blue eyes on Katherine and inquired of whom she had been taught.

"My grandmother taught me," Katherine replied. She could see the disdain hidden behind Priscilla's polite surprise, and it rankled her. She lifted her chin. "My grandmother, Lady Rockwell, was an excellent musician. She was far superior to any tutor I have known."

Priscilla narrowed her eyes, but said nothing. She turned once again to Sarah and bestowed another heavenly smile on her. Katherine sighed inwardly, tired of Miss Grant's flippant airs.

In due course their visit ended, and Sarah invited Priscilla to join them for dinner soon. Priscilla simpered her thanks, but Katherine almost wished she had found an excuse to decline. The two ladies set off; one in rapturous spirits over her new magazines, the other with grateful relief at their departure.

Once in the carriage, Sarah sighed with delight. "Is not Miss Grant a charming young woman? I am glad she has come back to India, for now we shall have such fun! She is very fond of company and dancing, and I daresay there shall be twice as many balls and parties now that she is here."

Unwilling to disappoint her friend, but unable to make such commendable remarks, Katherine said nothing. But this did not satisfy her friend.

"What is your opinion of her, Katherine?" Sarah pressed.

Not wanting to offend Sarah, Katherine hesitated. "She *is* very beautiful, but there seems something wanting in her manner of address. Did she not seem a bit proud by your estimation?"

Sarah was thoughtful. "I suppose she *is* a bit proud. But I imagine one cannot help being so, when one is raised in London," she said good-naturedly. Katherine smiled.

"Dear Sarah, I do not believe it is possible for you to speak ill of anyone."

"Indeed, you are mistaken," Sarah said, smiling wickedly. "For what good is there to be said of Captain Strong?"

Chapter 18

The seasons were changing, and as Sarah had predicted, the heat became nearly unbearable. Clouds rolled in from the coast, bringing with them torrential rain unlike anything Katherine had ever experienced. The first storm of the season struck a few nights after the ball, and Katherine had lain awake, terrified that the house was being torn asunder. But it was still standing when daylight broke through the clouds, and while she was at first relieved, her relief did not last long. Suffocating humidity permeated the bungalow, and Sarah and Katherine now spent nearly all their time indoors. The doors and windows were shuttered to keep out the heat, and a servant was always employed in waving the *punkah* in the sitting room. The only relief afforded them came when a shower burst forth just as the sun was setting. The rain served to cool the air somewhat, and without the sun to raise the temperature, it was relatively pleasant. Sarah and Katherine spent many evenings on the portico in the cool, damp air following such storms.

Lieutenant Marcus Bradford was now a regular visitor at the

bungalow. He came down several times a week, and his preference and regard for Katherine continued to grow. Katherine herself began to grow fond of him, and though she did not entertain such wild assumptions as Sarah often indulged in, she thought it indeed possible that he might offer for her, and began to consider marriage instead of employment as a means of providing for her future comfort and distancing herself from Charles.

Almost all intimacy between Charles and herself seemed now dissolved. He was polite, considerate, and attentive, but she was always "Miss Greenwood" now, and their walks and private conversations had disappeared as well. Once, while playing the piano in the library, she suddenly looked up and found him standing in the doorway, watching her. She met his gaze but he drew back quickly, and she had not seen him for days afterward. Katherine's heart ached, and even while her mind insisted it was all for the best, she yearned for the friend she had lost.

Late one morning, a carriage pulled up in front of the house. Sarah was in the kitchen, concocting a rub that supposedly eliminated freckles, and Katherine was in the library learning some new music when Wilson came in and announced that Miss Priscilla Grant had arrived. Katherine walked slowly to the parlor and found Miss Grant sitting primly on a chair, her gloved hands folded neatly in her lap. She stood as Katherine entered the room.

"Miss Grant, what a pleasure to see you," she smiled politely.

Priscilla returned all but the smile. "Thank you, Miss Greenwood. Is Miss Mendenhall not at home?"

Sarah entered the room just at that moment, having been summoned by Wilson first but needing to scrub her face clean of her homemade beauty ointment.

"Miss Grant!" she exclaimed, smiling widely. "How very kind of you to call."

Priscilla smiled benevolently at her. "I have been wanting to call on you all week, but the rain has prevented my coming," she replied.

"Yes, it has been raining torrents, has it not?" Sarah mused. "But then, I suppose it always does this time of year," she finished brightly.

"How is your family?" Katherine inquired politely.

Priscilla indicated that they were well, and Sarah rang for tea. A servant came in bearing a tray of soft biscuits and mint sandwiches, and the ladies ate while they visited. In the midst of their refreshment the door opened and Charles stepped into the room.

He stopped abruptly, clearly surprised to find them all assembled. He composed himself quickly however, and smiled as he bowed to Priscilla.

"Miss Grant! What an unexpected pleasure," he said cheerfully. Priscilla nodded and smiled demurely.

"Surely my presence is not *entirely* unexpected, Charles," she said suggestively. His face flushed but he forced a laugh.

"As coquettish as ever, I see." He glanced quickly at Katherine and found her watching him intently. His face flushed again.

"Come Charles, will you not join us?" his sister invited. "I daresay you have other items of business to attend to, but do be civil and sit down."

Charles chuckled. Seating himself next to Sarah, he cleared

his throat. "You are right, my dear sister, I do have business to attend to." He continued, ignoring the pouty look she gave him. "I was actually on my way to find you, to inform you that I shall be expecting a visitor shortly."

"Oh? And whom else might we have the pleasure of seeing today?"

"Colonel Whittaker. He promised to call the first fine morning we had, and I expect him at any moment." Here he glanced at Katherine again, but seeing that he was observed by Priscilla he immediately turned his attentions to her. With false animation he asked, "Miss Grant, how was your voyage? Are you pleased to find yourself once more in Calcutta?"

She laughed. "Come now, Charles, there is no need for small talk between us. We were quite intimate the last time I was here, were we not?" She smiled coyly at him, but he was not to be drawn in.

"It has been quite some years since then, Miss Grant, and much has changed, I assure you." His manner was abrupt, and his tone harsher than he intended.

Her smile faded. She glanced at Katherine, who was busy looking anywhere but at Charles, and her eyes narrowed. Charles saw her look and cleared his throat. He forced a smile. "That is to say, Sarah and I were unaware that we would be granted the privilege of your company again, Priscilla. To what do we owe the pleasure of seeing you again in Calcutta?"

Katherine's head snapped up. *Priscilla?* She watched Charles closely, hoping that she had misheard him. But there he sat next to Sarah, enjoying Priscilla's smiles, laughing at her wit, and completely and thoroughly ignoring Katherine. He seemed to

159

have eyes and ears only for Miss Grant, and since Sarah was equally enthralled in their conversation, Katherine sat quiet and alone, feeling absolutely wretched. It was one thing to wish for Charles to find an elegant, worthy young lady to pay his addresses to; it was quite another to witness it firsthand. Finally she slipped out of the room and made her way to the library, where she could at least find some solace in her music.

She sat down in front of the instrument and sighed, her heart aching on so many levels. She glanced at the music she had left on the stand. It was a recent piece by Frederick Chopin, his *Arpeggio*. It had arrived for her the previous week, and she had been struggling to play it ever since. Her hands were small, and it was difficult for her to play some of the intervals. She started in the fifteenth measure, where she had left off, and began to play.

The chords sounded broken, in more ways than one. Frustrated with her inability to play the music, she thrust it angrily aside. Restless, she glanced around the room, never lingering too long on any one aspect. Finally her eyes came back to rest on the instrument before her. She closed her eyes and delved into her memory, trying to find a piece of music to help lift her spirits. She went through various composers in her mind, and finally decided upon Mozart. He had been a true master, and she loved his piano sonatas immensely. She rifled through the stack of sheet music on the chair beside her until she found his piano Sonata No. 1. Placing the music before her, she began to play.

The music started quickly, its brisk pace helping to fill Katherine's mind and block out the thought of Charles and Priscilla in the other room. It was bright and cheerful, and by the time she had reached the second movement she felt in much better control of her emotions. She enjoyed the slower, more thoughtful configuration of this section of music, but the third movement brought back the faster rhythm and lighter mood which she craved. Her fingers flew over the keys, pounding the chords at the end. A laugh burst forth from her mouth as she finished, and she took a deep, cleansing breath.

"You never cease to amaze me."

She looked up into the bright, admiring eyes of Lieutenant Bradford. "Lieutenant, what a pleasant surprise! I did not know you had arrived."

"Only just. I heard that Colonel Whittaker had some business here, and I offered to keep him company on the drive." He winked at her, and she laughed. What did it matter that Charles was paying his addresses to Priscilla? She was courted by a handsome, uniformed, admiring young gentleman, and right now her heart was glad of it.

"Would you care to take a turn about the grounds, Miss Greenwood?"

She grimaced. "It is almost noon. The heat is nearly unbearable as it is."

He smiled. "Then let us sit on the back porch. There we shall be sheltered from the sun, and perhaps a welcome breeze will cool your flushed cheeks."

She blushed, and his smile widened. Narrowing her eyes in mock severity she said, "I believe you find enjoyment in making me blush, Lieutenant."

"Of course I do," he replied, unashamed. "You are never prettier than with a flush of color against your ivory throat."

She gasped, astonished at his forwardness. But he laughed,

and his eyes were warm as they gazed into her own. She could not help but smile at the adoration she saw in his look, and taking his arm, she agreed to accompany him.

Charles sat tensely in his chair, angry and annoyed. He was angry with himself, he was angry with Priscilla Grant, and he was angry with Colonel Whittaker, who sat across from him in Charles's private study. Charles had been startled by the sudden appearance of Priscilla Grant, and he had allowed his regard for Katherine to overcome his sensibilities and put them both at risk. He had acted quickly in order to take Miss Grant off her guard, but he noticed Katherine's dejected appearance once he engaged her in conversation. In that moment, it took every ounce of strength he possessed not to throw himself at Katherine's feet and beg for her forgiveness and her love. He knew he had been treating her abominably of late, and he feared that his assumed disregard might destroy any lingering affection she still held for him. He saw her slip out of the sitting room, heard her struggle on the piano to find refuge in her music, and he had very nearly gone to her then.

But then Colonel Whittaker arrived with Lieutenant Bradford. Charles should have known that Marcus would take advantage of the opportunity to attend the colonel to the plantation, but he had been so preoccupied with preparing for the harvest that he had forgotten to request Colonel Whittaker's presence alone. Almost as soon as the men had joined the party in the sitting room, Marcus excused himself "to attend to Miss Greenwood, in the library." The music had stopped, laughter was heard, and Charles had been forced to listen to a detailed explanation of Miss Grant's recent millinery conquest while the woman he loved was courted and charmed by another.

Now Charles sat in his study, trying to listen politely to the colonel's ceaseless prattling. Anxious to have the visit concluded so that he could dispose of Marcus Bradford, he and the colonel had left Sarah and Priscilla chatting in the sitting room while they retired to Charles's study. Their business completed, he had hoped that the colonel would excuse himself to return to his men. But the older gentleman seemed content to while away the late morning hours in drowsy conversation. Charles felt as though he was going mad.

Finally the colonel stood. "I shall be sending a load of men and supplies down to Balasore at the end of the week," he said. "I can have your message delivered to Mr. Cooper then, and you should have your reply within a fortnight."

"Thank you, Colonel."

He nodded in acknowledgment, and the gentlemen left the room just as Marcus and Katherine emerged from the library, having come back inside. Katherine was looking up at Marcus, her face aglow, her arm linked in his. Marcus had the air of one who had finally found himself in possession of a treasure long sought. Charles felt ill.

"Lieutenant," the colonel barked.

"Yes, Colonel," Marcus saluted, stepping away from Katherine.

"We shall take our leave now. The regiment cannot wait all day. You know how Captain Strong is..." He raised an eyebrow and gazed at Marcus sternly. Marcus bobbed his head quickly, and the two men turned to leave. The lieutenant turned back to Katherine, his face softening as his eyes fell on her.

"It was a pleasure to spend the morning in your company," he murmured, raising her hand to his lips.

"Thank you for coming to call," she replied, smiling shyly up at him.

Marcus gazed into her eyes for a long moment, then, realizing that Charles still stood near his study door, watching them, he dropped her hand and bowed. Turning to Charles, he bowed again. "Thank you for your hospitality, sir," he said.

Charles merely nodded, his face serious. With one last smile to Katherine, Marcus walked out the door and into the waiting carriage.

Katherine watched it drive out of sight, purposely keeping her eyes on it as long as she could, to avoid looking into the eyes she felt boring into the back of her head. Finally she turned.

Charles stood perfectly still, watching her gravely. Katherine knew his face well enough to be able to read his emotions, and what she saw nearly made her cry out. His eyes held the same haunted look she had struggled to define so long ago, and the sadness buried just under the surface wrenched her heart in two. She took a step towards him, and opened her mouth to comfort him, but before she could even form the words he turned and was gone.

Chapter 19

Priscilla stayed for dinner, but Charles buried himself in his study and refused to come out. Sarah apologized for her brother's lack of civility, and Priscilla very prettily excused him with a wave of her dainty hand. Confident after the forenoon's tête-à-tête with "dear Charles," she was not worried about one missed dinner appointment. Judging from the anxious looks Katherine kept shooting towards the door, Priscilla was actually glad that he was not in attendance. Though she was not entirely sure of Charles's own feelings on the matter, she felt certain that Katherine had her cap set for Charles, and Priscilla knew there was nothing so irresistible to a man as a woman who fancies herself in love with him.

She did not stay long after dinner, as she had another engagement for the evening, but it was decided that the three young ladies would meet again the next morning. She smiled angelically at Sarah as they said goodbye, and managed a civil farewell to Katherine. Once she had gone, Sarah turned to Katherine with a bright smile.

"You know how much I adore you, Katherine dearest, but I am sure you will agree with me that it is lucky for us that Miss Grant has come back to Calcutta. Is she not diverting?"

Katherine laughed lightly and evaded her question. "I believe you would find a hurricane to be a rather fine amusement, Sarah," she teased. "Anything out of the ordinary will do for you."

Laughing, Sarah linked her arm with Katherine's. "I must speak to Cook about the menu tomorrow. Shall I meet you in the library when I am finished?'

"Thank you, but I believe I should like to lie down," Katherine said with an apologetic smile.

"Are you unwell?" Sarah asked, her brow furrowed.

"No, I am merely tired."

Sarah nodded. "I understand. Please send for me if you need anything at all," she said gently. Katherine smiled gratefully at her before moving towards the hall.

Alone in her room, Katherine pulled out the advertisements she had saved. She read them through again, contemplating each position and imagining her life in such a situation. But she could not do it, and after the morning spent with Lieutenant Bradford, she did not think she needed to. Taking a deep breath, she tore them up and threw them away. She only wished her feelings for Charles were as easily discarded.

Charles opened the door to his study and listened. Nothing. He stepped into the hall and listened again, but there was nothing but stillness. As he stood there, the door to the sitting room

166

opened and Wilson came out. Seeing Charles hesitating in the hallway, he bowed and stepped towards him.

"Can I be of assistance, sir?"

Charles looked beyond his steward to see if anyone would be following him out of the parlor. Wilson noticed this and said, "It is only your sister therein. Miss Greenwood has retired to her room."

Charles's face relaxed, then suddenly grew concerned. "Is Katherine unwell?"

A hint of a smile appeared on his steward's face. "I believe she was merely tired. She is still getting accustomed to the Indian heat."

Charles nodded. "Yes, of course. Thank you, Wilson."

Wilson bowed, and Charles stepped past him into the sitting room. Upon his entrance, Sarah looked up, and the cook, with whom she had been conversing, discreetly excused himself.

"Are you come to keep your dear, lonely sister company?" Sarah asked. Charles smiled at her.

"I am sorry. I know I have been neglecting you."

"Yes, you have. But with Katherine here I do not miss you so much," she answered with a teasing smile.

"I am glad to hear it." He sat next to her on the sofa, and taking her hand said gently, "I hope this will be the last time I have to go away for some time."

"What! You are leaving again?" Sarah cried out. "Charles! What is taking you away so often?"

"I do not have to leave for some time yet. It is business, Sarah. You know that is the only thing that draws me away from the plantation."

"I know," she sighed. She looked up at him wistfully. "I only wish you did not have to go at all."

Charles gathered his sister into his arms. He knew that underneath Sarah's cheerful exterior was a heart still broken from their family's loss. He kissed her on top of the head. "Let me make it up to you," he said gently. "What can I do?"

Sarah pulled away and looked at him shrewdly. "Do you really want to make it up to me?"

"Indeed, I do." He grinned. "Would you like a new parasol?"

She shook her head. "I want to go to Barrackpore Park."

"Barrackpore Park!"

"Yes."

He looked at her suspiciously. "Why Barrackpore?"

"Because I have always wanted to see it," Sarah confessed dejectedly. "But it is too far for me to travel alone, and you are always so busy..." Her voice trailed off, and she looked down. Her loneliness pricked at Charles's heart, and he took her in his arms again. He held her for a moment, then drew back and smiled at her.

"Then we shall go to Barrackpore."

Sarah's face lit up. "Truly, Charles? Are you truly in earnest?"

"Truly, Sarah."

"Oh, thank you, Charles!" She threw her arms around his neck. "I cannot wait to tell Katherine—she will be delighted! And of course we shall invite Priscilla Grant and Lieutenant Bradford as well. We shall be such a merry party and have such a jolly time!"

Charles was alarmed. "Would it not be more to our taste if it were only ourselves and Katherine?"

"Of course not," Sarah scoffed. "Lieutenant Bradford knows all about Barrackpore and has already offered to show us the park. And it would be horribly rude to exclude Priscilla, now that we are all so chummy again."

Charles did not know what to say. The last thing he wanted was to provide further opportunity for Marcus to win Katherine's affections. He was not thrilled with the idea of having to handle Katherine and Priscilla both at once, either. But perhaps in a group the damage would be minimal. He finally nodded.

"I shall have to leave in a fortnight. Let us plan for Barrackpore before then."

Sarah squealed in delight, and Charles returned to his study to consider what he had just agreed to.

Chapter 20

The proposed excursion to Barrackpore was met on every hand with delight, and the following Tuesday was determined to be the best day for their pleasure, providing that the weather was fine. On Monday afternoon a fierce rainstorm blew in, and Sarah wrung her hands and fretted all throughout the evening. But Tuesday morning proved to be fine, and although it was still very warm, the rain had cooled the air considerably.

The carriage ride to Barrackpore would take more than two hours from the plantation, and Katherine, Sarah, and Charles left as the sun was coming up. Mr. Grant had offered the young people the use of his new barouche and a team of horses, which was ready and waiting for them when they drove up to the house.

Priscilla came outside in a flowing dress of pale green gauze, with a smile and eyes only for Charles. He bowed politely and helped her into the carriage. It was decided that Charles would drive instead of sending a servant with them, and after the ladies were settled and their picnic had been loaded, they set off for the regimental barracks.

Marcus was waiting for them outside the officers' quarters when they arrived, but as he climbed into the barouche Priscilla cried out. "This will never do! Here we are, all comfort and gaiety in the carriage, while poor Charles must sit alone. Let me join him that he may have his share of amusement during the drive."

It was not at all what Charles himself would wish, but Marcus was already handing her up, and she sat down next to him with a self-satisfied smile. Determined to ignore the sight of Priscilla sitting next to Charles, Katherine fixed her eyes on Marcus, who sat directly across from her. Marcus was pleased to have Katherine's pretty face before him, and the seating arrangements appeared satisfactory to all except Charles.

The drive to Barrackpore led them north through the streets of Calcutta, and Katherine watched the city pass by with great interest. The tall, pillared buildings along Strand Road soon gave way to mud huts and grass lean-tos. A beautiful Hindu temple rose out of the midst of these as they traveled northward, its domed roofs and high pinnacles reaching into the heavens. The streets throughout town were crowded with natives, as well as several British soldiers and their Indian counterparts. Cows, carts, dogs and palanquins pushed and shoved one another in the melee, and if it were not for Charles's expert driving skills they may never have made it out of town. After half an hour, the buildings of Calcutta thinned to only a few small huts with woven grass roofs, and soon their carriage was the only evidence of British influence to be seen at all.

Once outside the city, the countryside spread around them in exotic splendor. Groves of palms and "parrot trees" gave way to wide expanses of grassland and shrubs. Katherine never tired of the Indian landscape. She knew that her grandmother had loved India as well, but Katherine often wondered if it had taken as strong a hold in her grandmother's heart as the people and land had in her own.

"You seem quite captivated with the view, Miss Greenwood," Marcus ventured. Katherine turned to smile at him.

"England is a land of many beauties," she replied, "but the greatest beauty I have beheld in my life I have found here, in India."

"I believe I must agree with you," he said with a significant look. Katherine looked away, embarrassed.

"How far is it to Barrackpore from here, Lieutenant?" Sarah asked.

"We should arrive within an hour, I would imagine."

"Is it really as splendid as I have heard it described?"

Marcus smiled. "I am not quite sure how you have heard it described, but it is a very fine park."

Sarah sat back, a dreamy smile on her face. "I am sure it is wonderful. Oh, I am so happy!" she finished with a sigh. Marcus and Katherine laughed.

The remainder of the drive passed uneventfully. Katherine did her best to ignore the trilling laughs and simpering smiles Priscilla showered on Charles, and she mostly succeeded by watching the landscape around them. The sun continued to climb and the heat continued to rise, and the ladies put up their parasols to protect their complexions.

They arrived at Barrackpore by mid-morning, and the first view they had of it was very fine. The entrance to the park had a large gate, which was flanked on either side by half a dozen smooth Roman pillars. Tall trees hung over the road leading into the park, and beyond the gate they could see a wide expanse of grass, and more trees. Sarah was nearly beside herself with anticipation.

They passed through the gate and drove into the park a short way. Marcus directed Charles to the main stables, and they parked the barouche in the shade of a large tree. Charles climbed down from the carriage seat, then helped Priscilla to the ground. She promptly took his arm, so it was left to Marcus to help Sarah and Katherine out of the carriage. A native servant was given charge of the horses, and soon they set off.

They meandered through the park for a short time, until they came in sight of the menagerie. Katherine and Sarah expressed a wish to see the animals, so the five of them continued in that direction. The enclosures where the animals were kept were long, low buildings, divided and fronted with metal bars. The first one they came to had a collection of colorful birds inside. Parrots with plumage of green, yellow, and red perched on branches and boxes throughout the cage. On the floor of the enclosure were pheasants, partridges, and tiny quail, their dark plumes bobbing as they ran from one place of cover to another.

"Katherine, look!" Sarah exclaimed, pointing behind her.

Katherine turned to see a fully grown peacock parading slowly across the lawn, its long train dragging silently behind as it walked. Katherine was delighted.

"What a beautiful bird!"

"Have you ever seen a peacock before?" Marcus asked. She shook her head.

Grinning, he cupped his hands and emitted a loud sound,

much like a cat when it meows. Katherine was startled, and the bird was startled, too. It turned towards the sound and fanned its tail, raising the covert feathers perpendicular to the ground and showing off his gorgeous plumage. Katherine gasped.

"How beautiful! Such brilliant coloring!" she exclaimed. "I understand now why they are called the birds of paradise."

Marcus smiled. "A peacock on display is truly a glorious sight."

Priscilla fanned herself under the shade of her parasol. "It is abominably hot standing out here in the sun. Charles, dear, can we not walk down to the lake? Let us leave them to admire the bird while we seek someplace cooler."

Charles hesitated. "I am sure that my sister and Miss Greenwood are warm as well." Turning to the others, he asked, "Shall we not all walk towards the lake? There are many fine species of birds thereabouts as well."

"I should very much like to see the rest of the menagerie," Sarah said.

"Miss Greenwood? Would you like to see the menagerie or join us at the lake?" Charles's tone was polite, but his eyes were beckoning to Katherine, willing her to follow them. She hesitated.

Marcus leaned down and whispered conspiratorially in her ear. "There is a tiger in the menagerie," he said. Katherine looked up at him with interest.

"A tiger?"

He nodded. "And elephants."

That decided it. Katherine turned to Charles with an apologetic smile. "I believe I shall stay with your sister and Lieutenant Bradford, if you please."

Disappointment flashed in his eyes, but Charles merely nodded. Although still clinging to his arm, Priscilla had already taken a step away from the others, and he had no choice but to follow her to the lake. Marcus offered his arm to Katherine, which she gladly took, turning away from the sight of Charles and Priscilla. Sarah took Marcus's other arm, and the three of them went to explore the menagerie in greater depth.

Beyond the birds there was an enclosure containing a few varieties of monkeys. Sarah enjoyed the little brown monkeys that clamored from tree to tree, chattering excitedly, while Katherine liked the large gray monkeys with the black faces best.

"It looks as if they stuck their faces in the fireplace," Marcus said with a laugh.

"Where are the tigers?" Katherine asked, turning to Marcus.

"They are in the next building. Shall we go and see them?"

"Yes, please," Katherine said, her eyes bright with interest. "I have not seen one since my arrival, and then only from a distance."

Marcus was taken aback. "You have seen a tiger?" His face grew serious. "I hope you were not out walking alone."

Katherine laughed. "Oh, no. It was before I even set foot in India. We were traveling upriver in the ship before landing in Calcutta, and I saw one creep out of the jungle."

Marcus breathed a sigh of relief. "I am glad it was at such a distance. But let us satisfy your curiosity and see the beasts up close."

"I think I would rather stay here," Sarah said hesitantly. "The large cats frighten me; I would much rather enjoy the little monkeys and birds."

Katherine smiled at her friend. "Then we shall stay with you. It would be quite rude to take away your escort for my own selfish desires."

Sarah smiled gratefully at her friend, and the three of them continued to admire the animals in the surrounding enclosures. After half an hour, they walked towards the lake to see the waterfowl.

The lake was not far, but when they arrived they could see no sign of Charles or Priscilla anywhere. Katherine pushed her curiosity away, determined to enjoy Marcus and Sarah's company, regardless of what she thought Charles and Priscilla might be doing. Soon they were strolling along the lake's perimeter, admiring the variety of ducks, loons, and geese that swam on its surface. A graceful white egret stood in the shallows, and little gray and brown grebes bobbed to the surface before diving under the water again.

"Oh, Sarah, look!"

Katherine pointed across the lake, where two grown elephants, led by a pair of Hindu men, stopped to drink from the cool water. Marcus smiled.

"Would you care to ride an elephant, Miss Greenwood?"

Katherine stared at him, but Sarah clapped her hands in delight. "Oh, yes, we must! I have some money in my reticule; let us ask them for a ride."

Marcus led the two young ladies around the lake and slowly approached the massive animals. The native men who controlled them watched as they approached, and hailed Marcus in Hindustani as they drew near. He replied in their native tongue, indicating that they would like to purchase a ride on the elephants.

"You speak Hindustani?" Katherine asked, surprise coloring her tone.

Marcus smiled roguishly. "Yes, but I only learned it so that I could impress beautiful young ladies who desire to ride on elephants." He winked at her.

Katherine laughed. "I must defer that compliment to Miss Mendenhall, since it was she and not I who expressed a wish to ride the animals." Her companions laughed.

One of the elephant drivers commanded the smaller of the two beasts to kneel, which it did. Even kneeling, the seat of the *howdah* was seven or eight feet above their heads. Marcus grinned. "It looks as though you may need some help up."

Katherine looked at Sarah helplessly. "How are we supposed to get up there?"

Sarah narrowed her eyes and tilted her head thoughtfully. She approached the animal and put a dainty foot on its knee, grasping the lead rope and pulling herself up. Katherine gasped, then laughed.

"Sarah! What on earth are you doing!"

"I am mounting this elephant, of course," she said as she scrambled her way onto the *howdah*. She looked triumphantly down at her friends and laughed. "Well, Katherine? Are you coming?"

Katherine took a deep breath, then stepped up to the elephant and placed her foot where Sarah had. Suddenly she felt strong hands around her waist, and Marcus lifted her gently up until she could reach the side of the *howdah* and Sarah's outstretched hand. She pulled herself up and into the seat behind her friend. Blushing furiously, she turned and looked down at Marcus.

"Thank you, sir."

"My pleasure," he replied with a grin.

Sarah could hardly keep still in her excitement. "Oh, Katherine!" she exclaimed. "I feel just like a princess!"

Katherine laughed nervously. "Most princesses of whom I am aware ride in fine carriages drawn by horses; they do not cling precariously to the side of a seat strapped to the top of an enormous elephant."

Sarah waved her hand impatiently in the air. "In England, yes. But in India—oh! I have seen the processions of Moghul princes and queens, each of them riding nobly atop an elephant with a *howdah* made entirely of gold, with silks and cashmeres draped around them." She sighed dreamily. "I have always wanted to ride on an elephant, but I knew that Charles would never approve."

Katherine opened her mouth to reply, but gasped instead as the huge beast rose to its feet. Her hands clung to the back of Sarah's seat as her heart began to race. Perspiration beaded on her brow, and for once it had nothing to do with the heat. Sarah laughed exultantly.

"Katherine, is this not wonderful? I feel as though I could touch the clouds!"

Marcus called up to them. "Are you alright, Miss Greenwood?"

Katherine merely nodded, afraid that if she opened her mouth she might scream. The native driver barked an order and the elephant slowly began to walk. Katherine felt as if she might faint.

The huge beast moved slowly around the lake with the two

ladies perched on its back. Marcus walked alongside, anxiously watching Katherine's face. Slowly her color returned, and she began to relax. Sarah was all smiles and laughs, and after several minutes, Katherine's own nervousness subsided.

"Are you alive back there, Katherine?" Sarah called, turning over her shoulder.

Katherine managed a wan smile. "I believe so. Are you enjoying yourself?"

"Indeed I am, though I wish you were having as delightful a time as I."

Katherine laughed softly. "I am well enough. Now that I am not so frightened of falling headlong off this beast, the view *is* quite lovely. Why, there are Charles and Miss Grant!"

The couple in question were walking sedately along an avenue of trees, but turned as the shouts of "Halloo!" and Sarah's frantic waving caught their attention. Charles cried out in surprise, and he and Priscilla quickly made their way towards them. The Hindu driver directed the elephant to stop, and it knelt down in order to let the ladies dismount.

Priscilla stood several paces back, engaged in a somewhat angry conversation with Marcus, but Charles walked right up to the side of the elephant and addressed his sister. His face was full of surprise, but his eyes were merry.

"What is this? I leave you for an hour in respectable company, and I return to find you astride a giant wild beast." He reached up and helped her down from the *howdah*.

Sarah laughed, patting the rough gray skin of the elephant's leg. "No indeed, this gentle creature is more civilized than many a man I have met, my own brother not excluded."

He chuckled, then turned to help Katherine down. Her pale face and trembling hands at once arrested his concern. "Katherine? Are you well?"

She smiled faintly. "Yes, thank you. It has been an interesting experience, though I confess to be glad it is over."

His gentle eyes searched her own. "I am sorry I was not here. I would not have let Sarah persuade you into something you found so frightening."

Katherine shook her head. "It was not Sarah. Lieutenant Bradford suggested it first."

"Bradford?" Surprised, Charles turned towards the man in question, who, along with Sarah, was trying to mollify Miss Grant's heated outburst about the impropriety of such an exhibition. Anger flashed in his eyes and his face grew dark. Turning back to Katherine, he said, "I am sorrier still that I missed an opportunity to protect you from such foolishness."

Katherine drew back, surprised. Was it possible... could Charles be *jealous?* His behavior certainly made him appear so. Katherine did not know what to think. She had thrilled to hear her Christian name spoken by his lips once more, but it only confused her further. Her heart was racing and her head was beginning to ache; she wanted to be away from this man who knew her so well and made her feel so much. She withdrew her hand, which he still held in his own.

"Thank you, Mr. Mendenhall, for your help," she said quietly. His head snapped up and he blanched a little, but he smiled to hide his discomposure.

"Of course, Miss Greenwood. I am happy to be of service." He was quickly withdrawing into the formal, aloof host to whom she had grown accustomed, and she almost wished she had not spoken. But her course was set; her mind almost entirely made up. She turned her eyes towards her choice and walked quietly to Marcus's side, leaving Charles standing alone.

"Such a display of indecency, I never thought to see! I cannot believe it of you, Miss Mendenhall. I am sure you were influenced by those who have no interest in your well-being, and whose opinions matter little." Her sharp eyes turned accusingly on Katherine, who bristled under her gaze. But Sarah rose quickly in defense of her friend.

"Katherine had no influence over my decision, it was entirely my own," she said with spirit. "And, if the truth be known, it was *I* who persuaded *her* to ride."

Priscilla looked such horrified astonishment at Sarah that Katherine could not help but interject. "It may have been a bit impulsive, but I do not think it was at all improper. Sarah and I have sense of what true propriety demands; we would not have indulged had we felt it would reflect badly on either of us."

Marcus gazed admiringly at Katherine for her eloquent explanation, but Priscilla's look was venomous. Charles, who had joined them, stepped in to diffuse the situation.

"It is nearly noon, and the sun is hot. Shall we not return to the carriage for some refreshment?"

The others readily agreed, and Priscilla haughtily took Charles's arm again. Sarah, who stood near him, took the other, and Katherine quietly fell into step beside Marcus as they made their way back towards the entrance of the park.

Chapter 21

The midday sun was hot, and the gentlemen spread out a picnic for their party in a small grove of trees near the river's edge. The ladies fanned themselves underneath their parasols while Charles unpacked the basket. Marcus poured each of them some cool lemonade, and the meal continued in relative comfort. The food and drink served to refresh the young people, and any tension remaining from their morning outing evaporated.

After they had rested for a time, Marcus stood and addressed Katherine. "Well, Miss Greenwood? Shall we have a look at those tigers?"

Katherine eagerly accepted his invitation, and she rose to accompany him. Charles stood as well.

"Why do we not all go?" he said with forced animation.

"Oh no, Charles, please. I do not like the big cats. They… they frighten me," Sarah said timidly. Priscilla sniffed.

"I have no desire to waste the afternoon with wild beasts," she said. Katherine wondered if she meant the animals in the enclosure or herself. Marcus laughed.

"It seems as though Miss Greenwood and myself will have a look at them alone, then," he said cheerfully. Katherine blushed.

Charles watched her face, his expression serious. "Is that agreeable to you, Miss Greenwood?" he asked quietly.

Katherine forced herself to meet his gaze. She looked into his piercing green eyes, and slowly nodded. Then she turned, took Marcus's arm, and walked in the direction of the menagerie. Charles watched them go, feeling as if a dagger had been placed in his heart.

Katherine did not look back.

The tiger contained in the menagerie was a massive beast, with huge paws and a giant head. Katherine watched it from the safety of the path with awe; half wonder, half fear. It was lying in the corner of the enclosure, watching them with lazy eyes. Suddenly it yawned, and its enormous jaws opened, revealing rows of sharp, white teeth.

Marcus leaned down. "Not a beast you would care to meet on a pleasure stroll, is it?" he asked. Katherine laughed a little breathlessly.

"No, indeed." She was silent for a moment, watching the cat with bright eyes. "It is a beautiful creature, though."

"I was thinking the same thing," Marcus said, gazing at her.

Katherine blushed. She glanced around, and her heart began to beat faster. A few other people had been walking around the menagerie when they arrived, but for the moment, at least, they were alone.

"Katherine," Marcus said, his voice low. He had never called her by her Christian name before, and she felt a shiver run down her spine, despite the heat. She looked up into his brilliant blue eyes. He was watching her intently, and she began to tremble.

"I have never met such a remarkable young lady. You captured my attentions almost from the moment we met, and I confess that now you seem to have captured my heart."

Katherine's heart and mind were racing, and she looked away to gather her thoughts. She had never intended to marry for love; marriage was a duty, and as long as she felt some affection in the case, she did not mind marrying for convenience. Marcus was exactly the sort of man whom she had always expected to marry: handsome, intelligent, affectionate; she was fond of him, and was convinced she could not have chosen better for herself had she tried. But now that she knew what it was like to love, to feel so connected to a man that she felt as if half her heart must beat within his chest... she did not know what to do.

"Katherine," Marcus said again, his voice gentle. She looked up into his eyes; so trusting, so confident, so full of love and admiration. Was she ready to accept his hand? Had she made her final decision? Her mind calmly but firmly assured her that she had, but her heart was traitorously crying out for Charles.

"Katherine!"

Startled, Katherine turned towards the sound. Sarah, Charles, and Priscilla stood a fair way off, having just come around the corner of one of the menagerie buildings. "Katherine!" Sarah called again, waving.

Katherine blushed furiously, though she knew they could not have been overheard, and even Marcus's cheeks had a flush to them. The trio were not drawing near; Sarah's fear of the tiger obviously too great to bring them closer. But the moment had been shattered, and Katherine was glad for the interruption. Marcus offered her his arm, and they turned to join their friends once more.

Sarah was smiling as they walked up. "I was almost afraid you had been eaten," she teased. Katherine laughed to hide her embarrassment.

"No indeed. I was merely caught up in the beauty of the animals."

Sarah shivered. "How is it that they do not frighten you?"

Katherine smiled. "To be honest, riding atop that elephant frightened me far more than the tigers or leopards."

Sarah laughed. "I am glad we did it." She glanced at Priscilla, who was deep in a somewhat hushed conversation with Charles. Lowering her voice, Sarah added, "And I don't care what Priscilla says, I would do it again in a trice!"

Katherine smiled at her friend, and Charles turned towards them. His demeanor was calm, but she knew him well enough to see that his serene expression was a forced one. She wondered what he and Priscilla had been talking of.

"Charles, dear, I really do feel that we ought to be going," Priscilla said with an anxious look at the sky. A breeze had sprung up, and as Katherine looked around she could see dark clouds rolling in from the south. If they did not hurry, they might be caught in a heavy downpour on the drive home.

"I fear that Miss Grant is right, as always," Charles said with a nod in her direction. Priscilla beamed. "We shall have to finish our tour of the park another time."

The others agreed, and they all walked back to the carriage house by the main entrance. They found the horses stamping restlessly, but still in the care of the Hindu servant they had employed on their arrival. Charles began to hand in Sarah when Marcus spoke up.

"Mr. Mendenhall, would you care to ride in the carriage on the return trip? I would be happy to drive, and I daresay Miss Greenwood would greatly enjoy the view from the upper seat."

Charles's eyes flashed towards Katherine's face, but she was looking away. Since no one else seemed to object, he bowed his head in acquiescence. Marcus, with a triumphant glint in his eyes, handed Katherine up into the driving seat, then sprang to her side. The others were already seated, and in a very short time they found themselves riding out of the park and down the main road.

Since they were heading south towards Calcutta, it seemed as if they were driving directly into the storm. Katherine looked nervously at the dark clouds in the distance.

"Do you think we shall make it?" she asked anxiously.

Marcus smiled at her. "We had better, or we shall all get dismally wet."

She laughed lightly. "That is not much comfort, Lieutenant. I am wearing my new bonnet and do not want it ruined by the rain."

"Well, we cannot have that now, can we?" He winked at her, whipping the reins across the horses' backs, and they sprang into a faster trot. The lush green landscape flew past them as the storm drew ever closer.

They pulled up in front of the Grant's estate just as the first drops began to fall. Jumping to the ground, Charles barked in

Hindustani to a nearby servant to have his horses and carriage brought immediately. The dark young lad hurried off in the direction of the stables. The ladies quickly sought shelter under the deep covered porch, and the gentlemen soon joined them.

"It looks to be a long one," Marcus said with a worried look at the sky. "Shall you attempt to make it home before it gets worse?"

Charles nodded. "There is no telling how long these monsoons last once they get started, and I would rather be safely at home before the floods make the roads impassable."

Sarah touched his arm nervously. "Do you really think it wise for us to go, Charles?"

He turned to her with a smile. "It will be all right, Sarah,"

"You are all very welcome to stay until tomorrow, when it is sure to be fine," Priscilla looked up at Charles through her lashes as she extended the invitation. Katherine turned away.

"I must return to the fort by nightfall," Marcus said.

"Then it is settled. We shall leave you at the barracks on our way back to the plantation." Charles finished speaking just as their carriage pulled up. Katherine felt sorry for their driver, who would surely be drenched within minutes. But she climbed inside the carriage, glad for a roof over her own head at least. Sarah, Marcus and Charles joined her, and soon they were on their way.

The army barracks were not far, and it was not long before they arrived at the spot where Lieutenant Bradford was to leave them. Marcus thanked Charles for the use of his carriage and gave Katherine a significant look as he climbed out. She blushed, hoping the others did not see, but judging from the knowing look Sarah gave her, Katherine assumed that they did. Her cheeks burned, and she trained her eyes on the rain dripping down the windows. She did not venture a look at Charles, and he said nothing.

They made it home within an hour, before the roads became too wet and muddy. Wilson was outside with an umbrella to meet them.

"I wondered if you would be caught in this storm," he said as they made their way inside. "I shall have the tea things brought in immediately."

"Thank you, Wilson," Charles replied. "Though we are not wet through, I believe we should all like to change into drier clothes first." Wilson nodded, and the party separated.

Katherine was the last to enter the sitting room after changing her apparel. She took her time getting dressed, and made sure that her emotions were well under control before joining them. Sarah smiled at her as she entered the room.

"Here you are!" She handed her a cup of tea as Katherine sat down. Charles was standing with his back to them, looking out the window at the downpour. Katherine smiled at her friend.

"How did you like Barrackpore, Sarah? Was it everything you wished it would be?"

"I confess to be disappointed that we did not see all of the park," she sighed. Then, brightening, she added, "But I never dreamed I would get the chance to ride on an elephant! That almost makes up for it."

Charles chuckled under his breath, but he did not turn. Katherine watched him out of the corner of her eye, wondering what his thoughts were. Was he thinking about the lady in whose company he had passed the majority of the day?

"And you, Katherine? How did you find Barrackpore?"

Sarah's question brought Katherine out of her reverie, and she smiled. "I enjoyed it very much. The grounds were beautiful, and the menagerie so very interesting."

"I am sure it was not only the animals that captured your attention at the menagerie," Sarah said with a sly smile. Katherine ignored her, and Charles turned, clearing his throat.

"Well! I am glad we had a fine day for our excursion. And I am glad to be discharged of my debt to my fair sister." He acknowledged her with a smile and a bow of his head. "Now, if you ladies would excuse me, I have business to attend to." He smiled at them; a calm, brotherly air in his manner as he nodded at each in turn. His eyes did not linger on Katherine's, and she watched him go with a somewhat heavy heart.

It was clear to her now that Charles's mind was made up. Miss Grant would no doubt soon be mistress of the little plantation, and all that remained of her own somewhat questionable future was whether or not she could convince her heart to love another. Marcus was kind, intelligent and handsome, and his regard for her was obvious. Could she not learn to love him in return? She was fond of his company, and his future was promising... what more did she need? She reasoned with herself that there was nothing else to consider, but as she crawled beneath the mosquito netting surrounding her bed that night, her heart and mind wandered to the room across the house where another pair of eyes, their vivid green hue masked by the darkness, stared unseeing at the ceiling.

Chapter 22

It was now mid-September, and the indigo harvest was well under way. Charles was busy from morning till night, overseeing the workers and coordinating duties with his steward. At the end of another long, hot day, Wilson found him dozing in the chair behind his desk. He set his master's supper down gently, trying not to disturb him, but Charles stirred and opened his eyes. He sat upright, rubbing his hand across his face.

"You will work yourself to death, Master Mendenhall," Wilson reproved him gently. Charles chuckled humorlessly.

"What choice do I have, Wilson?" He looked up at his steward with haunted eyes. "The woman I love is beyond my reach, and now I am on the brink of losing my home, my land, and my living. What am I to do? Tell me, Wilson, how shall I bear it?"

The old servant watched him thoughtfully. "What about Miss Grant?"

"What about Miss Grant?" Charles said warily.

Wilson cleared his throat. "I thought you had an agreement of some kind with her," he ventured softly. "Last year you spoke of the possibility of uniting your families, and saving the plantation from seizure. Is that not the reason Miss Grant has returned to Calcutta at last?"

Charles was silent, staring out the window at the fading light. Finally he turned. "I do not doubt that Miss Grant is of a similar mindset as you seem to be. And yes, Wilson, you are right. I did speak of marrying her." He shook his head. "But London has spoiled her; I have seen enough evidence of *that* since her arrival. And while I confess to have thought of marrying her last year for the sake of saving the plantation, I simply cannot abide the thought of marrying her now, knowing my heart belongs to another." His eyes grew dark, and he ran his hands through his hair in agitation. Dropping his head in his hands he moaned, "Lost, lost! It is all over."

Wilson walked around the desk and laid his hand gently on Charles's shoulder. "Miss Greenwood may be lost to you, but the plantation does not have to be."

Charles stood, angrily stepping away from his steward. "I cannot marry Miss Grant. I will not subject myself to her arrogant, assuming airs for the rest of my life. But even if I did, what is that? This house, my plantation, will forever be haunted with the memory of Katherine. I have lived within its walls, tormented by the ghosts of my parents and brother long enough. I could not bear to have her memory and not her person linger here —I would go mad!"

Wilson was silent, his face grave. Finally he cleared his throat. "Then you must sell the remainder of the harvest for more than is owed, and ask for her hand."

Charles turned to look at him. "I told you, she is promised to another."

"Are you sure of that, sir?"

Charles met his steely gaze for a long moment, then dropped his eyes and sat back down. "No," he said quietly. "But I am certain of Lieutenant Bradford's regard for her. She, too, seems to favor him."

"Has she confided anything in your sister?"

"I do not think so. But Sarah is convinced it will be a match yet. What hope do I have?"

"There is always hope, Master Mendenhall," his old friend said firmly. "Do not despair. If your happiness rests on Miss Greenwood alone, then let us do all within our power to bring about the elimination of your debt so that you may marry her."

Charles smiled at his steward. "Thank you, old friend."

Wilson nodded. "I will send a message to Colonel Whittaker at once, to discover if there is any word from Balasore."

"Yes, I am surprised I have not heard from him. I wonder what has caused the delay?"

"You know the heavy rains make the roads nearly impassable."

Charles was nodding. "Yes, yes, you are right. Very well, I shall speak to the colonel. Do not bother to send him word; I will call on him tomorrow."

"Very well, sir." Wilson bowed and left the room, but as the door opened Charles heard the sounds of the piano floating on the soft evening air. He stood and made his way quietly towards the library.

Katherine was sitting before the instrument, her dark, glossy hair shining in the candlelight. Her face was serene, and a smile hovered about her lips. Charles watched her silently from the shadows, thinking her more beautiful than ever before. With every keystroke he felt his heart swell with love and desire until he wondered that it did not burst. He knew that he must win her, no matter what the cost. She had mended the hole in his heart, but he knew that if he lost her to another, his heart would not survive being torn asunder a second time. He backed slowly away, her delicate face etched in his memory, and quietly returned to his study.

Charles was gone before the sun was up, and he returned home shortly after the ladies had dined. He went directly to his study and called for Wilson.

"It is as you suspected—the roads prevented the regiment from returning until yesterday," he said as his steward entered. His eyes grew bright. "But such news the colonel has brought me! Listen to this," Charles held up a small piece of paper and read, " 'I should be most happy to purchase three hundred pounds of indigo dye, and, providing it is of highest quality, will pay £100 sterling upon its arrival. Signed, E. Cooper.' "

Wilson smiled. "That is very promising, sir."

"Promising!" Charles laughed. "Wilson, it is deliverance. I will oversee the last of the indigo cultivation and then I shall take it to Balasore myself."

His steward nodded. "Very good, sir. Shall I inform your sister?"

"No, she already knows that I shall have to leave again. I will talk to her when it is time for me to go."

Wilson bowed, and Charles dismissed him. He was nearly beside himself with joy and relief, and he could not sit still. He grabbed his coat again and headed back outside, making his way to the distant indigo fields.

Katherine watched through the window as Charles strode purposefully across the lawn. He had not spent much time with them since their excursion to Barrackpore, but Katherine was finding the separation to be a welcome relief. Her heart still ached at times, but it was better than the constant confusion and rivalry she felt within herself whenever Charles was around. She took a breath and turned to Sarah, who was poring over one of her fashion magazines.

"Shall we not go into town today?" she asked.

Sarah looked up. "Is there something in particular you wish to do there?" She raised an eyebrow and smiled. "Or someone you wish to see?"

Katherine laughed. "The former. I should like to pick up some new music."

Sarah laid aside her magazine. "And I should like to pick out some fabric for a new gown. My pink muslin is completely worn out, and I would like to have a new one made before Miss Grant's party next week."

The ladies took their gloves and parasols, and took along another servant to accompany them in addition to their driver. The music store on Chowringhee Road was their first stop. The low white building had a deep porch and arched wooden doors at the entrance. Katherine browsed through the stacks of music inside, stopping to read a few measures here and there, humming the notes softly to herself. Sarah watched her for a time, then asked, "How do you do that?"

"Do what?"

"Read the music without an instrument before you."

Katherine smiled. "My grandmother insisted that I know the notes of the pianoforte so well as to be able to hear the music in my head before I sit down to play."

"I cannot believe it—it reads like a foreign language!" Sarah replied, picking up a piece of music before her. "Only French is easier," she added as an afterthought.

Katherine laughed, and took her purchases to the front. She glanced inside her reticule. She had a little more than three crowns left, and it worried her. Sarah saw her concern and gently touched her arm. "Would you like me to pay for the music, Katherine?" she asked softly.

Katherine reddened, but smiled to hide her embarrassment. "Thank you, but no. I have enough; I was only thinking of how much I have spent already."

"You will not likely need to worry very much longer," Sarah said as they returned to the carriage. "An officer's commission pays very well, I understand."

"Sarah!"

"Why do you look at me like that? It is nearly a settled thing, is it not?"

"No, indeed," Katherine said, her voice more forceful then

she intended. She took a breath to steady her nerves, and attempted to speak more gently. "You may pretend to know what Lieutenant Bradford's intentions are, but I assure you that there is no understanding between us."

"*Yet*," Sarah replied, laughing. "Dearest Katherine, you cannot pretend any longer that Lieutenant Bradford has been paying his addresses to you for any purpose other than matrimony. And when you are married, you will not have to worry any longer about the burden you feel you are to Charles and I (though I have assured you that you are no such thing), nor that ridiculous idea you had as passing for a servant."

Katherine was silent, and Sarah frowned. "You will accept him when he offers for you, will you not?"

Fortunately, they arrived at the large bazaar on Grand Street, and Katherine did not have time to reply. The ladies alighted from the carriage, and were soon inside the spacious building.

Stepping into Taylor's Emporium was like stepping inside of London. Everything there, from the crystal chandeliers hanging beneath the vaulted ceiling, to the tall Roman columns resting upon the polished marble floor, was fashioned after European taste. Everything sold in the emporium was as well. Porcelain china, fine jewelry, fabric, lamps, shoes, silverware; it was the number one place to shop in Calcutta for a taste of England.

Sarah lost no time in searching out a large selection of muslins, silks, and brocades. She sifted through the fabric with a critical eye, finally narrowing her choices to two: a creamy yellow silk with tiny rosebuds printed on it, and a pretty blue muslin that just matched the color of her eyes. Turning to Katherine, she asked, "What do you think? The cream silk or the blue muslin?"

Katherine fingered the folds of fabric. "They are both very pretty. What is your own opinion?"

"The silk is light and airy, which I prefer, but I am afraid the color washes me out."

"I agree. Get the blue; it will hold up better, and the shade is lovely."

Sarah promptly dropped the silk and took the bolt of blue fabric to be purchased. She paid the merchant and handed her bundle to the Indian porter who accompanied them. The ladies once again climbed inside the carriage and were soon on their way to the dressmaker's.

They traveled around Tank Square to Strand Road, where the milliner's shop and the dressmaker whom Sarah frequented were both established. Taking her newly purchased muslin, she and Katherine entered the shop. Madame Lafleur was a Frenchwoman, and one of the best seamstresses in Calcutta. Her Anglo-Indian assistant looked up as the ladies entered and greeted them cordially.

"I would like to speak to Madame Lafleur, if you please," Sarah asked politely.

"She is with another customer at present. Would you like to wait for her?"

Sarah indicated that she would, and they were directed to a pair of chairs near the front window with a small table between them. A young Hindu girl brought them some tea, and Sarah and Katherine partook of the refreshment gladly. After a half hour, the gauzy white curtains separating the back room from the entrance parted, and Priscilla Grant walked out.

"Miss Mendenhall! Miss Greenwood! How lovely to see you," she simpered. Katherine and Sarah rose, and the ladies curtsied to one another.

"I hope you have not been kept waiting long," she continued. "I am in need of several new gowns, and Madame has been so good as to help me with them." She smiled at Madame Lafleur, who had followed Priscilla out of the back. The seamstress looked somewhat irritated but was trying to be cordial.

"Your dresses will be ready *très bientôt, Mademoiselle,*" she said to Priscilla. Priscilla smiled serenely at her, and while Madame Lafleur smiled back, Katherine noticed a muscle in her jaw twitching.

Priscilla turned back to Sarah. "Are you having a new gown made up for the party?" she asked archly.

"Yes, indeed. I have just purchased this blue muslin; is it not nice?" Sarah replied, eagerly holding out the fabric for Priscilla's opinion.

Her delicate eyebrows arched, but Priscilla smiled. "Yes, very pretty." She waved a hand vaguely at the room behind her. "I brought Madame a selection of silks and brocades that Papa brought me from Paris, but this will be quite pretty, I think."

Katherine saw Sarah's smile falter, and it made her angry. How dare she insult her friend so! Katherine watched to see if Sarah would reply with something witty in return, but she was silent. Seething inside, Katherine forced herself to smile at Priscilla. "No doubt your dresses will be very fine, but as Charles himself prefers an airy muslin to a stiff brocade, I am sure that Sarah will look lovely in the blue."

Priscilla's smile grew hard, and she tossed her head haughtily at them. "We shall see what *dear* Charles prefers on Wednesday next. Good day to you," she said as she swept out of the shop.

"*Bon débarras!*" Madame Lafleur said, rolling her eyes. Then, turning towards Sarah, she said with a smile, "My dear! I am 'appy to see you. And Miss Greenwood, 'ow do you do?"

Katherine returned her smile, and Madame Lafleur took the fabric from Sarah. "*Très joli*, it is very pretty. You would like a dress for Miss Grant's party, no?"

"Yes, if you please," Sarah replied, then she hesitated. "But if you are too busy…"

Madame Lafleur waved her hand impatiently. "Ach! Never too busy for *ma préférée*," she said, smiling at Sarah.

She whisked her away to the fitting room, and Katherine sat down once more to wait. In a quarter-hour Sarah was finished, and Madame Lafleur sent them away, promising that the gown would be ready by the beginning of the next week.

It started to rain on the drive home, but thankfully the shower did not last long. When at last they arrived, they found Charles waiting for them in the sitting room. Katherine thought he looked tired, but he smiled warmly at them.

"Did you have a nice time in town?" he asked as they sat down. The sitting room was hot and humid, even with the giant *punkah* in motion. Sarah fanned herself.

"Yes, we did. Katherine purchased some new music, and I ordered a new gown for Miss Grant's party next week."

Charles's expression froze, and Sarah frowned. "You are coming with us, are you not?"

He hesitated. "I would like to, of course…" His eyes flicked to where Katherine sat. "But I have business to attend to

199

tomorrow, and I am afraid I will not be back in time. I did warn you," he defended as Sarah began to protest. "But it will be my last trip of the season, I assure you."

Sarah sighed. "Very well. We shall go to the party ourselves, and we shall not miss you one jot." Her face took on a teasing look. "Although Miss Grant certainly will."

She laughed as Charles narrowed his eyes at her, but since Wilson arrived at that moment to announce dinner, the conversation ended.

$\mathcal{Chapter}$ 23

Katherine arose early the next morning. There had been a shower during the night, and the air was fresh and crisp. She dressed and went into the sitting room, where the doors leading onto the portico had already been opened to let in the cool morning air. She sat outside, enjoying the quiet stillness of the early dawn, the silence broken only by the occasional call of some bird of paradise.

The front door opened and Charles strode out, buttoning his jacket. He stopped when he saw Katherine sitting nearby. She saw him hesitate, but then he walked over to where she sat. He smiled down at her.

"I am learning that I am not the only early riser in my household anymore."

Katherine smiled, gazing out at the view before them. "I have always loved the dawn. It brings a peace to my heart that I feel no other time of day."

"Yes," Charles sat on the chair beside her own, looking in the direction of her gaze. "The twilight of evening is beautiful, but it does not always bring peace. We are forced to reflect, and the choices of the day are not always satisfying. But the beginning of a new day is fresh and open; it is left to us to decide how we will fill its hours and with what attitude we approach them." He turned and smiled at her. "It is filled with brightness and hope."

Katherine felt the familiar ache in her breast as she looked into his warm eyes. Once again, he had understood her more perfectly than anyone else ever had.

Charles looked out past the lawn, to where the early morning sunlight reflected off the muddy puddles left in the vacant fields. "I am going away for a time," he said quietly, not looking at her. Katherine watched him, his profile rendered even more handsome in the soft light. "I believe I have found a buyer for the remainder of the harvest, and I must travel to Balasore to sign the contract and complete the transaction."

"Where is Balasore?"

"It lies about 150 miles southwest of Calcutta, near the coast."

"Must you travel so far?"

"Yes." He hesitated, then finished in a rush. "Our harvest last year was weak, and it is extremely important that I sell our crop this year for as much as I can. We are comfortable here, Sarah and I, but..." He laughed nervously. "One cannot live on hopes and good wishes alone."

He looked at her, his eyes dark and serious, his gaze fixed on her own. His face was so familiar, his voice so beloved. She looked into his eyes and felt her heart come alive. Katherine might be loved and adored by Marcus; she might even marry him, and may grow quite fond of him, but she knew that her heart would always belong to Charles.

And she knew that he could not be hers.

She had nothing but love to offer him, and it was not enough. Charles was making it perfectly clear that he required money, and a marriage to Miss Grant was accompanied by a handsome dowry. Perhaps if he loved Katherine as greatly as she loved him... but she now knew that was not the case. She did not blame him; she knew herself the horror and hatred that poverty could bring to a home. But, oh! To have it thrown so carelessly at her! To have it explained in such clear terms! Her face grew warm. She had not been guarded enough in her manners to him, and he had been forced to put her in her place once more. She felt ashamed and humiliated, and Katherine had to look away lest her tears betray her.

Charles watched the blush on her cheeks fade, the brightness in her eyes grow dull, and his heart dropped. He was too late. He was convinced that her heart had been won by Lieutenant Bradford, and she was no longer his to win. His face flushed, and determination coursed through his veins; he would not concede! He loved her more fiercely than Marcus ever could, and he was determined to win her hand and her heart. And there was no time to be lost.

He stood abruptly. "Good day, Miss Greenwood," he said with a brisk bow. Katherine merely nodded, her face impassive. She watched him walk briskly to the waiting carriage and get inside. The driver turned the vehicle around and soon it was out of sight.

Katherine stared down the lane long after Charles had disappeared. She felt painfully hollow inside, like the familiar ache of hunger when one has not eaten for a day. He was gone, and her heart along with him.

Slowly she stood, pacing the length of the porch before turning back inside. She went to her room and sat down on the bed. Looking around her, she remembered the first morning she spent at the bungalow. Then, she had been full of hopes and dreams, of plans and preparations, with eyes wide open to the wonders of the new land before her. But now she felt almost lifeless. India had been her dream, and she had exulted in the freedom she felt having attained it. Now her life spread before her, and though the course she had set for herself lay in crimson-clad splendor at Marcus's side, her heart jostled painfully down the rutted dirt road to Balasore.

She sighed. She knew that in time her heart would heal, but never completely. The disappointment of first love leaves scars that no time can completely eradicate, but she was willing to help it along as best she could. Lieutenant Bradford was a welcome distraction, and she was glad that Charles would be away for a time; hopefully his absence would be long enough to convince herself she could be happy as a regimental wife.

A soft knock on the door made her turn, and Bhavani stepped inside.

"Is it time for breakfast?" Katherine asked. The girl nodded.

"Thank you, Bhavani. I shall be right there."

Bhavani bobbed a curtsy and retreated. Katherine stood, glanced at herself in the glass, then followed her out of the room.

The next several days passed in relative quiet. Most of the storms of the season were past, and the frenzied air that had permeated the bungalow since the onset of the harvest began to fade away. The air became cooler, and Sarah did not lie about in languid dissipation any longer. Sometimes there were callers in the morning, or she and Sarah went out; but Katherine's afternoons and evenings were most often spent in the library.

Katherine threw herself into her music. She mastered Frederick Chopin's *Arpeggio*, playing it with gusto. Beethoven, Bach, Schubert, and Mozart; she played until her fingers were sore and her heart was full. It helped her to have an occupation, and it relieved her mind from the wonder and worry of what her future would hold.

Lieutenant Bradford called on Monday, and made sure they were planning to attend Miss Grant's party on Wednesday. Furthermore, he secured Katherine's hand for the first two dances, should dancing be admitted during the course of the evening.

"I am sure there will be dancing," he said with a twinkle in his eye. "For what other amusement for young people is there?"

The day of the party arrived. Charles had been gone almost a week, and Katherine had made great strides in training her heart not to think of him. She and Sarah pulled up in front of the Grant's massive estate, each anticipating the evening with delight. The manicured lawns and symmetrical gardens had been carefully cultivated by the Indian *malis*, and the inside of the house shone with polished brilliance.

Katherine wore a white silk gown with clusters of red rosebuds on it. Her mahogany hair was braided and wrapped around her head, with tiny jasmine blossoms woven throughout.

Sarah walked beside her, looking as bright as a summer sky in her new blue muslin. Her rich chestnut hair was curled and piled atop her head, with a few ringlets framing her angelic, albeit somewhat freckled, face. Their eyes and cheeks were bright with anticipation, and Katherine smiled, determined to enjoy herself.

The party consisted of several officers and all the young people belonging to the principle families of Calcutta. Priscilla stood next to her parents, looking serenely around the room as her guests milled about. Sarah and Katherine made their way over to her, and the ladies curtsied at one another in greeting. Priscilla held out her hands to Sarah and smiled broadly.

"My dear Miss Mendenhall!" she exclaimed. "I am so happy to see you! Is not your brother with you?" She looked behind them expectantly, where others were entering the room. Sarah shook her head.

"Alas, it is as I feared, and Charles has not returned yet," she replied.

"It is no matter," Priscilla said airily. "I dare say he will soon give up his wild ways of scampering about the country and settle down." She smiled knowingly at them.

After being introduced to Priscilla's parents, Katherine and Sarah meandered around the room for a few minutes before being prevailed upon to play a game of Lottery Tickets. Sarah took a seat at the table directly, but Katherine declined, expressing a wish to observe rather than participate. She watched the first few rounds with interest, but when a familiar figure in a scarlet uniform approached her, she turned from the game with a smile.

Marcus took her hand and raised it briefly to his lips. "Miss Greenwood, you are a vision," he said with feeling. She smiled, and he led her to a pair of chairs apart from the rest. They sat down, and passed almost an hour in quiet, pleasant conversation. Priscilla was prevailed upon to play the harp, and after her another young lady was called upon to play the pianoforte. Marcus turned to Katherine with a smile.

"Would you care to favor us, Miss Greenwood?" he asked.

Katherine shook her head. She had no desire to make a spectacle of herself in Miss Grant's presence. Marcus took her refusal in stride.

"Then let us join the set—you have promised me at least two dances tonight."

Katherine readily agreed, and soon they had joined the small number of ladies and gentlemen dancing in the parlor. She enjoyed the lively country dance, and laughed in delight as she and Marcus turned around the room. Sarah was coupled with another officer, and she gave Katherine a satisfied look as they happened by each other. The evening seemed to be passing pleasantly for both of them.

When they sat down to supper, Katherine found herself seated beside Marcus on one side and Priscilla on the other. She smiled politely, and tried to make conversation with her hostess, but received very little more than short, cordial answers in return. Katherine had nearly given up trying to enjoy her company; Priscilla Grant simply would not be liked. But when Marcus excused himself after the meal to visit with another officer, Priscilla leaned in and spoke to Katherine in a low voice.

"I am happy to see you have gotten over your infatuation with Charles."

Katherine stared at her. "I beg your pardon?"

Priscilla laughed darkly. "Come, come, Miss Greenwood. You do not need to pretend with me." She eyed her shrewdly.

Katherine blushed and looked away. "I do not know what you are talking about."

Priscilla ignored her reply, and assumed a casual air. "Lieutenant Bradford is quite a catch, though what he sees in you is beyond me. You *are* a bit pretty, but without family or fortune to speak of, I am surprised that he has formed a serious design on you."

Katherine was speechless in her anger and embarrassment. She opened her mouth to tell Priscilla just exactly what she thought of her, but Miss Grant continued. "Indeed, I told Charles after your escapade in the park that I was glad he, at least, was safe from you."

Katherine reigned in her anger. She took a sip of water to compose herself and said, "I am surprised that you felt him in danger enough to warn him."

Priscilla's eyes flashed. "Charles was never in any danger from *you*. He and I have been intimate for years, and not even the scheming plans of a presumptuous young chit such as yourself could remove his affections or absolve our understanding. It will not be long before you are out of his house and nothing but a distant memory; *I* will see to that myself."

Katherine grew pale, but it was the matter revealed and not the insults expressed that made her blanch. It was as she had suspected. Charles was promised to Priscilla, and even if Katherine *did* have a fortune, no amount of love for her would cause Charles to withdraw his promise to Priscilla; he was far too much of a gentleman for such conduct. Her head was swimming and her heart felt like lead. Priscilla watched her listlessness with an air of triumph, and soon she stood and stalked haughtily away. Katherine sat in stunned silence, unaware of her surroundings.

"Katherine? Are you alright?"

Sarah's voice brought Katherine out of her stupor. Her friend was standing beside her, watching her face with anxious concern.

"I… do not know," Katherine said weakly.

"Then let us get you some fresh air. It is quite stuffy in here."

She led Katherine through the crowded rooms and out the open back doors to the garden. A few couples were strolling around the moonlit grounds, their soft voices floating up to them on the still night air. Katherine sat down on a bench near the balustrade and Sarah fanned her face.

After several minutes Katherine's color returned, and Sarah began to relax. Katherine smiled up at her.

"Dear Sarah, what would I do without you?"

Sarah smiled at her softly. "Are you feeling better?"

"I am."

"Good." Sarah exhaled heavily. "For a moment I thought you would faint! What has troubled you so?"

The encounter with Priscilla pricked at Katherine's raw heart, and she shook her head. "I was only surprised by something I heard."

Sarah narrowed her eyes at her friend. "Well, whatever you heard, I hope you will dismiss it, for nothing that distresses you so is bound to be true."

Katherine laughed humorlessly, but did not reply.

"Are you ready to go back inside?"

"Yes. Thank you, Sarah."

They returned to the house and the jovial crowd therein. Marcus soon joined them, and Sarah went off to dance again. Katherine tried to push aside the conversation from supper, but Priscilla's words played over and over in her mind, tormenting her.

"You seem out of sorts, Miss Greenwood," Marcus remarked, looking at her with concern.

Katherine managed a small smile. "I am only a bit tired."

He regarded her thoughtfully. "I fear that you find company tiresome."

"Not all company."

He grinned. "And dare I hope that I belong to such an untiresome set?"

She smiled wanly. "You do, Lieutenant."

"I am glad to hear it."

As Marcus handed her up into the carriage at the conclusion of the party, Katherine reflected on the evening. She had arrived in high spirits, and before supper she had enjoyed herself immensely. But Priscilla had ruined the night for her. Her arrogant manner and pretentious claims made Katherine's cheeks burn with anger and humiliation. And while the information Priscilla relayed regarding herself and Charles had confirmed Katherine's suspicions, it was not entirely a surprise. She had always known that Charles was destined for another. Now, at least, she knew for certain, and she could lay aside her girlish dreams and face her future with determination.

She sighed. Matters of love were so very complicated. Why did her heart insist on loving Charles when Marcus was her choice? She reflected on that statement. *Marcus is my choice*, she thought again. Marcus was charming, handsome, gentle, and kind, and Katherine knew that he loved her. That alone meant a great deal to her. To be loved by such a man was a great compliment, and she felt the honor of his attentions fully. Her heart beat strangely as she thought of becoming his wife, and it cried out for Charles even while her mind continued to rationalize her choice to marry another. She tightened her grip on her feelings; her heart *would* obey her—it must! Like Sarah, she felt certain that Marcus would make an offer for her hand very soon. And this time, Katherine knew what her answer would be.

Chapter 24

Marcus came to call early the next morning. The ladies had just finished their breakfast when his arrival was announced, and Sarah gave Katherine a knowing look as they entered the sitting room. For once, Katherine did not blush. She knew what Marcus would say, and she knew what her answer would be.

But Marcus did not stay long, he merely wanted to see that Katherine had recovered sufficiently from her distress the prior evening. When he had been assured that she was well, he was content to pass a quarter-hour in their company. Determined to bring about the proposal she felt was inevitable, Sarah invented some task that drew her away from them, and soon Katherine was left alone with the lieutenant.

He chuckled as Sarah quit the room. "It seems as though Miss Mendenhall is anxious to leave us alone."

Katherine fidgeted, embarrassed. "I am sure her business could not be delayed."

Marcus smiled but did not speak, and Katherine became more and more nervous as the silent minutes ticked by. To hide her embarrassment, she said, "It was so very kind of you to call. I thank you for your attentions last night; as you can see, I am quite recovered."

"I am glad to hear it." Marcus shifted in his seat, and for the first time Katherine detected a hint of nervousness in his manners. Her heart fluttered and she clasped her hands together, preparing herself for what she was sure he would say.

Marcus stood and paced to the window. He stared out at the view for a moment, then turned to face her. "Katherine," he said gently, walking to stand before her. "Dearest Katherine," he said again, sitting next to her on the settee. She turned slightly, willing herself to look into his face. His eyes were bright and his complexion ruddy, and he glanced towards the door to ensure that it had been closed. As he did so, his eyes landed on the clock above the fireplace, and he laughed quietly to himself.

"No, no, this will never do." He looked into her eyes, and a smile lit up his face. He picked up her hands and kissed first one and then the other. "I am afraid that my addresses must wait. I am obliged to return to my regimental duties at present, but may I call on you tomorrow, and request an audience alone?"

Katherine's heart stuttered in her chest, but she smiled and answered in the affirmative. He thanked her, bowed, and took his leave. As he left, he asked Katherine to give his regards to Miss Mendenhall. "For I am sure," he said, trying to hide a smile, "that she is lurking in the hallway, ready to pounce on you as soon as I leave."

He was right. As soon as the carriage bearing him drove away, Sarah emerged from her hideout in the library, and insisted that Katherine satisfy her curiosity.

"He did not propose," Katherine said, and smiled as Sarah's mouth dropped open. "But he is returning tomorrow morning, and has asked to see me alone."

"Well, that is as good as a proposal in my book," Sarah said with a grin. "Dearest Katherine! I am so happy for you. Such a handsome young man! And a lieutenant besides," she sighed dreamily, and Katherine laughed. Sarah smiled, but narrowed her eyes at her friend. "You *will* accept him, will you not?"

Katherine took a deep breath. "Yes, I will. He is a good man, and he loves me. What reason have I to refuse?" But even though Sarah seemed content with her answer, Katherine herself squirmed inside.

Because I love another man.

She dismissed the thought, pushing it far into the back of her mind, and tightened her grip on her heart. Turning to Sarah, she smiled. "I believe I shall read for awhile. Would you care to join me in the library?"

Sarah shook her head. "I thank you, but no. While I *did* invent my errand earlier, I really must speak to Wilson this morning about airing out the rugs." Katherine laughed, and the two friends parted.

Nearly two hours later a large, comfortable carriage pulled by four gray horses stopped in front of the house. Katherine was in the library, absorbed in *Gulliver's Travels*, and knew nothing of their visitor, but Sarah observed the carriage's arrival from her position in the sitting room. She saw one of their servants open the door and two ladies alight from the vehicle. They walked up the steps and into the house, and Sarah stood as the door to the sitting room opened and her Aunt Ellen was presented to her.

Aunt Ellen was a tall, robust woman with a round face and a ready smile. Her hair was streaked with gray and there were an abundance of wrinkles around her eyes and mouth. She entered the room before her companion and held her hands out to Sarah. "My darling niece! How you have grown! As much in good sense as in beauty, I hope?" she asked. Sarah laughed in response and embraced her aunt.

"If I shall grow to be half as clever as you it shall be enough," she replied.

Aunt Ellen patted her fondly on the cheek. "You shall grow just as clever as your dear old aunt, but perhaps not so round." She laughed at her own wit and turned to her companion.

"Margaret, come and meet my favorite niece."

Sarah giggled. "I am your only niece, Aunt."

"All the more reason for my partiality!" she laughed. Her companion moved forward until she stood beside her. She was somewhat older than Aunt Ellen, and taller and thinner. Her hair was silver, and so pale it was almost white. She carried herself with a great deal of poise, and Sarah stood up straighter as she was presented to her.

"Margaret, this is my niece Sarah Mendenhall." Then, gesturing to her friend, "Sarah, this is Margaret Greenwood, Countess of Rockwell."

Sarah's hands flew to her mouth as she drew in a breath. The two women stared at her, surprise evident on their faces. Sarah laughed and began to explain.

"Oh, forgive me! I did not mean to be rude, it is only... I cannot believe it! Lady Rockwell! How delightful! It is too much... I cannot believe it!" She bobbed a curtsy, her smile stretching from ear to ear.

Lady Rockwell chuckled. "My dear girl, I am only a countess. There is no need to carry on so."

"Oh, it is not that! It is... oh, I cannot tell you! It is too much! You must excuse me, I beg you will excuse me..." And out of the room she ran.

Aunt Ellen, who had been staring at her niece with a look of bewilderment, now turned to her friend. "I am sorry, Margaret—I do not know what has come over the child!"

Lady Rockwell was amused. "She did seem very surprised at my coming."

"Oh, I do not doubt she was surprised, but why should she react in such a way? It is very peculiar."

"Indeed it is," Lady Rockwell agreed.

The door to the sitting room stood partially ajar; Sarah, in her haste, had not shut it behind her. Now she pushed it open, leading another young lady into the room. Sarah curtsied at the two older women, who had turned at her entrance. "Aunt Ellen, Lady Rockwell, may I present my dear friend, Katherine Greenwood."

Katherine jumped as Sarah said "Lady Rockwell," and as she turned her eyes towards the women before her, her heart nearly stopped. One was completely unknown to her; Katherine could only assume her to be Aunt Ellen. But the other—oh, the other! Her face was as dear to Katherine as her very own. For a moment she stood perfectly still, staring; then, with a strangled sob, she ran towards her grandmother and threw her arms around her.

"Katherine?" the older woman asked, stunned. Katherine clung to her neck, sobbing.

"Yes, Grandmother, it is I, it is I."

Lady Rockwell mechanically put her arms around Katherine. Then, as the surprise wore off, and Katherine's sobs subsided, she pulled her granddaughter away from her to look at her face. Katherine smiled at her, tears of joy streaming from her eyes. Lady Rockwell studied her. She had not seen Katherine for four years, and Katherine had grown taller. Her figure was more defined and her cheeks were not as round, but the same dark, intelligent eyes looked back at her. Lady Rockwell's face softened in a smile.

"It *is* you!" she cried, embracing her granddaughter again.

Sarah watched their reunion with tears in her eyes and a smile on her face. She sighed, and turned to her aunt.

"Aunt Ellen, is it not wonderful?"

Her aunt chuckled. "It certainly is a surprise. I had no idea of Margaret's granddaughter being anywhere near here."

"How do you know Lady Rockwell?" Sarah asked with interest.

"Margaret and I have been friends for years, and knowing that I was leaving for India soon to visit my son, she asked to accompany me in order to search for her granddaughter. But we seem to have found her before the search even began!"

Katherine drew away from her grandmother, surprised. "You came looking for me?" Her grandmother nodded. "But how did you know I was here?"

Aunt Ellen interrupted before Lady Rockwell could answer. "I believe that story would be best told on a full stomach," she hinted to Sarah.

Everyone laughed, and Sarah rang the bell for dinner.

Chapter 25

"It was a day I shall never forget," Lady Rockwell said.

The ladies were gathered around the dining room table, the remains of their meal being carried off by the servants. Katherine sat holding her grandmother's hand, a look of pure joy on her face.

"I had almost given up hope," Lady Rockwell continued. "My barrister, Mr. Yates, assured me there was nothing to be done. When Katherine's mother remarried, she and her daughter," she nodded at Katherine, "became the responsibility of her new husband." Her voice turned cold. "And unless I agreed to turn over my entire estate to him, he would not let you return to my care."

Katherine gasped. "Did he ask you to do that?"

Lady Rockwell nodded. "Yes, he did. Shortly after you left. But of course it was not in my power. The estate is entailed to a distant cousin, but even if it could have been sold or given to him..." She hesitated. "My darling Katherine, I knew that it would do you no good."

Katherine nodded. "I understand, Grandmother, and I do not blame you at all." She smiled, and the woman beside her smiled back.

"So what did you do?" Sarah asked. Her chin was propped between her hands and she leaned forward eagerly.

"I waited. For nearly three years, I waited." Turning to Katherine she asked, "Did you not receive my letters?"

Katherine sat up. "No, indeed. Did you write to me?"

Lady Rockwell nodded. "Every week."

Tears filled Katherine's eyes as she looked into her grandmother's face. "Mr. Fletcher forbade me to write to you. But he must have confiscated your letters, for I never saw them. I thought you had forgotten me."

Lady Rockwell patted Katherine's cheek. "I could never forget you, *meine Liebling*," she said fondly. The endearing nickname made Katherine's tender heart swell with emotion, and tears of joy streamed from her eyes. Lady Rockwell continued.

"When several months had elapsed without a reply, I began to worry. I sent Mr. Yates to discover where you were, and how you were getting along." She scowled. "That wicked man has got what he deserved."

Wiping her eyes, Katherine frowned, confused. But before she could ask what her grandmother meant, Lady Rockwell continued.

"I heard what your stepfather was doing, and I was furious. But there was nothing I could do. Mr. Yates insisted that the law was entirely on his side, and that your life might be in even greater danger if I intervened. So I continued to wait. I was counting the days until you came of age, and I hoped that when you did you would return to me. Or," she hesitated, "I hoped you would escape."

She looked pointedly at Katherine, who drew in her breath. "The ring."

Lady Rockwell nodded. "I did not dare explain it to you; you were still so young. But I hoped and I prayed that you would be able to keep the ring safe, and that one day you would understand its purpose."

Tears rolled silently down Katherine's cheeks. She looked up into her grandmother's face. "I did not want to sell it. It was all I had left of you."

Katherine's grandmother smiled. "I am glad that you did, my dear. Else I may not have found you."

"What do you mean?"

Lady Rockwell pulled out her reticule and withdrew a silk handkerchief tied with a bit of ribbon. She laid it on the table and began to untie it. Sarah and Katherine leaned in closer, while Aunt Ellen sat silently by and smiled. Finally the string was undone and the kerchief unfolded. Katherine gasped.

It was her father's signet ring.

Lady Rockwell picked it up gently and turned it over in her hands. She smiled tenderly at Katherine and handed her the ring. It was large and heavy after the style of signet rings at the time, and once again Katherine beheld her father's initials engraven in an elaborate design around the family crest. She examined it with wonder.

"Almost one year ago, I received a very strange visitor," Lady Rockwell said. "A man by the name of Richard Abrams came to call. I tried to turn him away, not being at all familiar with that name, and him not being sent by anyone I knew. But the man insisted on seeing me, and convinced my butler to carry the message that he had something of value that he believed belonged to me."

Katherine was nodding. "Abbot and Abrams. I went to their shop."

Lady Rockwell smiled. "I believe it was Mr. Abrams that helped you. He told me that a young lady had come into his shop the prior week with a very valuable ring. He recognized the crest and wondered if it had been stolen. I assured him it had been a gift, but that I would be glad to purchase it back from him."

"But how did you know that Katherine had gone to India?" Sarah asked. Katherine and her grandmother exchanged looks.

"Where else would I go?" Katherine smiled.

Lady Rockwell nodded. "I was almost certain that you had traveled here. But I did not know to which port you were bound, and I could not follow immediately." Her face grew serious. "I knew that your stepfather would come looking for you."

Katherine shivered, and her grandmother squeezed her hand.

"When I told him that I knew nothing of your whereabouts, he flew into a rage. He was convinced I was hiding you. I had to have a constable haul him away."

"What happened to him?"

Lady Rockwell drew herself up and said severely, "I do not know nor do I care how he spent the remainder of his days. All I know is that he got himself killed in a drunken brawl last February and left your mother destitute."

Katherine stared at her, stunned. Lady Rockwell met her gaze, and her face softened.

"He is gone, Katherine."

Katherine felt numb. She stood, pacing to the door and back again. She sat back down. So much had happened in the last hour that she could hardly make sense of it all. Sarah reached across the table and took her hand.

"Katherine dearest, are you all right?" Her voice was gentle and full of concern, and as Katherine looked into her eyes she suddenly came to her senses. Drawing a deep breath, she tried to smile at her friend.

"I am well, thank you, Sarah."

Aunt Ellen chuckled. "It looks as though your head is spinning, Miss Greenwood."

Katherine turned to her and smiled. "It is. I cannot believe it. Any of it." Her face grew serious again, and she looked at her grandmother. "Is he truly gone?"

"He is," she said stiffly.

"And my mother?"

"She has gone to Bath. I understand that her father's family is taking care of her there," she said a bit more gently. Katherine nodded.

"I am glad to hear it."

Lady Rockwell studied her. "Yes. Well, I have no doubt she is better where she is now." Katherine was quiet, reflecting on all that had occurred.

Aunt Ellen stood. "Well, my dear," she said, addressing Sarah, "would you kindly show me to my room? Lady Rockwell and her granddaughter might wish to converse a bit longer, but I should like to take a nap."

Sarah led her aunt out of the room and down the hall. Once

they were alone, Lady Rockwell turned to Katherine.

"Now, tell me everything."

Katherine told her grandmother about selling the ring and buying passage to India. She related to her the friendship she had formed with Elizabeth Jones, and how her connection to Wilson led Katherine to the kindness and generosity of the Mendenhalls. She spoke of her excursions to town, the first time she saw an elephant, and about discovering music again. When she finally grew silent after speaking for an hour, her grandmother eyed her speculatively. "And where is Mr. Mendenhall, of whom you have been speaking so warmly?"

Katherine blushed. "He is away on business at present."

"Hmph," came the reply. But Lady Rockwell was watching her granddaughter closely, and Katherine was painfully aware that her cheeks were pink and her manner agitated. Not wanting to explain the twisted web of romance in which she currently found herself entangled, she stood and gestured to the open door.

"Would you like to hear me play?"

Lady Rockwell's grave face relaxed, and she smiled. "That would be lovely, my dear."

Katherine led her into the library across the hall, and drew up a chair next to the piano. Her grandmother sat down, an expectant air in her manner and a soft smile on her face. Katherine seated herself in front of the instrument and began to play.

She played all of her favorites; everything she knew her grandmother would recognize. Beethoven's *Für Elise*, Mozart's *Turkish March*, Schubert's *Serenade*—for over an hour Katherine played as if she and the music were one. Lady Rockwell closed her eyes, listening intently. Finally, when the last notes of Bach's

Italian Concerto died away, and she was sure Katherine was not going to play another, she opened her eyes. They were bright with tears, and a smile hovered about her lips. "Thank you," she said simply.

Katherine's heart swelled within her, feeling as though she was overflowing with joy. She embraced her grandmother again, and the two women held each other for a long time. Finally Lady Rockwell drew back.

"You have improved, Katherine," she said with a smile.

Katherine smiled back. "It has been wonderful to have an instrument so readily available again."

Lady Rockwell laughed. "That is not entirely what I meant." Her face grew serious. "I was afraid that the years of neglect and abuse would have spoiled you; that you would have grown vulgar and coarse. I am happy to find that you have not only maintained your dignity, but you have become a bright, intelligent, worthy young lady. I am proud of you, my dear."

Katherine's eyes welled up with tears. "Thank you, Grandmother," she said. "I have always wished to please you, and I am glad I have not disappointed you."

The old woman smiled. "You are far from a disappointment. Tell me," she asked with a questioning look, "are you happy here?"

Katherine was surprised. "Of course. Sarah is my dearest friend; she and Charles—that is, Mr. Mendenhall," she blushed at her carelessness, "have been so very kind to me. Everyone has." Her eyes grew bright. "And India! It is everything I ever dreamed it would be, and so much more."

Lady Rockwell chuckled. "That does not surprise me. I grew

very fond of India myself, when I first came. But have you no wish to return to the land of your birth? What of England, Katherine?"

Katherine hesitated. "I... do not know."

"Why ever not, child? Is there something holding you here?"

Katherine thought of Charles, and Marcus, and Sarah—in that order. "Not exactly. But... if I should return to England, where shall I go?"

Lady Rockwell drew back, surprised, but then she laughed. "I see that I was not clear before." Smiling at Katherine, she said, "Now that your stepfather is gone, there is nothing preventing you from coming back with me. Your mother will consent, I am sure, and I had hoped that I could find you and convince you to return and live with me once more."

Katherine threw her arms around her grandmother, laughing in delight. "Oh, Grandmother! Of course I will come home with you! Of course... that is..." She suddenly hesitated, pulling away.

"What is it, Katherine?"

Katherine was silent. Her grandmother cleared her throat.

"Is there a young man? This Charles Mendenhall?"

Katherine blushed. "No, indeed, Grandmother. That is... he is not the young man." Embarrassed, she stood, wringing her hands in agitation.

"There *is* a young man: Lieutenant Marcus Bradford. He is an officer in the regimental army stationed in Calcutta. He—that is, we—have grown quite fond of one another, and I do believe he will ask for my hand." She paced the room, not looking at her grandmother as she became more and more embarrassed. Lady Rockwell watched her with some amusement.

"You *believe* he will ask for your hand?"

"Yes. He nearly has, on two separate occasions, only he was prevented each time. But he will be here tomorrow, and has requested an audience with myself, alone." Her face flushed crimson and she sat down again, staring at her hands as she twisted them in her lap.

Lady Rockwell nodded slowly. "I see."

She was then silent, but when Katherine offered no other explanation, she ventured, "And you wish to accept his offer?"

"I do not know!" Katherine blew out her breath, dropping her face in her hands. "I do not know what I shall do now." She raised her eyes and looked at her grandmother. "I confess, I had meant to accept him. I had no other choice. I could not continue to impose on the Mendenhalls in this manner, and he is a kind, honest, gentleman-like man. What reason had I to refuse?"

"Do you love him?"

Katherine was silent.

"Katherine," Lady Rockwell said more firmly, "*do you love him?*"

Katherine looked at her grandmother and slowly shook her head. "No, Grandmother. But *he* loves *me*."

"Ahh, I see," Lady Rockwell said quietly. She watched Katherine closely. Finally she stood.

"Well my dear, I do not envy you the sleepless night you shall have," she said with a twinkle in her eye. "If your young man is due here tomorrow, you will have to decide what course to pursue before he arrives." Katherine looked up at her, and Lady Rockwell laid a hand gently on her cheek. "Whatever you decide, Katherine," she said softly, "is all right with me. As long as you are happy, I will be happy, too."

Katherine's eyes filled with tears again, and she kissed the wrinkled hand pressed against her face. She stood and took her grandmother by the arm, and they left the library together.

Chapter 26

"Lieutenant Marcus Bradford to see you, Miss Greenwood."

Katherine looked up as Wilson announced her visitor. She stood, smoothing the folds of her skirt as she waited. Her heart beat erratically in her chest as Marcus entered the room. He bowed low, smiling at her as if she were the very sun in the sky. She smiled back nervously.

"Do sit down, please."

He sat in the chair she indicated, and Wilson quietly closed the door. Sarah had insisted that Katherine spend the morning alone in the sitting room, while she, Aunt Ellen, and Lady Rockwell passed the morning hours in the library. Katherine had heard their laughter, as well as Sarah's feeble attempts to play the pianoforte. She smiled as she thought of her grandmother standing nearby, directing and critiquing, while Katherine had been forced to sit in solitude, carelessly sewing stitches in her embroidery as she waited nervously for Marcus to appear.

And now he sat beside her. She noticed that he seemed less nervous than yesterday, which only added to her own uneasiness, and she tried to push aside the knot growing ever larger in her stomach. Finally he cleared his throat.

"Katherine, I am sure you know the reason for my visit," he said. She nodded, which he took as encouragement. "Almost from the moment I met you, I have come to regard your company above anyone else of my acquaintance. Your beauty, your talents, your modesty; every virtue that you possess combine to make you the loveliest creature I have ever met. I lie awake at night thinking of you, and when I dream your face is always before me."

He paused, and gently took her hand in both his own. He bent down and brushed his lips against the back of her hand, then looked into her eyes. "I have little in the way of worldly wealth to offer you at present, but I lay before you my heart, and I pray that you will do me the honor of becoming Mrs. Marcus Bradford, and consent to be my wife."

He was confident, but not arrogant. His confidence stemmed from the encouragement she had given him; from the proof in her behavior over the last several weeks that she welcomed, and even at times encouraged, his attentions. The knowledge that she must now be the means of destroying the happiness she had helped to create stabbed her to the core.

"I am sorry," she said quietly, forcing herself to look in his eyes. "But I cannot accept."

His smile faded, and his face flushed. Surprise, hurt, sorrow, and even a hint of anger played across his features as he struggled to compose himself. He stood and crossed to the window, looking out into the wild tangle of green. Katherine sat in awful anticipation for several minutes, waiting for him to speak, until she could bear his silence no longer.

"I am very, very sorry," she began, feeling utterly wretched. "I know that my behavior to you has been... encouraging. You must believe me that I never had any intention of hurting you."

"How else am I to take your refusal?" he asked without turning.

"I am sorry. I truly have a high regard for your merit and worthiness, and I am not unaware of the honor your affections and proposals are. I can only venture to say that... my circumstances have changed." She knew what he would think: that she had only been encouraging his attentions in order to secure her own comfort; that she had no regard for him at all. But the complete truth was too complicated to explain, so she said no more. Her eyes filled with tears. "Please, forgive me," she said softly, dropping her eyes.

Marcus stood, silent and motionless, for several minutes longer. Finally he turned. "And is there no hope you can offer me?" he asked. Katherine thought she detected a hint of bitterness in his voice, and it cut her to her core.

"I am sorry," was all she managed to say.

He turned abruptly and strode to the door. Grasping the handle, he pulled it open and then turned to face her. His expression was fierce, but behind the anger that flashed in his eyes she beheld a deep, mortal sorrow which almost made her cry out.

"I would not have thought it possible," he said in a low voice. "To be so entirely mistaken in my estimation of your regard." He took a breath, struggling for control. "But it is done. I have been made a fool, but at least my folly is discovered in time. Good day,

Miss Greenwood." He strode out of the room, shutting the door forcefully behind him.

With a sob, Katherine dropped her face in her hands and wept.

About a half hour after Marcus left, the door to the sitting room opened and Sarah peeked in. Alarmed at the sight of Katherine crying, she exclaimed, "What is this? Katherine! What is the matter?"

Katherine tried to quiet her sobs, but they wracked her body in great shudders which she could not control. Sarah ran to her side, embracing her.

"There, there, dearest, do not cry. I am sure it is not so bad as it seems." She held her tightly, stroking her hair and hushing her sorrows, and in time Katherine calmed down. When at last her sobs subsided, Sarah spoke again.

"I am sorry that the lieutenant did not propose," she said gently. "I do not know what he can be about, but I am sure that he will speak soon."

"He did propose," Katherine replied miserably. Sarah drew back, a look of shock on her face.

"What! Then what can this mean?"

"I have refused him," Katherine explained, her tears beginning afresh. "He asked for my hand, and I refused."

Sarah frowned. "Then I have no pity for you. How can you tell me you have refused him, after your behavior to him all this time? After you told me yourself that you planned to accept him?"

Katherine shook her head, tears streaming down her face. "I cannot marry him, Sarah. Not now. How can I attach myself to a man I do not love?"

"You were ready to do so yesterday."

Her words stung, and Katherine winced. "Yes, I was. But now that my grandmother has returned, now that I can have a life with her again... Sarah, even you cannot blame me for allowing Marcus the opportunity to find and marry a woman who loves him in return."

"I doubt he sees the kindness in your refusal," she replied archly.

Katherine was hurt. She had not anticipated a lecture from Sarah, and finding that her friend so thoroughly disapproved of her actions left Katherine feeling utterly alone. She stared at her hands, her head down, her cheeks wet with tears. Finally Sarah sighed.

"I am sorry. I know that I am being horrid, but I was so surprised at your declaration and, I confess, greatly disappointed." She looked at Katherine, and her expression softened. "Are you sure you cannot accept him?"

Katherine shook her head emphatically. "I will not marry where I do not love; not when I have a choice."

Sarah sighed, but nodded. "Very well. I am sure he is heartbroken, for I have never seen a man so in love before, but I hope that Lieutenant Bradford will someday recover." Her words were of little comfort to Katherine, but at least her friend was no longer angry with her.

"Come," Sarah directed, taking Katherine's hands and pulling her to her feet. "Your eyes are all puffy and your nose will swell if you do not bathe your face." Taking Katherine's arm, she led her out of the room.

"I am sorry to have caused you pain, my dear," Lady Rockwell said to Katherine.

They were alone, sitting outside after dinner. Katherine shook her head and tried to smile.

"It was not you, Grandmother," she said. "And although Lieutenant Bradford is hurting right now, I think that in time he will come to forgive me."

Lady Rockwell nodded, but her face was full of concern. "Are you quite sure of your choice, Katherine? England is far away… you will never see him again."

Katherine nodded firmly. "Yes, I am sure. I do not love him, Grandmother. And although he is a good man, I would rather spend my life with you, whom I already love and adore."

"Very well," Lady Rockwell sighed. "As long as you are sure."

"I am," Katherine replied. She hesitated, picking at a stray thread on her skirt. "But… I should like to leave for England as soon as possible."

Lady Rockwell raised her eyebrows, surprised. "So soon? I thought you would like to spend some time with your friends before we sail."

Katherine was silent, and her grandmother watched her closely. She wondered if there was more than a rejected suitor behind Katherine's desire to flee India. "Is there a particular reason you wish to return to England so quickly?" Her suspicions were confirmed when Katherine blushed.

"No, not particularly," she said. "I will be sad to leave my friends, and this beautiful land as well. But I shall be sad no matter when we leave. I should still like to sail for England as soon as we are able," she said again.

Lady Rockwell nodded slowly. "Very well. We can be ready to leave in a week."

Katherine was startled. Charles had already been gone almost a fortnight, and she was not sure when he would return. She was still mortified whenever she thought of their last meeting, and she wanted to be far away when he at last returned.

"Can we not leave any sooner?" she asked anxiously.

This time it was Lady Rockwell's turn to be surprised. "What! Is a week not soon enough for you?" Her eyes narrowed. "What are you running from, Katherine?"

Katherine turned crimson. "Nothing, Grandmother. I only thought that there might be a ship sailing from Calcutta in a day or two."

"Hmmm," her companion murmured. She was watching Katherine closely, her granddaughter's agitated manner evidence that something was amiss. But since Katherine offered no other explanation, she finally nodded. "Very well. I shall speak with Ellen and discover when the next ship sails for London."

Relief washed over Katherine, and she smiled. "Thank you, Grandmother," she said with feeling. She stood, then bent down to kiss her grandmother's cheek. "I shall tell Sarah directly, and begin to pack my things."

Lady Rockwell watched her go, troubled. Katherine had never been a secretive child, but her grandmother was sure that there was something she was not telling her. And though it might take some time, Lady Rockwell was determined to discover what it was.

Chapter 27

"Oh Katherine, how shall I do without you?"

Sarah's eyes and nose were red from crying. Aunt Ellen and Lady Rockwell had arrived only three days earlier, and Sarah had looked forward to a long visit before even thinking of saying goodbye to her friend. But Katherine had informed her the night after their arrival that she and her grandmother were to sail for England immediately, and the suddenness of their departure made the separation even more unbearable. Yesterday had been a tumultuous combination of shopping and packing, and they had all been too busy to think of the painful goodbye that must shortly be said. But the morning had arrived, and Sarah was thoroughly miserable. She blew her nose on her aunt's handkerchief, having already soiled her own, and tried in vain to stop her tears. Despite her efforts, they leaked out her eyes, streaming down her face and ruining her second-best morning dress.

Katherine's eyes were also wet, and she embraced her friend, who began to sob again.

"There, there, Sarah," she tried to console her. "You did very well without me before I arrived; I am sure you will adjust to life without me again." This did nothing to comfort her friend, who cried even harder. Aunt Ellen, who stood nearby, patted Sarah gently on the shoulder.

"Come child, this will never do. Would you like Miss Greenwood to carry the image of your reddened face with her all the way to England? It is not goodbye forever. I dare say you shall see her again."

"Indeed, you shall," Katherine declared, trying to smile. "You have always wanted to see England, so you must come visit me."

Sarah sniffed and dried her eyes, trying bravely to smile through her tears. "I should like that very much," she said, but even as she spoke her lip began to quiver. "But I do not know when Charles will wish to make the journey."

Aunt Ellen snorted. "Who said anything about waiting for Charles? I shall take you there myself," she declared. Sarah turned to her with a joyful cry.

"Oh Aunt Ellen, will you truly?"

"Indeed I will," she said again. "I can only tolerate India until the heat becomes unbearable, and trusting that our journey will not be delayed for any reason, you shall see Miss Greenwood again within a year."

Sarah sighed. "It seems an eternity when you say it like that. But it will be a wonderful event to look forward to." She smiled, and Katherine was glad to see that she had at last managed to stop crying.

Lady Rockwell approached Sarah and gave her a gentle hug. "Miss Mendenhall, thank you for your kindness to my dear Katherine," she said. "I am more grateful than words can express for your generosity. Should you ever need anything, I hope you will send me word."

Sarah's cheeks turned pink with pleasure, and she returned her smile. "It has been a delight, Lady Rockwell."

"You two will never get away if you continue in this fashion," Aunt Ellen chuckled. Katherine sighed, and turned to her grandmother.

"Are you ready?"

"If you are, my dear."

Katherine embraced Sarah one last time, promising to write as soon as she reached her home in Leicestershire. Aunt Ellen waved jovially as the two women climbed into the carriage, and soon they were jostling along the familiar road to Calcutta.

Katherine was silent on the drive to town. She gazed out the windows at the passing landscape, silent tears filling her eyes and spilling down her cheeks. Dark, barren fields once filled with indigo plants flashed by as they passed, and Katherine ached at the sight. Only a few weeks earlier they had been full of life and color, but now they lay empty and desolate, like her heart. India had changed her. She had come to this strange, new land as a timid young girl, but the spicy sweetness in the air had stirred something within her. She had blossomed under the Indian sun like a delicate flower. But even more than India, Charles had changed her. He had awakened within her the ability to love. He had coaxed her heart into blooming without her even being aware, but now she found herself wrenched from the safety of his love, like an indigo plant that is plucked for the harvest.

"You are very quiet, my dear," Lady Rockwell ventured to say when they at last turned into the docks. Katherine dried her tears and tried to smile.

"I shall miss this land," she said, gazing about her at the lush, tropical landscape. "There are so few dreams in this life that are as sweet in their reality as we hope them to be, but India has surpassed all my expectations. I shall miss it so."

"Your grandfather, God rest him, left his heart in India every time he traveled home," she said, watching Katherine out of the corner of her eye. Katherine knew what her words implied, but she said nothing.

Two native servants had been sent with them to carry their trunks, and these men led the way through the crowded docks to the ship on which Katherine's grandmother had purchased their passage. It was a large vessel, commanded by a Captain Whitworth, and filled with cargo and passengers bound for England.

Lady Rockwell and Katherine were led to the small private cabin they would be sharing during the voyage. They stowed their valises and returned to the deck to wait until the ship was ready to leave. Within an hour all was in readiness, and the first mate called for their departure. Lady Rockwell turned to Katherine, who stood facing the bustling town of Calcutta. Her grandmother reached out and gently touched her arm.

"Come," she said quietly. "Let us go home."

Katherine nodded, but as her grandmother walked slowly away, Katherine turned and looked out over the green expanse of teak and parrot-trees, past the balustraded roofs of the British homes along the esplanade. Her heart traveled beyond her view, down a rutted dirt road lined with grass huts and indigo fields, to a small plantation where nearly everything dear to her remained.

Her grandmother said they were traveling home, and indeed, Lady Rockwell was. But Katherine knew that home was not the country for which she was bound, but the land she was leaving behind.

It was nearly dark by the time the carriage finally rolled up in front of the bungalow. Charles was weary in body and mind, but his spirit was alive with triumph. His journey to Balasore had been more successful than he anticipated, for not only did he sell the refined indigo dye from the remainder of his harvest, but the purchaser, Mr. Cooper, was so pleased with the quality of dye that he agreed to purchase whatever remained the following year as well. Charles had completed his business and begun his return trip as soon as possible. It took several days to make it back to Calcutta, where he stopped only long enough to deposit the money in the bank and see Mr. Kerns. Mr. Kerns agreed to have the papers drawn up by a lawyer in town, and the long-awaited freedom that Charles had yearned for for years was at last within his reach.

He was anxious to see Katherine; the thought of her had sustained him every mile of his long journey, and his heart beat with restless anticipation to behold her again. He entered the house and made his way to the sitting room, where voices floated on the still night air like lilies on a pond.

The two women sitting near the open patio doors turned as he entered the room. Glancing swiftly around, Charles saw they were alone; Katherine was not in sight. He frowned, but as Aunt

Ellen stood and crossed the room to embrace him, he managed to smile.

"My dear Charles, how long it has been!" she exclaimed. He bowed and smiled at her broadly.

"Aunt Ellen, it is good to see you in such excellent health."

"Oh, I am always in good health," she replied with a twinkle in her eye. "I simply listen to what my doctors say and then I do the opposite." Charles laughed.

"And how do I find my dear sister?" he asked, crossing to her and squeezing her hand. She smiled weakly up at him but said nothing. Concern lit his features, and he sat down beside her.

"This is a rather disheartening welcome," he said, trying to be cheerful. "What is the matter, Sarah? I hope you have not been unwell?"

"No, I am well, Charles. It is only..." Her voice trailed off and her eyes filled with tears. Alarmed, Charles seized her arm.

"Sarah! What is the meaning of this! Tell me at once!" Dread filled his stomach as he realized that some danger may have befallen them in his absence. "Where is Katherine? Is she all right? What has happened?" He nearly shook her in his frenzied attempt to discover the meaning of her tears.

Sarah shook her head, trying to compose herself. "Katherine is gone."

Charles grew pale, and his stomach turned. He stared at her blankly, willing her to say the words that would explain this misunderstanding. But she sat before him, silent tears falling from her eyes, and he knew they were true. Finally he spoke.

"Did she become ill?" he asked, his voice barely above a whisper. Suddenly he jumped to his feet. "Did Bradford...?" He could not bring himself to form the words. Was she lost to him forever? Had she married Lieutenant Bradford while he was away? He felt sick at the thought.

"No, no," Sarah was saying, shaking her head. "Lieutenant Bradford offered for her, but she refused him."

Relief flooded his mind and calmed his racing heart. She was not lost to him, not yet. And if she refused Lieutenant Bradford, she must still harbor some lingering regard for him. The thought gave him courage. But Sarah was still crying, and he grew uneasy once more.

"Then where is she?" he asked, looking around once more.

Sarah burst into tears beside him. She took a great shuddering breath and said, "She is on her way to England. She left with her grandmother this morning."

Chapter 28

Katherine stared out the window at the bleak, wet landscape. Springtime in England was wet and muddy, and it made Katherine miss the vibrant colors and arid climate of India. She smiled to herself as she considered the differences between the rain in England and the rain in India, and then she sighed. It seemed as if everything reminded her of India. When they had at last arrived in Leicestershire, Katherine was amazed to discover how many things she missed about the subcontinent. The food, the landscape, the city—she even found herself wishing for the drowsy comfort of the ever-present heat.

Upon her arrival home she had written to Sarah as promised, but even with the additional packet lines that could sail to India in twenty-two weeks, she knew it would be months before she received a reply. The distance weighed heavily on her heart and her spirits, and she felt much depressed.

Katherine missed not only her dear friend Sarah, but also

Bhavani and Wilson and the other native servants and merchants she had grown so accustomed to seeing. Naturally, she also missed Charles, but the pain she felt in remembering him was sharp, and she tried to avoid thinking of him too much. But it was not an easy task. As many things as there were that reminded her of India, there were far more that reminded her of Charles. It was the little, everyday things that brought him to mind the most: watching the sunrise, playing the piano, even sitting in companionable silence with her grandmother made her think of him, and she was forever rebuking her heart for crying out for him when he was certainly out of her life forever.

Life settled into an easy routine back in her grandmother's home, and Katherine tried her best to be happy and cheerful. But her heart had been touched by love, and instead of getting easier with time, Katherine found it became harder and harder to live without its source. Lady Rockwell sensed that Katherine was not happy, and it troubled her.

"Katherine, dear, you have barely touched your food," she announced one day over supper. "What is troubling you so?"

Katherine looked up into her grandmother's concerned face. She tried to smile, but only managed to sigh. Lady Rockwell grew stern.

"You have grown more and more reserved in recent weeks. Are you sure you would not like to go to London for the Season?"

Katherine shook her head. "Thank you, Grandmother, but no. I do not enjoy the crowds; I would much rather stay here with you, where we can be quiet and comfortable."

"Hmph. You do not seem very comfortable here. I have watched you, my dear, and I am worried about your health. Ever since we returned from India, you have taken hardly any notice of your surroundings, and seem to take no pleasure in anything, even your music," she said severely.

Katherine sat up straighter. "Forgive me, Grandmother. I do not mean to seem ungrateful. It is only…" She pushed a few peas around her plate. "I miss India far more than I imagined I would."

Lady Rockwell nodded. "I thought as much. Which is why I was surprised that you were in such a hurry to leave it." She narrowed her eyes, but Katherine said nothing. Lady Rockwell thought she knew what was at the bottom of Katherine's behavior, and she decided to try another tactic.

"I am sorry that we left before I had a chance to meet Mr. Mendenhall," she said casually. Katherine gave a little jump at the mention of his name, and then she blushed. Lady Rockwell smiled grimly.

"Katherine."

Katherine glanced at her grandmother, but looked quickly away. Her cheeks burned, and she knew that her charade was over.

Lady Rockwell said nothing for the remainder of the meal. She finished her broiled fish and creamed vegetables, while Katherine continued to push the food around her plate. Finally, when the liveried servants had born away the last of their supper, she turned to her granddaughter.

"Come, *meine Liebling*. Tell me what has happened."

They removed to the parlor, and Katherine poured out her heart to Lady Rockwell. She explained about meeting Charles, and finding in him a kindred spirit and a quiet friend. She told of their innumerable conversations, the gentle companionship he

246

offered, and the kindness he always extended. Lady Rockwell listened closely as Katherine told her how she felt when she realized she loved him, and the pain that followed as she tried to hide her regard for fear he would discover her true feelings.

"Have you any idea if he returned your affections?"

Katherine sighed. "I do not know. There were times when I thought he did, when we understood one another so perfectly..." Her voice trailed off and she shook her head. "But even if he did, I had nothing to offer him."

"Nothing to offer him!" Lady Rockwell scoffed. "My child, you underestimate the value of the virtues you possess," she said critically.

Katherine was silent, and her grandmother regarded her thoughtfully.

"What I do not understand," she said slowly, "is why you ran away from him once I arrived? You speak of having nothing to offer him; of being beneath his notice. But surely you can see the value in being once again under my protection. *He* could see the value in that, and would surely have taken notice of you."

Katherine was indignant. "Certainly, Grandmother. But do you think my regard for him would have remained, had he offered for my hand only after your arrival? To have my esteem thus tarnished; to find him a fortune hunter? No," she said with feeling, "that would have been worse than not being loved by him at all. I could not bear it."

Her grandmother nodded slowly. "I understand. But now you shall never know." She looked intently at Katherine. "Can you live with that, my child? Will you not always wonder?"

Katherine was silent for several minutes before she answered.

"It does not matter," she said softly. "He was sworn to another."

Lady Rockwell drew back, surprised. "What! You knew this, and yet you allowed your heart to be lost on him?"

Katherine's face flushed. "I did not know," she said defensively, "not until it was too late. I only discovered the attachment shortly before your arrival."

The disapproving look on her grandmother's face gradually melted away. The silence stretched between them, broken only by the chiming of the grandfather clock in the hall. At last Lady Rockwell stood.

"I am sorry, my dear," she said gently. "I know your nature, and I am sure your attachment was real and strong. But I hope that in time you will learn to let go, to remember your time in India with fondness and not with pain."

She bent down and kissed her on top of the head, then left the room. Katherine sat in the quiet darkness, alone with her memories, until the early hours of the morning. Only then, when she finally crawled between the satin sheets of her canopied bed, did she allow her heart to break open and her tears to flow.

In the weeks following, Katherine tried her best to revive her spirits. She read to her grandmother in the mornings, and in the afternoons she gave herself up to her music. She practiced for hours on end, and the music helped to heal her wounded heart. There were still times when she allowed herself the self-pity of lost love; when she cried into her pillow at night, longing to wake and see Charles smiling at her over breakfast. But she was learning to let go, and to accept her new life. She began to smile again, and Lady Rockwell was happy to hear her laughing before long.

One afternoon, Katherine and her grandmother were resting in the drawing room after a morning of receiving callers. Katherine's head was aching, and Lady Rockwell suggested that she retire to her room.

"You do not look well, Katherine," she said. "You should go lie down."

"Thank you, Grandmother, but I am well. I feel restless when alone in my room; I would rather be with you."

The old lady smiled and nodded at the book sitting on the settee next to her. "Then come here and continue *Don Quixote* for us, it was just getting interesting."

Katherine had been reading for about twenty minutes when the butler entered and announced that they had a visitor. Lady Rockwell dismissed him with a wave of her hand. "We are taking no more callers today, Lawrence," she said, returning to her embroidery. Her butler bowed and left the room, but a few minutes later he returned.

"I am sorry, madam, but there is a young gentleman who insists on seeing Miss Greenwood. He gave me his name and refuses to leave until he has spoken with her."

"Then call for the constable, Lawrence. We shall not be troubled further," Lady Rockwell said severely. But Katherine called out to the butler before he left the room.

"What name did he give?" she asked, curious.

"Mr. Charles Mendenhall."

Chapter 29

Katherine stared at the butler, stunned.

"Charles Mendenhall?" Lady Rockwell repeated, as surprised as her granddaughter.

"Yes, madam. Shall I show him in?"

She turned to Katherine, who sat motionless beside her, a vacant expression on her face. "Katherine?" she asked gently. "Would you like to see him?"

Katherine looked at her grandmother, and slowly shook her head as if in a daze.

"No... yes. Oh, I do not know! How can it be Charles? What is he doing here?"

Lady Rockwell chuckled. "Even I believe I know the answer to that question." She looked meaningfully at Katherine, who blushed scarlet and stood, clearly agitated.

"But what shall I say to him? How shall I receive him?" She paced across the room and back again, wringing her hands. Lady Rockwell watched her for a moment, then turned to the butler.

"Tell Mr. Mendenhall to wait. We shall call for him directly."

Lawrence bowed and returned to convey the message, shutting the door behind him. Lady Rockwell went to stand beside Katherine, who now stood gazing out the window at the dreary May landscape. Lady Rockwell put a hand on her arm, and Katherine turned to face her grandmother. She was pale and trembling, and Lady Rockwell looked at her with concern.

"My dear, you do not have to face him," she said gently, but Katherine shook her head.

"No, I will see him. If he has come all the way from India to speak with me, the least I can do is hear what he has to say."

Her grandmother nodded. "Very well. Would you like me to stay with you?"

Katherine hesitated. She did not know precisely what Charles wished to discuss with her, but she was quite certain that some things she would prefer to hear in private. "I think I would like to see him alone, if you do not mind."

"Of course. I shall tell Lawrence to send him here, while I wait for you in the parlor."

Katherine nodded. When her grandmother had withdrawn, she took a deep breath and returned to sit on the sofa. Her heart beat wildly, and her stomach was doing nervous little flips. She fidgeted, pulling at her gown and smoothing the folds of her skirt. The gentle *tick, tick* of the clock on the mantel was the only sound in the room as Katherine sat, waiting.

Charles stood in the foyer, restless and nervous. His journey from India had been long, and he had rested very little since his arrival in England. As soon as the ship docked in London, he hired a coach to convey him to Leicestershire, a journey of more than a hundred miles which took five days to complete. He found an inn near Sutton, and began his inquiries about the Greenwood family at once. After passing another sleepless night, he hired a second carriage to transport him to the estate. He was weary in body and spirit, but his mind could not rest until he had seen Katherine.

He glanced around. The opulence of the estate staggered him. The domed ceiling stood three stories over his head, and two massive staircases leading to the second and third floors ascended from either side of the entrance. High paned windows stretched nearly from floor to ceiling, and ornately carved moldings framed each doorway he could see. Gilded mirrors, crystal vases, velvet curtains; the very air he breathed seemed richer. Charles had known that Katherine's grandmother was wealthy, but he had had no idea of the enormity of her fortune until now. Standing just inside the massive front doors he suddenly felt like a pauper, and for a moment he considered himself a fool for even thinking that Katherine would be willing to give all of this up for a small indigo plantation in the heathen nation of India.

He straightened as the butler who had admitted him into the house returned. "I am sorry, sir," he said. "But Lady Rockwell and her granddaughter are not accepting callers at this time."

Charles set his jaw, determined. "I have traveled more than six thousand miles to see her, and I will not leave until I am admitted into her presence." The butler raised his eyebrows, and Charles took a breath, striving to compose himself. "Please—I am sure that Miss Greenwood would consent to see me if you tell her that Mr. Charles Mendenhall wishes to speak with her."

The butler hesitated, but at last he nodded. "Very well. Wait here, please." He turned and disappeared once more down the long hallway.

Charles blew out his breath. What if Katherine refused? Had he come all this way in vain? *No*, he thought emphatically. *I will not lose her.* But as the minutes stretched by he began to doubt. Had he alienated her so completely that she would refuse to see him ever again? Is that why she had left India so suddenly? He felt ill at the thought. Charles heard steps approaching from the hallway, and he looked up expectantly as the butler came into view once more.

"Lady Rockwell has asked that you wait here, and they shall summon you directly."

The relief Charles felt was almost tangible, and he smiled for the first time in weeks. "I will wait all day if I must," he said with a wry grin.

"I do not believe that will be necessary," the butler replied stiffly.

Charles's smile faded. He had never met Lady Rockwell, but if she was as stuffy as her old butler there may be some difficulty with her. Was Charles expected to see them both together? He grew nervous at the thought. He already felt himself base in addressing Katherine after his treatment towards her, but how was he expected to explain himself with her grandmother looking keenly on?

A bell rang, and the butler retreated once more. He was only gone a few minutes before he returned.

"This way, sir," he directed.

Charles followed him down the long hall past several rooms. Had he not been so nervous, Charles would have found pleasure in admiring the tapestries and portraits that lined his path. At last the butler stopped in front of a large, heavily carved door with a solid brass handle. He opened the door, stepping inside the room and announcing Charles's presence. Charles's heart was pounding so loudly he felt sure the servant would hear it as he passed. He took one last, deep breath and walked into the room.

The butler closed the door quietly, and for a few moments Charles and Katherine stared at one another. Charles's courage nearly failed him as he watched Katherine rise gracefully from her place on the sofa. She wore an elaborate gown of creamy silk, with blue forget-me-nots embroidered all over the large, full skirt. Her dark hair was done up in the latest style, and a string of pearls were clasped around her throat. She had grown pale, and was a bit thinner than when Charles had seen her last, but her overall appearance was so gentile, so utterly beautiful that he thought himself a fool once more.

"Mr. Mendenhall," Katherine said at last. "Will you not sit down?"

Charles mechanically took the seat she offered, but as her lovely eyes rested on his own he sprang to his feet once more.

"Miss Greenwood, I do not know what you think of me," he began, clearly agitated. "Indeed, I do not know what I think of myself after my behavior towards you. But you must understand; I *will* have you know that I love you, have always loved you, and have come to England to beg you to accept my hand in marriage."

Katherine's face flushed, and she dropped her eyes to her hands in her lap. Pain and anger filled her heart; how dare he solicit her hand in such a manner! He was a fortune hunter; there could be no other explanation. The anguish she felt in finding herself so mistaken in his character was almost more than she could bear. It was silent for several minutes while she struggled to compose herself, and Charles waited in tortuous suspense for her to speak. When she at last looked up, her steely gaze chilled him to the core.

"I thank you for the compliment, sir, but I cannot accept your offer," she said icily.

Charles took a step back, feeling as though he had been struck. She looked at him with such contempt, he knew at once that some misunderstanding had come between them.

"What has happened?" he asked, his voice barely above a whisper.

Anger flashed in her eyes. "That is a question I should like yourself to answer," she replied.

Charles reddened, and he turned to pace across the long room. Katherine watched him go, the distress she felt in both mind and heart so exquisite she could hardly breathe. The tension in the air was thick, and the silence stretched between them in agonizing stillness. Finally Katherine stood and addressed him.

"I am sorry you took the trouble and expense of coming all the way to England," she said. He turned slowly around as she began speaking, and he watched her intently. "But I beg you will excuse me; I am not feeling well and should like you to leave."

"No," he nearly shouted, quickly crossing back to her. "I will not leave; not until I have been satisfied that you understand me."

"I understand you perfectly, sir," she said acidly. "You were very generous to allow me to remain in your home, to treat me with the kindness and charity with which you did. But had you any true regard for me, you would have acknowledged it openly before now. Instead, you have declared yourself only *after* my grandmother arrived in India, only *after* I had returned with her to England. Oh, yes," she said bitterly, her eyes filling with tears. "I understand very well how much the granddaughter of a countess is worth."

Charles stared at her, appalled. Was this her opinion of him? Did she think him a fortune hunter? He suddenly saw himself in view of her declaration, and it disgusted him. He shook his head.

"No, Katherine, you are wrong. Please allow me to explain."

"I will not," she said again, turning away. Her will was weakening in his presence, and when he uttered her name her resolve nearly crumbled.

"I know what you think of me," he said more gently. "You see me as a fortune hunter. You think that I am only asking for your hand now that you are once more under your grandmother's protection. But that is not true. Katherine," he said, his voice stronger, "I have loved you almost from the moment I met you. I will admit, your presence was at first unsettling, and I avoided you for a time. But from the first moment in the library, I knew that you had the ability to touch my heart in a way I did not know was possible."

He blew out his breath, frustrated. "I was a broken man. When my parents died, they left me with such a wounded soul, such gaping holes in my heart that I never thought I would feel whole again. But then you arrived, and your own spirit was suffering such that I felt a kinship with you. You understood my pain; you understood *me*," he said gently.

Katherine turned and looked at him, her gaze no longer hostile but confused. She wanted to believe him, but did she dare risk her heart? She shook her head, the memory of his cold, indifferent manner warring against the hope that had sprung up inside her. But she did not turn away, and the sight of her face gave him courage.

"It was the music that brought us together," he continued with a smile. "But every moment I spent in your company endeared you more and more to my heart. You were so genuine, so vulnerable; I found my own wounds healed as I listened to your voice, and before I even knew what I was about, I was headlong in love with you."

Katherine returned to the sofa and sat quietly, listening to him. He ran his hands through his hair, becoming agitated once more. "But there were... complications." He continued in a rush before she could misconstrue his meaning. "I had nothing to offer you. The plantation has been mortgaged for many years—I entered into the agreement in order to pay the debts resulting from the deaths of my parents and brother. You must understand; I was in a desperate situation when you arrived in India, and the final payment to my lender was due in October, or my entire living would be lost. I knew I could not make an offer for your hand when I was in such a precarious situation. What if the harvest was weak? What if I did not earn enough to make the final payment? I was already gambling with Sarah's and my own future security; I would not risk yours as well."

He crossed to the sofa and sat down beside her. "That is why I was so often away. I was determined to find a buyer for the second harvest, and thus pay off the mortgage. I knew I had to be free of my debt before I could declare myself to you." His voice became husky with emotion. "Believe me when I say that nothing else could have drawn me away from your side," he said with feeling.

Katherine was silent, contemplating all he had said. She wanted to believe him; her heart was begging her to have faith in him. But something troubled her. Finally she looked up. "What of Miss Grant?" she asked quietly.

"What of Lieutenant Bradford?" Charles countered. Katherine blushed. Slowly she stood and paced away from him, measuring her steps and her words carefully.

"Your behavior was so confusing," she explained. "There were many times when I thought—I hoped—that you cared for me. But you were gone so frequently, and your manner so erratic that I did not know what to think. I knew that without family or fortune I had little to recommend myself to you, so what was I to do? I was not fit to be a servant, and I had no money on which to live. I knew I could not impose on your charity forever, so when Lieutenant Bradford began to show a preference and a regard for me, was it not natural that I encourage his attentions?"

Charles was silent for several moments, but at last he nodded. "It was, and I do not blame you for encouraging him." He took a deep breath and smiled. "I am only glad that you went away before he had a chance to secure your hand."

Katherine laughed self consciously and looked down. "I did not leave quite soon enough. I had to refuse him."

Charles chuckled. "Yes, Sarah told me as much." He regarded her thoughtfully. "Will you tell me why?"

Embarrassed, Katherine kept her eyes cast down. "I felt wretched about it at the time. I had encouraged him, and I *did* plan to accept him, but when my grandmother arrived in India, I found that I could not bring myself to do it. I did not love him, and he deserved more than a marriage of convenience." She turned to face him. "And what is your explanation, sir?" she asked as she sat down again, anxious to have the attention drawn away from herself. "Why did you break your engagement to Miss Grant?"

Charles raised his eyebrows, surprised. "I was never engaged to Miss Grant."

She stared at him. "Whatever do you mean? I... I thought you had an understanding with her."

Charles hesitated, choosing his words carefully. "The Grants are one of Calcutta's finest families, and like many of our peers, they chose to send their children home to England for their education. The first time I remember meeting Miss Grant was when she came to visit Calcutta the year she was fourteen." His cheeks turned red and he shifted uncomfortably in his seat. "I was nineteen, and I confess to have been infatuated with her at the time—all the young men were. But I do believe she had a preference and a regard for me as well." He drew a deep breath and looked unflinchingly into Katherine's eyes. "At the time, the plantation had already been mortgaged and I was deeply in debt, and I am sorry to admit that I entertained the thought of marrying Miss Grant in order to secure the capital needed to pay off my lender. But there was never a formal understanding between us.

259

We never spoke with one another about uniting our families, and though it appeared that Miss Grant returned to Calcutta in the hope of rekindling our courtship, in the end, like you, I would not settle for a marriage of convenience."

The room was quiet, and the *tick, tick* of the clock was the only indication of the passage of time. Lost in their thoughts, they were suspended in time, waiting for their fates to collide.

Charles took her hand, and his voice was low with emotion. "When I arrived home from Balasore, I thought all my troubles were over. I barely stopped to rest for fear I would be too late, and your hand secured by Lieutenant Bradford. Can you imagine my surprise, and shock, when I discovered that you had fled the country? I was nearly beside myself. I was forced to remain in Calcutta until the papers could be drawn up which satisfied my debt to Mr. Cooper. But let me assure you, Katherine, that I was on the first available boat to England when my business was concluded."

He smiled into her eyes, and reached up to brush his hand across her cheek. "I love you more deeply than you can ever imagine," he said. "You are the only reason I have for living, the only reason I would ever leave my home and travel halfway around the world. I do not have much to offer you. Indeed," he glanced around the room and his countenance fell, "I would not blame you for refusing to give all of this up a second time. But knowing now the whole of my history, and at the risk of being rejected twice, I once again ask for your hand in marriage."

She looked up at him, and the intensity burning in his eyes removed all her defenses. Her heart burst forth from the restraints she had placed upon it and filled her soul until she thought she would overflow. Tears filled her eyes, and Katherine smiled. "Mr. Mendenhall, I can only venture to say that if you love me half so well as I have always loved you, I shall consider myself the luckiest girl in all of England to accept your hand."

Charles's face lit up in a brilliant smile, and he stood, drawing Katherine to her feet. She gasped as he picked her up by the waist and swung her around.

"Charles!" she cried out, laughing. "You have lost your senses. What if someone should see you?" she said, thinking of her grandmother waiting down the hall.

"What of it?" he replied, grinning at her crookedly as he set her down. He took both her hands in his own, kissing first one and then the other. He looked into her eyes, and she once again knew she would follow him anywhere. "I have won my fair lady, and I do not care if half the kingdom were to look in upon us; my affections will not be contained." With that, he wrapped his arms around her and bent his head to hers.

Katherine had never been kissed by a man before, but she knew that the love between them made her first kiss the most passionate, devastating kiss she would ever experience. Her love for Charles filled her heart and mind with such intensity she felt as if she would burst into flame. She wrapped her arms around his neck and kissed him back with every fiber of her being. With his arms around her and his lips pressed against her own, Katherine threw off her defenses and melted into him.

When Charles at last drew back, Katherine clung to his shirtsleeves, not willing to break their embrace. He chuckled under his breath, kissing her gently on the forehead. "My dearest, darling Katherine," he whispered. Her face was flushed and she sighed in contentment. He brushed his hand along her cheek, and it felt like fire on her skin.

"Yes, Mr. Mendenhall?" she said, gazing up at him with a look of complete devotion. He smiled and took her hand, kissing it lightly.

"Would you object to having the marriage performed as soon as a license can be procured?" he asked.

Katherine drew back, surprised. "What about your sister? Sarah would never forgive you for being married without her present."

"She would never forgive me for traveling to England without her, either," he replied with a twinkle in his eye. It took Katherine a moment to understand his meaning.

"Sarah is here? Oh, Charles!"

He laughed at her delight, and nodded. "Yes, Sarah is here. She stayed in London while I came in search of you."

Katherine threw her arms around him. "I am so happy she has come. And since she is here, I have no objection to becoming Mrs. Charles Mendenhall as soon as may be." She sighed, a look of pure happiness on her face.

Charles laughed and took her in his arms once more. He looked down at her face, smiling into her deep brown eyes. "Thank you," he said simply.

She smiled, and he bent to kiss her lips once more.

Epilogue

They were married before the blossoms of May had faded with the heat of June. Sarah was Katherine's bridesmaid, and never was a girl of eighteen more delighted to be so. Lady Rockwell took a fancy to her, and when Katherine and Charles sailed back to India at the end of the summer, Sarah remained behind in Leicestershire as a companion to the countess.

When the Mendenhalls arrived in Calcutta, they found that Colonel Whittaker and his regiment had been reassigned to Bengal, news which Katherine was relieved to hear. And Miss Priscilla Grant, it was discovered, had suddenly arrived in India the summer before in order to escape a scandalous affair she had been involved with in London. When word of her disgrace reached the close-knit English community in Calcutta, she and her family had removed from the city, and by the time Katherine and Charles arrived, were living quietly in a northern town at the base of the Himalayas.

The little bungalow became a treasured escape from the cares of life. Love grew within its walls and permeated the lives of everyone who crossed its threshold. Music and laughter poured from its open windows and doors, spilling out into the hot, humid air. The bright Indian sun shone down upon the dark, glossy leaves of the little indigo plants which, like the love between Katherine and Charles, grew and flourished year after year.

THE END

Acknowledgments

First and foremost, I would like to thank my Heavenly Father for blessing me with the time, talents, and will to make this dream a reality. All that I do, and all that I am, is because of Him.

My husband, John, who is the love of my life. He is my sounding board, my cheerleader, my biggest fan, my confidante, and my very best friend. Thank you for your love and support over the months and years it has taken me to get to this point. None of this would ever have been possible without you.

For my sweet children: Caleb, Elina, Audrey and Mira. Thank you for not complaining when you ate cold cereal and peanut butter sandwiches for days in a row, for dealing with a tired, crabby mommy on those days after I was up too late working on my book, and for loving me, encouraging me, and helping me to fly. I love you more than words can say.

To my fantastic friends and family members who read, critiqued, helped and encouraged me from the very earliest drafts. Kimberlee Burch, Annalee Woolf, Jared Odd, Angela Smith, Christine McKinnon, Amy Payne, Debbie Hong, Amber Gunnell, Melissa Ahmed, and Maxine Odd, you guys rock! Thank you for all the advice, suggestions, corrections, and encouragement. You are loved and appreciated so, so much.

I would also like to thank my wonderful, loving parents, Dana and Miriam, and my rockstar brothers Konlin and Zack, who never laughed at the cheesy stories and cliché poems I wrote as a child and teenager. Thank you for your faith in me—I love you all so much!

For Mr. Dennis Sandmeier, my high school English teacher, who recognized my passion and abilities when I was most vulnerable and impressionable. Thank you for helping to guide my writing and for pushing me to stretch myself, even when I didn't want to be stretched. Nothing can measure the magnitude of impact a devoted teacher can have. Thank you for being a positive influence in my life.

To all the members of the United Authors Association, and especially those in the Utah Valley Writers chapter. You were the driving force behind my picking up the pen to finish this book after a decade-long hiatus. Thank you for your suggestions, critiques, and encouragement. I am grateful for all the meetings and resources you make available to writers like me.

And finally, I would like to thank my beloved grandfather, Robert George. He did not survive to see this book in print, but he knew my writer's heart because I inherited it from him. He called me his "little brown-eyed Emily," after Emily Dickinson, one of our favorite poets. Grandpa, thank you for believing in me. Thank you for sharing your talents and wisdom with me. Thank you for loving and encouraging me through all the hard times when I was growing and developing my skills as a writer. I hope I have made you proud.

Turn the page for an exclusive peek

at Shaela Kay's next book

Scoundrel IN Disguise

Prologue

5 years earlier
Surrey, England

The horse's hooves beat a thundering cadence, spewing rocks and dirt behind him as his rider drove him ever faster. The pounding of the horse's gallop was nearly as loud in Rex's ears as the beating of his heart, and even though each hoofbeat brought him closer to his destination, every second seemed like an eternity. In another half mile he would turn down the drive, and the lights of the house would guide his way instead of the nearly full moon that had been his companion since London. He whipped his horse ever onward, determined to bridge the distance between him and his beloved Mary in as little time as possible.

He yanked on the reins, and his horse stumbled as he turned off the road and down the drive. As soon as they were clear of the large oak tree that marked the entrance to the estate, Rex spurred his horse faster, confused that he could not see the lights of the house shining through the trees. Surely the entire house would be ablaze, anticipating his arrival.

But no. As he crested a small hill and came clear of the copse, his heart sank. Only a solitary window glowed in the corner of the massive building, and Rex knew that could only mean one thing.

He was too late.

Nearing the house, he pulled up on the horse's reins, forcing the beast to skid to a stop. Rex swung his leg over the side and was running to the door before his mount even had a chance to get his footing. He burst into the house, turning down a corridor to the left and nearly running over the old butler in his haste. The servant's grim face said it all.

Mary.

The house was silent as the two men stared at one another. Rex's chest was heaving as he strove to catch his breath, fighting for air to ask the impossible question. But before he could form the words, the older gentleman shook his head sadly.

"You are but two hours too late, sir. She is gone."

Rex heard the words as if from the end of a long tunnel. He knew what they meant, but his heart shied away from the pain in their meaning, refusing to accept what his mind understood. Mary was gone. She was dead. He would not see her smile, nor hear her laugh ever again in this life. He shook his head slowly, trying to stop himself from crashing into the wall of pain he felt himself spiraling towards.

"Dr. Jones has gone, but he said he will return tomorrow," his butler offered. Rex remained silent. "Come," the older man said gently, taking a step towards the stairs. "She has left you something."

Rex watched his old servant slowly climb the massive, curving staircase. The butler paused and looked back, as Rex mechanically put one foot in front of the other, following him to the second floor. They turned down a corridor and stopped at the very end, where the faint glow of candlelight could be seen issuing from underneath a heavy oak door. The butler opened it, standing to the side to let his master enter first.

Rex stepped inside, and the woman standing by the far window turned. Slowly she approached, holding out the small bundle in her arms as she reached his side. Rex held his arms out automatically, taking what she offered. A whisper of a cry sounded from the tangled blankets, and he looked down into the tiny face of a newborn child.

The minuscule human stretched its weak arms out, its tiny face twisted in soundless displeasure. Rex stared at the child, reeling at the weight he suddenly felt upon his shoulders. He looked up at the woman standing beside him.

"She left the child… for me?" he asked, his voice as unsteady as he felt.

The woman nodded. "Mary gave the babe a name before she died."

"And it is?"

"Her name is Caroline."

Chapter 1

August 1833
Leicestershire, England

It was a lovely wedding. Katherine wore a beautiful gown of ivory lace, with rosebuds woven in her hair and a train nearly five yards long. She and Charles were married in May, and Sarah smiled to herself as she thought of how happy she had been that day, seeing her only brother marry her dearest friend. The happy couple chose to spend their honeymoon at the estate in Leicestershire where Katherine had been raised—a decision which pleased not only Sarah, but the countess as well. Lady Rockwell knew that her granddaughter would be returning to India with her new husband at the end of the summer, and she was anxious to spend as much time with her as possible. Sarah, too, was glad for the three months to spend with the two people she loved most in the world before being separated from them indefinitely.

But August had come at last, and with it the ship that bore the two young lovers away. A week had now passed since their tearful parting, and the depressed air that had hovered in the house in the days following their departure had dissipated. Sarah's was not a melancholy disposition, and her natural cheerfulness soon lifted her spirits, as well as those of Lady Rockwell.

Sarah came down the stairs to breakfast one morning, humming to herself as she took the seat across from her hostess.

"You seem cheerful this morning," Lady Rockwell observed.

Sarah's smile faltered. "I am trying to be. I miss Katherine and Charles, but I have had *such* a headache from crying so much, that I am determined to be done with it. No amount of tears will bring them back, so what is the point in carrying on so?"

"It is natural to miss them. Your brother especially."

Sarah nodded. "And I am sure that your ladyship misses Katherine."

A lump rose in the old woman's throat, but she forced herself to smile. "Yes. *Meine Leibling.* I feel as if she only just returned with me to England. But now she is gone to India again." Her voice drifted off, her thoughts following her granddaughter on the long voyage around the tip of Africa to the hot, humid subcontinent. She shook her head, as if to dispel the melancholy air that clung to her words.

"*Meine Leibling.*" Sarah repeated the unfamiliar words, and the countess smiled.

"*Sehr gut, Fräulein.* German suits your tongue quite nicely."

"Where did you grow up, Lady Rockwell? Katherine told me it was somewhere in Prussia."

"Strausberg."

"*Strausberg.*" Sarah repeated, trying to mimic the throaty sounds. "Is your family still there? Are you never lonely?"

The countess laughed softly. "How could I be lonely when I

have you for company?"

Sarah smiled fondly at her. She had been overjoyed when Lady Rockwell extended an invitation to stay with her in England. Having spent her entire life in India, Sarah had yearned for the sights and sounds of a true English home, and had dreamed of spending a season in London ever since she was a girl. Now, at the tender age of eighteen, she was finally getting her wish. Her blue eyes sparkled with anticipation as the meal began.

A liveried footman stood behind each of their chairs, serving them from the vast array of dishes on the table. Lady Rockwell ate her food with calm elegance, and Sarah attempted to follow her example. When the servants cleared away the last of the china at the conclusion of the meal, Sarah breathed a sigh of relief.

"I am afraid I shall never grow accustomed to the formality of dining here," she said with a laugh.

Lady Rockwell raised her eyebrows as they made their way to the sitting room. "I hope you are not in earnest, Miss Mendenhall, for there are a great many more formalities with which you must accustom yourself, if you are to spend the Season in London."

"Is it really so very different from India?" Sarah asked doubtfully.

"Of course it is," Lady Rockwell replied, seating herself comfortably on the sofa. "You may have been raised in the home of a British gentleman, but you resided in a heathen nation. No matter how proper you felt your social customs were in Calcutta, I can assure you that there will be far more expected of you whilst you are here."

"Such as?"

Lady Rockwell ticked them off on her fingers. "You are never to walk out alone, except in the garden next to the house. You must always wear a hat and gloves when you go out, and carry a parasol if you are walking in the park. A lady must always have a chaperon when she is in the presence of a gentleman who is not her near kin. You are never to dance with a gentleman you do not know or to whom you have not been introduced, and never," she looked at Sarah sternly, "are you to ask someone to call you by your Christian name."

Sarah hid a smile. She had thoroughly shocked Lady Rockwell upon her arrival when she asked that her hostess call her Sarah instead of Miss Mendenhall, and the countess lost no time in lecturing Sarah about the impropriety of such a request. The older woman lifted her eyebrows, and Sarah sighed in resignation.

"Very well," she conceded. "I shall do my best not to embarrass you."

"*Gut.* I have high hopes for you, Miss Mendenhall. With my name and connections, there is a very good chance of your marrying well."

Sarah shifted uncomfortably in her seat. "Of course I wish to make an eligible match, Lady Rockwell. But I do not want to be married right away. After all, I am only eighteen, and this is my very first Season in London! I want to thoroughly enjoy myself, without any thought of matrimony or matchmaking or eligible young men."

"Indeed! Though surprised to hear such a declaration, I confess that it eases my mind considerably. It will probably be to your advantage not to take thought of marriage just yet. Let London get under your skin first; you will be older and wiser next year and will have plenty of time for that sort of thing then."

Sarah smiled, but a knot was beginning to form in the pit of her stomach. Though she had accompanied Katherine and the countess to several dinner parties and private dances since her arrival, she had yet to attend a grand affair in London. She worried that when the time arrived she would not be fashionable enough, or that she would do something to embarrass herself or the countess.

Her fears were not unfounded. Sarah had been raised on a small indigo plantation outside of Calcutta, India, by her brother Charles, who was eight years her senior. They had been left alone in the world when their mother, father, and elder brother died in the cholera epidemic that swept through India in 1818. Without a mother to guide and direct her, Sarah had grown up to be sweet but rather impulsive, and she was by no stretch of the imagination an expert on the strict social customs of refined society.

Most of the well-to-do families in Calcutta sent their children to England for a formal education, but that particular privilege had not been Sarah's. Instead, she was educated at home by an elderly governess, whose own accomplishments were sadly lacking. Though Sarah had a firm grasp of grammar, arithmetic, history, geography, and other such mundane subjects as complete a well-rounded education, she had not been given any instruction in music or art, and very little in French and German. Free to pursue her own interests instead, Sarah had spent her spare time poring over the ladies magazines and newspapers that trickled in from London, hungry for the society that was hers by birth but not by means. As she matured, Sarah developed a keen eye for fashion and a natural style of elegance uniquely her own. But she knew that her début in London would not be a test of her appearance alone, but of her manners and accomplishments as well.

"Now, Miss Mendenhall," Lady Rockwell began, smoothing out the burgundy folds of her taffeta morning dress, "when I offered to let you stay with me, I knew that I was taking upon myself the responsibility of introducing you into the finest society. Your father was a gentleman, and as a gentleman's daughter, you are expected to conduct yourself with the utmost grace and decorum. Your manners are very pretty, but I find that your education has been sadly lacking. You will be expected to study and improve yourself while you are here."

"Yes, Lady Rockwell," Sarah said meekly.

Lady Rockwell laughed at her worried expression. "It will not be so hard as you think, *Fräulein*. Let us begin in the music room, and then we shall practice your French."

It was not the first time Lady Rockwell had made the effort to give Sarah music lessons. They had been attempting the pianoforte for several months, but her pupil was not making much progress, so Lady Rockwell decided to try the harp.

"Elbows up, Miss Mendenhall," she reminded, thirty minutes into their lesson.

Sarah bit back a retort. Her arms were tired and her fingers were sore, but she complied. The simple melody was indiscernible from the sheer number of incorrect strings Sarah plucked. She struggled through ten more minutes before dropping her hands to her sides.

"It is no use, Lady Rockwell—I shall never be able to play an instrument."

"Nonsense! You are doing quite well, I believe."

Sarah gently massaged her swollen fingertips, dismally staring at the music before her on the stand. The expression on the countess' face softened.

"*Voudriez-vous essayer quelque chose de nouveau?*" she asked.

"*Oui, s'il vous plaît!*" Sarah responded eagerly.

The countess laughed lightly. "Very good, my dear. Your French has improved."

Sarah flushed with pleasure, removing herself from her position at the harp. "What did you have in mind?"

"It is not something I can teach you, I am afraid," the countess replied.

Sarah's interest was piqued. What could she possibly learn that would require the skill of someone other than the countess?

Lady Rockwell ignored her curious glances, walking instead towards the doors leading to the library.

"I shall hire a tutor for you, but in the meantime, let us take some refreshment in the library. I have just received a copy of Frederic Shoberl's translation of *Notre-Dame de Paris*. Let us see what Monsieur Hugo has to say."

About the Author

 Shaela Kay was born and raised near Seattle, Washington. She studied Theatre and English at Brigham Young University-Idaho, but left her studies in order to be a wife and a mother. When she isn't writing, you can find her quilting, crafting, or homeschooling her four children. She and her husband John live with their family in a little house along the banks of the mighty Columbia River. Visit her online at www.shaelakay.com.